ROWDY

WILD AND MEAN, SHARP AND KEEN

CHRIS MULLEN

This is a work of fiction. Names, characters, and places are either products of the author's imagination or are used fictitiously. Any resemblance to actual persons, living or dead, locales, or events is entirely coincidental.

Copyright © 2020 Chris Mullen

Library of Congress Registration Number TX 8-885-227

MKT Publishing

ISBN 978-1-7352925-1-9

Cover and interior design by: *Mokaite* 莫

Thank you, Michelle Chester, founder and owner of EBM Professional Services, for your talent, support, and editorial work with *Rowdy: Wild and Mean, Sharp and Keen*.

ebm-services.com
chrismullenwrites.com

THANK YOU, JACK MULLEN – CREATIVE CONSULTANT, POET, TEACHER, GRANDFATHER, AND MY DAD – FOR YOUR GUIDANCE, IDEAS, VAST LITERATURE AND HISTORICAL KNOWLEDGE, AND FOR BEING MY #1 FAN.

THANK YOU, MARGIE MULLEN– TECHNICAL ADVISER, COOKIE PROVIDER, GRANDMOTHER, AND MY MOM– FOR YOUR INSIGHT, SUPPORT, AND FOR ALWAYS BELIEVING IN ME.

ROWDY

WILD AND MEAN, SHARP AND KEEN

CHRIS MULLEN

PROLOGUE

Rowdy sat on the front porch of his ranch house and surveyed the horizon. A sultry breeze swirled about the Circle R ranch, bringing a sweet smell of coming rain. A rider was coming in. At Rowdy's feet was Dog. Dog, more interested in identifying the scent flowing in with the breeze, had yet to sense the coming visitor. Rowdy watched the rider's image grow larger as it slowly sauntered closer. The rider looked toward the Circle R. A smile edged out of the corner of his mouth. It was Roberson.

Dog, growing tired of the mysterious smell, caught sight of Roberson and stood pointing in his direction. Quietly, he stepped forward and then shot off the porch, sprinting towards Roberson. Rowdy stood and watched as Dog escorted Roberson through the gate and up to the hitching post where he dismounted. He secured his horse to the post and looked up at Rowdy. Rowdy looked back. Neither said a word. A gust of wind blew between them, spraying dust along its path.

"Got a feeling about this one?" Roberson said finally.

"More so than the last time," Rowdy replied.

"The last time... should've been the last time." Roberson spoke as he climbed the stairs to the top of the porch. Dog followed

2

and reclaimed his spot next to Rowdy. Both men laughed as they shook hands, but Rowdy knew in the back of his mind that Roberson was right. He laughed anyway as Roberson sank into the chair next to him.

"I hear the deer are running bigger this year than they have in a while," Roberson said. He loved to hunt and jumped at every chance.

"I suppose we will see when we get there, but if this wind doesn't die down, we may catch the brunt of those storm clouds," Rowdy said, pointing at the sky beyond the ranch.

Roberson spat. Both men watched as bulging clouds spread out and up across the western sky, growing darker and more ominous by the minute.

"Danged if that isn't blowing our way!" he said.

"Come on," Rowdy said. "Let's put yer horse in the barn and head inside for some coffee. Maybe this thing will blow itself out and we can hit the trail in an hour."

The storm didn't blow out. It grew rapidly, sparking lightning flashes that trailed like spider webs across the sky. Booming thunder followed. Dog, still lying on the front porch, slowly stood up and headed inside for his favorite napping spot.

Rain began to fall, gentle at first. Wind whipped through the Circle R and the sky opened up. Rain swept in diagonally, splashing the ground angrily. The front door rattled against its hinges while the two men tipped back in their chairs and nursed their coffee.

"Looks like we'll be a while," Rowdy said.

Roberson, irritated that his hunting trip was delayed, let out a grunt.

Deafening thunder rolled across the plains as the rain showed no signs of letting up. Roberson stepped to the window and looked out.

"Dang!" he said, "This is gonna clean wash us out!"

"I've seen worse," Rowdy replied.

"Worse than this?" Roberson questioned. "Can't imagine."

Skeptical, Roberson looked out over the soggy terrain. Small streams of water ran rampant, carving miniature canyons into the ground.

Rowdy rocked back in his chair and a swift glimpse of the past rolled through his mind—Mississippi river water pouring over his skiff, supplies careening away down river, lightning flashing overhead, and roaring thunder echoed through him.

A crisp flash of lightning chased by its thunderous pursuer jolted Rowdy back to the present. Roberson turned around.

"Where did you see anything like this?"

CHAPTER 1

It had been two days since I'd escaped from home and although I knew it was something I had to do, I never imagined how bad things would turn so quickly.

I had one tin cup, a baker's pot, three strips of dried venison, a half-eaten can of beans, my brother's knife, one silver dollar, all of which were left over from a recent hunting trip with my brother. He had pulled me from my hiding place, raced with me to the river, forced me onto our small skiff, and pushed me out into the rivers current. With hardly a wave, he rushed back towards the flames. I don't know if it was the shotgun blast or the sight of him falling to the ground that shocked me the most. My heart pounded my chest and tears streamed down my cheeks.

"No!" I screamed out, reaching out to him, to home, as it slipped further from me.

Everything happened so quickly and now I was alone. I had no path except that which the river currents provided. I floated downstream away from my family's farmhouse watching flames and smoke fill the air as it burned. Away from the shouts and hollers of evil rapture. Away from my murdered father and older brother. Away from the band of men that raided our stead, shot my horse, and left me with scars that time would never fully heal.

"Why didn't I do something?"

I asked myself this question at least a thousand times as I lay on my back, the sun burning my face. I pounded my fist against the slats of wood holding me up as I gave myself to the mercy of the river. Tears of pain and frustration rolled off my checks and were lost in the waters surrounding me. I was an island, and I was alone.

CHAPTER 2

The first day passed slowly. It felt as if time itself was attempting to prolong my escape. My path before me was unknown, but I was going to put as much distance as I could between me and the place I used to call home. I floated for hours, brushing along the riverbank at times. My fingers dangled off the side of my skiff. The water was refreshing, but I felt no joy.

Around mid-day I heard distant laughing and splashing. As my skiff drifted closer, I floated by what looked like two friends playing. They would jump in the water, splash around, and then jump out again. Each trying to outdo the other, but both having the time of their lives. I was too tired to say anything and not ready to confront my reality. I was alone. No friends to laugh at or splash, no family to call my own.

One of the boys jumped in to splash his friend but caught sight of me. His distracted landing caused very little commotion in the water and was quickly the target of an uproar of laughter and finger pointing. All fun and games of course until he noticed the direction of the gaze on his friend's face. Wide eyed, the boys looked at me from the shallow water near the riverbank and watched as I slowly swirled past them and down river. One boy raised his hand

and cautiously waved. I hadn't the energy or willingness to return the gesture. I rolled over on my back, closed my eyes, and cried.

I lay there like a cast away at sea, scared and feeling hopeless. A light wind cooled my body, but the blazing sun scorched my face. I didn't care. So much had happened.

"A man acts like one because he has to. A boy acts like one when he wants to. What are you?" My father would say to me. What would he say now? I was 13 years old and was now in charge of my own survival.

Night brought little comfort. I hardly slept. When I did doze, the nightmarish scene of my father's last glance startled me back to my stark reality. The darkness on the river consumed me, swallowing me up in its murky void. I found some comfort in the stars above and stared up at the sky for what seemed like hours, watching the twinkling in the heavens and wondering if my father and brother were there. Were they watching over me? Was I safe from the men that killed them? Would I meet up with that gang again, and would I be strong enough to avenge what they had done to my family?

The second day was calm. I paddled some, all the while keeping my eyes on the shoreline for signs of trouble. I had not set foot on land, nor did I see anyone since drifting past the boys yesterday. The occasional water snake and numerous mosquitoes were the only hazards I had encountered to this point. I was just fine with that.

I gnawed on a piece of venison. It was tough and dry and was the last of the deer my brother and I had hunted only a week before. I hadn't had enough time to gather proper supplies for a trip like this and knew that I was going to need to replenish them soon. I learned to hunt and fish at an early age and had become quite good at building traps and making fishing spears. I could keep lying here or I could do…something. I sat up and looked around.

Using my brother's knife, I stripped a couple low hanging branches from a tree and as I floated by, sharpening the end of each one. I was determined to keep moving and decided to fish as I continued downstream, guided by the current once more. The river had started to widen a bit, and I decided to stay close to shore. I fished towards shallow water and took advantage of the shade from trees that hung out over the banks. The trees looked as if they were trying to reach for a drink but couldn't quite lean over far enough. Some were dead, their branches bouncing helplessly in the wind. My skiff and these dead trees were eerily similar in that there was no rhyme or reason to their movements. They were at the mercy of nature. The wind and the water decided their direction as my direction was being chosen for me.

By sunset I had speared two catfish and was looking forward to eating them for supper. Bright yellow and orange rays of light shone through the willow branches where my skiff was tied. I was not ready to stop, but this alcove was very inviting. It was dry and had a flattened area with enough room to make a small fire. I gathered twigs and branches and formed a small triangular shaped mound, using the smallest kindling first. I added a few dry leaves to help catch a spark but not enough to create unnecessary smoke. It took a while, and a bit of luck, but I was finally able to find a flame by striking the blade of my knife repeatedly against a rock I thought could possibly be flint. I pumped my fist in celebration as my fire grew. I cooked the fish on the riverbank and listened to the crackling beneath my catch.

The catfish didn't taste too bad and was just what my body needed. I was exhausted both mentally and physically. I needed to rest but convinced myself I had to keep going. But where? I stepped back onto the skiff and sat down looking over the water. As the beginnings of twilight began to appear in the sky, the hum of cicadas lulled me into a trance. I laid down, shut my eyes, and fell asleep. That was a big mistake.

CHAPTER 3

I awoke suddenly to a flash of lightning immediately followed by a deafening clap of thunder. The wind whipped through the branches of the willows that were so calming only an hour or so before. Now they thrashed about trying to escape the power of the oncoming storm. The skiff was pulled back and forth by the trees. The water had become rough. I looked to shore. The riverbank was too steep to climb and abandoning my gear, my lifeline, was not an option anyway. I reached for my brother's knife. Acting quickly to free my skiff, I cut the rope and was swiftly thrust down river. The small skiff twisted and bucked up and down. It was like trying to ride a horse that hadn't been broke. Lightning bolts stretched across the sky briefly lighting up the darkness around me. Thunder followed each strike and was intensifying. The wind howled. And then the rains came.

"Just hold on," I told myself.

I gripped the center slat with one hand and my brother's knife with the other. There was nothing I could do. I bounced along the river getting pounded by the downpour. Rain poured down my scalp, blinding me at times. I had to squint just to see the shoreline. I was now more than 30 feet away, with little hopes of steering myself to safety when the front end of my skiff collided with something large and hard sticking out of the water. The force of the impact cracked the front ties of my skiff, dislodging the slats. I had struck a tree that had been washed away from the bank, its roots and branches twisting and stabbing at the water. I was sinking. In a matter of moments, the storm and the river had taken almost everything I had.

"Help!" I screamed out, but there was no one to hear me. Thunderous laughter filled my ears. A flash of lighting crashed overhead and bolted for the tree line. In a blast of light and heat it struck the top of a tree, igniting it like a candle freshly doused with kerosene. I was in deep. I reached out to grasp the last bit of skiff that was somehow holding together. My arms ached. My hands were full of splinters. River water rushed into my mouth. I swallowed more than my stomach could hold. Out it came again, back to the swirling rampage, leaving a vomitus trail in its wake.

Is this it? I thought.

I continued to hold firm until the last shards of my skiff broke loose. Now fully vulnerable in the water, I was swept down river. Darkness surrounded me. The river pounded me. The rain did not let up. Through it all, the one thing that woke me, that blinded me with every flash, now gave me a glimpse of the only thing that might save me from drowning. The very tree that had destroyed my boat was only a few feet away. If I could somehow maneuver over to it, I might be able to pull myself up. Stretching out, I pulled at the water. Again and again, I tried to swim towards the tree. Lightning pierced the air again, allowing me a split-second look to see if I was any closer. I was not. In fact, it was pulling away.

My body ached. With one last effort I surged forward in its direction, giving everything I had.

Faster! I screamed inside my head. *Do you want to die in this river? Faster, NOW!*

Two strokes, three strokes, four.

I must be getting close. Just a little more.

I reached out and jammed my fingers against the log. It had to be it. As my thoughts were being read by the storm, a flash of lightning engulfed the sky, confirming that I had somehow reached the tree.

It was slippery. I tried to pull myself up, but the tree started to roll in my direction. I reached up with my right hand and pulled hard. My chest met the slippery bark of the tree and glided upwards and out of the water. I kicked my left leg up and secured my foot around a broken branch. With one final thrust, I heaved myself out of the water and onto the top of the log. My arms hugged tightly to the log while my legs draped on either side. The rain poured and the lightning flashed, but exhaustion prevailed. The last thing I saw was the smoldering shoreline being extinguished by the rain. Water dripped from my nose. Everything went black.

Visions of my father entered my dreams—carrying me on his shoulders when I was young, showing me the proper way to dry gunpowder, whipping me when I had taken a silver piece from the money box under his bed to buy sweets from a traveling merchant, and his outstretched arms lifting me up after I fell out of the tree by the brook back home. These dreams were so far away, and yet I was in fact being lifted out of the river.

CHAPTER 4

The mix of rain and river water that drenched my body was now replaced by a cold sweat. My body shivered as I lay covered by a woolen blanket. A musty smell filtered into my nose. I could hear voices nearby. Still only semi-conscious, I was unable to understand what they were saying. I moved slightly to reposition myself but quickly stopped as a sharp pain pierced my left side. I placed my right hand across my body, gently cradling myself.

The rain had stopped. It was still dark. A small lantern glowed near me, dimly lighting the room. There was a round window to one side and a wooden door at the other. The door, not completely closed, was outlined by light coming from just outside. I opened my eyes wider now, still shivering, and tried to sit up. I braced myself on the edge of the bed, still holding my left side. Pushing up, I was able to raise myself only to my elbows before I lost my balance. I half fell, half slid to the floor, making more noise upon impact than I wanted.

Pain throbbed from my side. I clenched my teeth to hold back a scream. Not knowing where I was or who had pulled me from the river concerned me. Were they friendly? The door to my room creaked open. A tall, dark figure blocked most of the light entering the room. I was about to find out.

"Easy, son." said the man in doorway.

His voice was low and raspy. He stepped closer and knelt beside me.

"Let's get ya back on the bunk, Okay? You're runnin' a fever, and the way I see it, you need to rest."

I was too weak to do anything. Using his arm for balance, I gingerly stood up just enough to slide back onto the bunk. I laid back and pulled the covers over me. My right foot stuck out. I took a deep breath and then exhaled.

"Where am I?" I asked. "How did you find me?"

"Yer onboard Delilah. We were tied down further upriver riding out the storm that blew through yesterday."

"Yesterday!" I exclaimed.

"Yep. You've been out for most of a day. Thought you'd pass but looks like you may actually pull through. Good, too. I'd hate to throw ya back in the river." He chuckled as he moved a chair closer to me and sat down.

"My name is Jim Hennessy. I'm the ship's captain, owner, and tradesman. Had this ship 'bout 12 years. I make runs up and down river, buyin' and sellin', but mostly transportin' goods from the south all the way to St. Louis. That's where the money is."

Captain Hennessy sat back in his chair. He was a larger man, but by no means portly.

"Anyway, I had just finished inspecting the tie-downs when I caught a glimpse of you floatin' down river on top of an old tree. Figured ya were probably dead, but something inside me told me to find out. I yelled for Mac to grab a pike and try to haul ya in. You were only about eight feet from Delilah when I first saw ya, but the current of the river outmatched our reflexes onboard. Instead of the pike, I pulled out my knife, cut the lines, and we took off after ya."

Knife... my brother's knife. Where was it? I had lost so much to the river.

Captain Hennessy continued about how they finally came along side of me and how Mac had pulled me off the log. He had tied himself to the starboard mast before jumping overboard. Mac grabbed me with one arm and pulled me from the log. He'd cradled me while Captain Hennessy pulled us back to safety.

"My things?" I asked. Aside from bits of bark and sand, my pockets were empty.

"Son, you were soaked to the bone," he said. "Only things on ya was yer clothes, and even then, you'd lost a shoe and ripped a giant hole through yer shirt. Bloody, too. Ya must have really gotten beat up. What on earth were you doin' out in that storm?"

"My knife? My brother gave it to me," I asked quietly as I was starting to fade out again.

The last symbol of any connection I had with my family was probably swamped in river mud at the bottom of the Mississippi. Captain Hennessy looked at me, stood up, and walked to a table across the room. He opened a drawer on the top and removed an object from it. He returned to my bunk, took my hand, opened it, and placed my brother's knife securely in my grasp.

"Can't never be too careful."

"Thank you," I said.

My eyes had grown very heavy. Captain Hennessy said

something, but I was already out. He doused the light and left me alone to sleep.

Night passed, and all things were quiet on the river. The moon began to shine through the breaking clouds. River water rippled against the side of the boat. Somewhere in the distance an owl hooted and took flight in search of its nightly meal. I dreamed again, but mostly in patchy segments. My father yelling for me to run, my brother tossing me onto the skiff and cutting the lines before I could object, tossing me his knife. Fire. Water. A vision of my mother from when I was very young. My mother? She had gotten sick and died before I could even walk, yet I could see her. Eyes as blue as the summer's sky, skin so soft. Her gentle hands on my forehead. A soft kiss followed by a whisper.

"Wake up."

Sun shone in on my room. It was early morning. My side throbbed less but was stiff and sore. Lifting the blanket and moving my tattered shirt aside, I finally looked at the site of my pains and saw that I had a gash from my ribs to my hip. The wound seeped fluid in small drops but had started to scab over. The skin around it was discolored. Purple and greens fanned out from each side. I lightly pressed my right hand against myself, testing the sensitivity of my injury.

What are you? echoed from deep inside.

The initial pressure made me wince. At that moment, I decided what I was. I swung my feet off the bunk and stood up. My clothes were worn. I was shoeless. I slowly stepped towards the small window. Mist from the river still lingered, blanketing the top of the water. A fish jumped near the shore. To the right, a group of cranes stood still atop the muddy banks of the Mississippi looking down on us in approval of our passing, barring we didn't disturb their meditative state. The cloudless sky was a stark contrast to the last time I looked at it. I turned and headed for the door. I opened it and stepped outside. Captain Hennessy stood at the bow of the boat. He squinted as he looked downstream. A dark-skinned man stood to one side of the boat. He held a pole in his hand, dipping it into the water, somehow working the river like a lion tamer training a lion. That must be Mac. Now we were traveling with the current. Mac pushed the pole into the water to guide our way.

Captain Hennessy called out to Mac. "A little to port. Sandbar ahead."

I walked to the edge of the boat and looked over. My reflection looked back at me. In its distorted liquid state, it seemed to taunt me, rather than reassure me that things were alright now.

I almost had you, my murky image seemed to say. *Just you wait, just you wait!*

Even now the river provoked frustration and confusion. Mac turned in my direction. He was a strong looking man. His shoulders had bulges coming out of every side. His muscular arms, a direct result of time he'd spent on the river. He was dark skinned but had light colored eyes. His head was shaved. A scar tracked its way along his left cheekbone from his nose to his ear. Mac looked at me but kept at his post, lifting and pushing, he guided the boat down river.

"Come over here, boy," Captain Hennessy shouted.

I slowly walked over. Captain Hennessy leaned forward and

spit into the water.

"So, yer up?" he said. "Finally decided to come back to the land of the living? I've seen some crazy things down near New Orleans that reminded me of you these last few days. Near death, talkin' in yer sleep, looking like yer eyes were open even though you were unconscious. If I didn't know any better, I'd say you were a voodoo witch doctor."

Captain Hennessy looked me cold in the eyes. Mac stopped and turned to look at me as well. I looked to one, and then the other, not understanding a word that was just said.

"BWAHAHAAA!" Captain Hennessy laughed. "Son, I'm only funnin' ya."

He continued to laugh, but I noticed at the same time Mac was not laughing at all. Only looking at me, or should I say, looking through me.

"Captain Hennessy, sir, where are we going?" I questioned.

"St. Louis, then south," he replied. "Where were you going?"

I hesitated and then told a partial truth. "I was heading to see my Uncle when I got caught up in the storm."

Captain Hennessy looked at me. A stern change took over his face. "You a run-a-way, boy?" he said.

I looked back at him and answered, "No sir. Just had some bad luck and now here I am."

"Seems to me you had some good luck. If Mac over there hadn't pulled you out, the river would have swallowed you up. You'd be second helpings to the bottom feeders here in the 'Big Muddy' by now."

"I guess you're right."

I turned to speak to Mac.

"Thank you. You saved my life."

Mac didn't answer. He hardly acknowledged me at all. I turned back to the Captain.

"How much farther is it to St. Louis?"

"'Bout a day and a half. Grab some chow back inside."

He pointed to the cabin door.

"Room next to where you were sleepin' and take a load off. I may need you to be good and rested for tonight. Gettin' close to St. Louis is good, but that also means we need to keep a watchful eye. Many a folk may decide they want what we got, even though we ain't got nuthin' at the moment."

His stern look now faded. He spoke in an even tone, watching the river all the while.

As I walked through the door, I glanced out over the water. The mist had risen, and the sun now began to stretch across the water. Thinking about what the Captain said, I stepped inside and shut the door. Instantly it hit me. River Pirates!

CHAPTER 5

I spent part of the day listening to stories Captain Hennessy told about his travels up and down the river. I watched Mac as he guided our way. He hummed as he worked. Delilah had a rudder in the back that was connected to a wheel with handles on either side. Captain Hennessy would turn the wheel one direction or the other when we needed a little more deliberate navigation but would otherwise leave it straight and harnessed in place while Mac kept us on course.

The breeze was light, and with summer approaching, there was a hint of warmth in the air. My fever had broken during the night and, except for the bruising and gash to my side, I was beginning to feel much better. A dragonfly swooped by, pausing mid-air to scan its immediate horizon, briefly looking at me. The colors on its small body glistened in the sunlight. It flew off, disappearing into the reeds that lined the shore.

I explored the boat from back to front. It was mostly empty of cargo but had room to transport plenty. Along one side was a wooden platform jutting out over the water. A burlap tarp that hung down from either side concealed what was beneath. Leaning over, I could barely reach the far side of the platform with my outstretched fingers. It was as long as I am tall and seemed to be a structural part of the boat, but not one that I could figure out.

"Come on up here, boy," Captain Hennessy called.

I jumped, fearing that I had overstepped the boundaries of what I could and couldn't do onboard. I walked to the bow where Captain Hennessy was standing, still wondering what lay beneath the tarps.

Captain Hennessy showed me how to act as the "spotter". The spotter's job was like a leadsman on a steamboat, though I wasn't in charge of any lines. I was to look for changes in the water, to keep an eye down river for current flow deviations, floating debris, and oncoming vessels. Finally, I had to scan the shoreline for signs of life or suspicious activity.

"You tell me if you see anythin' outta the ordinary, okay?" he said.

This was a job I could do. Sitting with my legs straddled over the bow of the boat, I spent the first few hours very engaged, making sure I paid attention to every detail. The way the water danced past the bow, how the trees swayed slightly in the breeze. I listened to the birds chirp back and forth, almost arguing at times. I gazed down river looking for anything and took in everything. I had never experienced my surroundings more than I did today. It was hypnotic.

I flashed back to the farm—the fight, the harsh words rolling off my father's lips, my brother walking towards the group of men surrounding him. His hand slowly rising, his fingers outstretched for my brother to stop, never once looking directly at him. I lay beneath the porch boards to our house. Childlike, I hid, too scared to move, too young to know better. The men around my father sneered at him as they drew their weapons. My eyes opened wide. A cold chill ran through my body, freezing any movements I wanted to make, and instantly, I screamed, "PA!"

He looked in my direction, knowing exactly where I was. Turning to my brother he yelled, "Get outta here!"

My brother paused, not wanting to leave.

"NOW!" he yelled again.

That's when I heard the first blast. My body jolted as if I'd heard the deadly shot for the first time.

"You okay, son?" Captain Hennessy called out to me.

I had lapsed into an emotional trance, reliving the terrors of the last moments with my father and brother. Tears trailed down my cheeks. My eyes were blood red, stinging now. I wiped my nose with the sleeve of my shirt and looked at Captain Hennessy. I had no reply, just a sad, alone in this world feeling that poured through my body. Captain Hennessy stood up and walked over to me. I looked up at him, helpless.

"Go inside. Take a load off. We'll talk later."

He reached out his hand to me. His grip was strong, and his hands were rough. He pulled me to my feet. My bottom lip quivered but I was able to muster a scratchy reply. "Yessir."

Evening came, and I sat down with Captain Hennessy to discuss what he called my "current situation". I had no choice but to tell all. Captain Hennessy listened to me talk. He would nod his head, never once interrupting but kept constant eye contact. When I was done neither of us spoke a word. An empty air seeped into the room dividing what was past and what was now reality. I looked at Captain Hennessy. He stood up, walked to the backside of his chair, and looked back at me.

"Tomorrow we land in St. Louis. We'll get you cleaned up and put a new pair of shoes on yer feet. You'll need 'em if you plan to stay onboard. Or if you prefer, we could have a conversation with the local Marshal's office. I'm sure they'd have a plan to git you squared away somewheres. Up to you really," he said.

He turned to leave the room but stopped as I spoke up.

"Captain Hennessy? If it's all the same to you, I'd like to stay on a while."

His back was facing me, but his answer was clear. "A-yuh," was all he said.

I couldn't sleep. We pushed through the night to make St. Louis by mid-morning. I lay on the floor near the table where we ate. I was no longer privileged to the "Captain's Quarters" as it seemed I was now a deckhand myself. I could hear Captain Hennessy snoring. I figured he was catching a little shut eye while Mac saw to our course out on deck. It occurred to me that through all our conversation I was never once asked my name, nor did I provide it. Was it that important? I knew who he was. Mac never seemed to speak, at least not that I have heard yet, but I knew what to call him, too.

Mac. Where was he from? How did he get the scar on his face? He'd probably never say, but my imagination had already come up with several scenarios. He had saved my life, but I was still cautiously curious about him. Was he just following orders? I wanted to find out more about him.

It was a quiet night. Calm. The ride was smooth. All the daytime chatter of bugs and frogs, fish jumping, and birds chirping had given way to the solitude of night. I decided to go on deck and try to talk with Mac. It would be just us for a while at least. Captain Hennessy would be waking soon to see us the rest of the way in.

The floor creaked as I walked. His snoring continued as I opened the door to the main deck but was immediately muffled as I shut it behind me. The air smelled sweet. I took a deep breath through my nose. The night sky danced above me. I looked around deck but did not see Mac. He was not at his usual post. I had only taken a single step when I was grabbed from behind. A hand was brought over my mouth and held tight. I couldn't breathe. Out of the corner of my eye I could see the steel blade of a cutlass slowly being brought over my shoulder. I was frozen with fear. The blade touched my cheek but did not leave its mark. Instead it continued, slowly moving out beyond my face.

Wake up Captain Hennessy, I thought.

Once again, my surroundings had gotten the best of me. "Always have a watchful eye," Captain Hennessy had said during the day as I practiced my spotting duties. But now? What was happening?

"Look."

This word was whispered into my ear.

"Look 'dare."

With one hand still pressed firmly across my mouth, the other holding the blade now pointed downriver towards the opposite shoreline. I looked past the end of the blade and saw the shadows of the trees swaying from shore. Nothing unusual stood out at first. As

I continued to scan the shadows, I saw what resembled a small skiff. Then I saw a second skiff moving along the shoreline away from us. Just beyond that, a dull glow was coming from shore.

"Dis be a bad ting."

It was Mac.

The first skiff had caught up to the second now and I could see three to four men on each. One man jumped to shore, anchoring the skiff while the others quietly waited. As if they had been counting the time, the entire gang of shadowy figures leapt ashore and charged towards the glow. Shots rang out. I could hear screams. The light from the glow flashed back and forth as bodies blocked its path from my sight. More shots were fired.

Captain Hennessy charged through the door behind us. Mac let go of me and turned to catch the Captain before he made any sounds loud enough to give away our position. He carried a long rifle in his hands but quickly regrouped himself as he and Mac came together. Mac turned back to me, placed his hand on my shoulder, and gently pressed down. We all crouched near the deck of Delilah barely making a sound. Mac had an intense look of concentration on his face. Captain Hennessy had a similar look, but also seemed to be planning our next move at the same time. We floated quietly along as the barrage of carnage continued onshore. A final shot rang out followed by grunts and cheers. A murderous victory was being celebrated as we floated safely by.

Captain Hennessy moved to the stern of the boat and continued monitoring the scene while Mac returned to his usual post. Instead of guiding though, he quietly helped propel us down river, quickening our pace by driving his push pole deep into the shallows and pulling it out again, repeating this until we were at a safe distance. Captain Hennessy returned to the bow, said something to Mac, and then walked over to me.

"River Pirates. We were lucky," he said.

He turned and walked to mid ship and looked out over the mysterious platform. A small nod of approval and a pat of his hand on the side of the boat suggested that he was satisfied, but with what? He returned to the bow and stood by Mac. Still holding the rifle in his hand, he said nothing. Mac continued his strokes at the water.

It'll be a long night for all of us, I thought. I sat down right where I was and leaned against the side of the cabin. A barrel blocked my view of the river to my right. I looked up at the sky again. The moon had started to rise. It was as if it had waited for us to get out of harm's way before making its arrival. Moonlight bounced on the water in front of us now. I closed my eyes and let out a sigh of relief. I didn't sleep. We would be in St. Louis soon, or so I hoped. I was ready for a new day. A new beginning.

CHAPTER 6

It was mid-August. Three years had come and gone since Captain Hennessy and Mac pulled me from the river. Sweat dripped from my forehead and ran down my nose. I had just finished securing the last of the cargo boxes we'd picked up in New Orleans. Captain Hennessy chatted with the wharf master while Mac prepared to shove off. This was by far the biggest load we had taken to date. Our cargo consisted of silks and furs from Europe, and uncut leather from Texas. We also secretly carried four barrels of gun powder and a two-pound canon. This made our voyage more hazardous, more desirable to hijack if word got to the wrong folks. Captain Hennessy had also added a new man to our crew. Pierre Lefevre.

It was not uncommon for us to pick up an extra hand or two when we headed upriver. Captain Hennessy had many connections and usually picked up help through someone he knew. Pierre was different. He had sought out the captain, looking to travel north. He was a loner, but they typically are. Pierre was a younger man, probably 23 or 24. He had a rough, unshaven face, but was considerably fond of his mustache. It was long and black, and it stuck out from his face on either side of his nose. He was a bit taller than me and seemed to instantly show his self-serving superiority, barking at me to do things, and always calling me, "z leettle boy".

Captain Hennessy returned to Delilah and gave the order to shove off.

"Upriver men!
Our fortune awaits around the bend.
The current will fight, we'll push through the night,
To your posts! Upriver men!"

Captain Hennessy smiled as he gazed upon our path.

Traveling against the current was hard work, but my excitement for the journey strengthened me every time. In addition to long oars placed at mid-ship, Delilah was equipped with a secret—a side-paddle wheel. Captain Hennessy always concealed this addition to Delilah when traveling with the current and whenever we were close to port. He waited to use it until we were on our way, out of sight from the dock's view. Captain Hennessy never threw caution to the wind and would always "keep a watchful eye" for this addition was a one of a kind on keelboats. Originally, the paddle wheel powered larger boats that steamed up and down the Mississippi from city to city, transporting travelers, gamblers, and goods. They moved rather slowly for their size, which made Captain Hennessy's design so unique. In smooth water we could catch and pass almost any larger steam powered paddle wheel on the river and could best just about any other river pilot trading and selling goods. Covered with a canvas tarp, the side paddle wheel sparked my curiosity when I first came onboard Delilah. I was sure it was a cannon or a weapon, placed to help defend the ship if attacked. As I remained onboard and learned my way about the river, I found out just how valuable it was.

With Pierre on the starboard oar and me on the port, we pulled at the water. Mac stood in front, manning the push pole. I never was sure what to call it but figured that was how Mac used it. We hadn't gotten very far on the first day when I had made my mind up about Pierre.

"Zis weather iz terrible! Zo hot!" complained Pierre.

No one answered. Mac turned slightly towards me, and I could see that he was grinning.

As we made our way upriver, Captain Hennessy walked from bow to stern, inspecting the load, grunting to himself as he inspected each tie and strap. He returned to the bow of the boat, pulled out his looking glass, inspected the horizon, and then scanned the shoreline on each side of the river. Satisfied, he turned to me.

"How we doin'?" he said.

"Good, Captain," I answered.

Pierre huffed and wiped his brow. Captain Hennessy walked over to Mac and spoke quietly with him. After a brief moment, he turned and said, "Let's fire up the boiler and let Delilah do some of the work."

I smiled. Pierre was unfamiliar with Delilah and had no idea what the Captain meant. Mac disappeared inside the main cabin. A few moments later we heard a chug and hum followed by a black smoke trail that drifted up from a concealed exhaust port in the mechanical cabin.

"Yeah!" I hollered.

Captain Hennessy smiled.

"If our luck holds out and the weather is good, we should

make St. Louis by Sunday after next."

Mac, Pierre, and I took shifts on the oars while the captain navigated our path from the steering column as we chugged and stroked our way upriver.

Captain Hennessy was always quick to estimate our arrival, but mostly overshot the mark every time. I think it was his way of raising our morale when he could say we were ahead of schedule. We made good time that first day after leaving New Orleans. Twilight started to settle in, and you could see the fading sun setting in the west. At the same time, night pushed its way upon us. A purple glow spilled off the horizon to the east and flooded its way across the sky. The heavens twinkled above, and the moon's reflection slowly appeared in the rippling water. It was a peaceful evening. Fireflies chased one another near shore. A beaver slipped into the water and swam parallel to us for a while. I caught myself counting the lights in the sky. Stars. Tons of 'em. And then, Pierre spoke out.

"Hey leetle boy! Why don't you jump een a catch zat beevare? Would be a uzeful thing." Pierre lifted his nose and twirled his mustache.

I could tell he was fishing for a response. I gave him none.

"Ju not know how to sweem? Iz too bad. Such a leetle boy."

I had been on the Delilah for three years and three months. I had met and worked with plenty of crewman while onboard. Some were rougher than others. Some were funny, and some were quiet. One even challenged me to a fight, but Captain Hennessy had stepped in before any rough housing began. Pierre was definitely in a class of his own, and I had a feeling that things were going to get worse.

CHAPTER 7

Delilah chugged into the night until Captain Hennessey gave the order to man the lines. We tied up in a familiar stretch of river, ate a late supper, and listened to the captain talk about his time on the water. I enjoyed hearing his stories even though I had heard some of them more than once. Mac was indifferent mainly because he was part of most of them. Pierre on the other hand rolled his eyes and pushed his bonnet down over his forehead, lying down on the deck. When the stories were all told out, Captain Hennessy stood up and looked out over the water.

"One done, more to go, the days, just like the river flow." His words were poetically captivating.

He was content on the water. In fact, we never stayed more than a night or two on shore. He turned and looked at Mac and me. Pierre was still lying on the deck. Sleeping or not, he reminded me of a drunken sailor passed out from a long night of drinking at the saloon. Useless. He was going to be "leetle" help tonight.

I volunteered to take first watch. Each crewman, captain included, would stay up for a time keeping an eye on Delilah and on the river. All the lanterns were extinguished. The captain kept a long gun on deck, but we hardly ever carried it as we surveyed our surroundings. It was better not to move at all. Sounds carried up and down river and it was to our advantage to be still, look, and listen.

I was halfway through my shift when I began to hear voices in the distance. *Is that singing?* I wondered. Although it was faint, I could hear a small group, maybe a family, singing, but the words did not make any sense to me.

"Past the water, following the moonlight son,
Along the water and you'll soon be home."

They repeated these words over and over. At first the group sang together, then taking turns, it sounded like a woman would sing, and then a man. I thought I heard children at one point. The singing lasted only a short time. The last echo of a man's voice trailed off melodiously with the breeze and they were gone.

Mac relieved me shortly after and I went inside to lie down. Closing my eyes those words rang in my head.

Past the water...you'll soon be home. Past the water...
you'll soon be home. Past the water and I'll soon be home.

I hummed the tune as I trailed off to sleep. My body needed the rest.

CHAPTER 8

We made good time each day but my patience for Pierre was dwindling. I'd had about enough of "leetle boy" and was about ready to show him how "leetle" I wasn't! Captain Hennessy seemed aware of my growing frustration but never intervened. I had grown with him and before him these past years, and although he would never replace my father, I looked up to him. My responsibilities had increased. His trust in me was measured by my abilities to follow through, produce, and not give in when things were tough, or times were bad.

What are you?

It seemed now I was being challenged to take care of myself. To stand up, make good decisions, and when appropriate, defend myself as I see fit. Captain Hennessy could see it, whether he would admit it or not, but I was becoming a man. Not quite 17, but a man, nonetheless. The river that almost killed me, that taunted me, was now the very thing that strengthened me. Each stroke of the oar, each pull of the line, every current that pushed at me sculpted my body, mind, and spirit. My legs grew strong. My arms and chest were solid, though not nearly as muscular as Mac. My awareness was sharp and focused. I was thirsty for knowledge. Captain Hennessy taught me the ways of the river. For now, that was my world.

I learned to read when I was younger, mainly because my father said that my mother would have wanted it. I devoted some time to reading each day but didn't have much of a selection to choose from. A couple of old schoolbooks that Captain Hennessy picked up a while back, along with a tattered bible he kept onboard, were my only choices. Occasionally I would find a newspaper near the docks after we finished loading and unloading cargo. I kept it rolled up in my back pocket, but unfortunately the ink would often smudge or get wet as I worked, so they never lasted very long.

All this time, and now it seemed my next step was to prove myself by standing up to Pierre? Was he worth it? I was about to find out.

It happened two days before we arrived in St. Louis. Mac had just secured the boat to an outcropping of trees near shore and I was stowing the oars for the night. Pierre was leaning against the railing, spitting into the water as I walked by.

"Go an' fetch me sum watare, leetle boy. I am thirstee."

"Fetch it yourself," I replied and continued past him.

Without turning around, he stuck out his left foot, tangling my feet beneath me. Trying to catch my balance I let go of the oars and found myself crashing to the deck. One oar bounced on the deck and slammed into my face just below my left eye. Blood gushed from my cheek. The other oar flew forward, ricochet off the arm rail, and slid into the water. I scrambled towards the edge trying to grasp it before it floated down stream.

"Look! Even now z leetle boy crawls like a babe." Pierre burst out laughing.

I was done! I turned on my knees towards Pierre, pushed up with my feet and charged. With my head and shoulders aiming low, I struck Pierre in the gut, knocking him off his feet. We landed side by side on the deck, but I was too fast. I leapt on top of him, pinned his left arm with my knee, and punched him in the face just below his right eye. My knuckles popped. Pierre grabbed my right shoulder and pulled me towards him, butting me with his head. Dazed for a moment, I lost my grip on him. Pierre stood up and quickly kicked me in my side. I landed against the cabin wall with a thud. He came again, but this time I caught his foot mid kick and twisted him to the ground. I stood quickly as did he. We were both soaked with sweat, our faces bleeding. By this time, Captain Hennessy and Mac heard the commotion and quickly crossed ship to us. Mac took a step to intervene, but Captain Hennessy held him back.

"They need to work this out once and fer all," he whispered.

Facing each other, I wiped the front of my face with my arm. Bloody sweat dripped from my wrist.

"Ju a tough guy, eh?" Pierre chided. "Le'ss juss zee how tough you are!"

Pulling a knife from his belt, he charged, stabbing at my chest. I quickly moved aside, the blade barely missing its mark. Pierre turned and lunged again. I caught his arm mid-air, and we wrestled to the side of the boat. The arm rail braced my stance but dug into my ribcage. Pierre smelled. His breath was hot against my face.

"Nutting but a…"

I wasn't about to let him finish. A surge of adrenaline welled up inside me. I brought my left knee up swiftly, landing a massive impact between his legs. Pierre howled and staggered back. I wasn't finished though. Still grasping his arm, I slammed it down against the rail. The force of the blow dislodged the knife from Pierre's hand sending it splashing to the murky waters of the Mississippi. I let go of his arm and faced Pierre. I landed a quick punch to his chest followed by a final jab to the bridge of his nose. Blood poured from his nostrils as he collapsed to the deck. I hovered over him like a lion guarding my kill. Waiting. Breathing heavily. Bleeding.

"Enough," Captain Hennessy shouted.

I turned to see him standing with Mac only a few feet away. I stepped away from the scene. My eye was throbbing. My knuckles were sore. The energy I expelled on this battle was now exhausted. Captain Hennessy walked up to me.

"You okay?"

"Yes, sir. I was only—"

He cut me off. "Later," was all he said.

Mac leaned over the rail and looked for the lost oar. It was nowhere to be seen. Shaking his head, he quietly walked to the stern of the ship, checking the load and continuing his duties. Captain Hennessy walked over to Pierre. Pierre sat on the deck, his left hand covered his nose.

"Get up," he said to Pierre. "We land in St. Louis in two days. This is the last of the rough housing onboard. Do your job, and you'll get paid when we arrive as promised. Pull a knife on anyone onboard again, well, I'll shoot ya myself and feed ya to the river. Hear me?"

Pierre grunted as he stood. Blood dripped from his mustache. Beads of sweat covered his brow and slid down his cheeks. A red lump had formed on his forehead where he had butted me. He was a mess.

"Go clean up and finish yer duties. Now!"

Captain Hennessy turned and walked to his captain's chair by the steering column and sat down.

The rest of the evening was uneventful. Pierre and I kept our distance, but I could hear him mutter something in French when I walked past with Mac to get something to eat. I talked briefly with the captain just after dark. He stood at his usual spot at the bow of Delilah, looking out over the water. I wanted to explain my side of the situation. As always, Captain Hennessy listened without interrupting.

When I finished, he responded, "You've always had a smart way about ya. Yer quick to learn and hardly ever complain. Till now I can't recall you ever fightin' a man. Ya use yer head an' mostly that's the best thing to do. But there comes a time when a man will find it necessary to take a stand, either for himself or for someone else. Pick yer battles, don't let 'em pick you. Once ya commit, see it to the end and make sure that ya leave a mark of remembrance so that it is known that you are not to be taken lightly."

He looked at me as a father might look at his son. Was he proud? Disappointed? I couldn't exactly tell, but I knew that I had done the right thing. I thanked him and headed off to my bunk. I had the third watch tonight and wanted to get as much rest as I could. As

I turned to walk away Captain Hennessy said one more thing, something that stuck like mud on a boot that would never let go.

"Ya sure were a rowdy fella today."

I turned to look at him.

"Rowdy. Heh-heh."

"Night Captain," I said.

He nodded and turned back to the rail once again. Looking upriver, I heard Captain Hennessy whisper one last thing as I walked away.

"That's my boy… Rowdy."

CHAPTER 9

I woke up with a start, realizing that it was past my time to watch over Delilah. I quickly, but quietly readied myself and made my way on deck. Mac took the first watch and Pierre was assigned the second. Captain Hennessy's rhythmic snoring disappeared behind the cabin door as it closed behind me. Everything was quiet. I slowly walked a few steps away from the door, looking towards the watch post. Pierre wasn't there. I looked down one side of Delilah and then the other for him, but I could not find him anywhere. Pierre was gone.

A lost man could mean several things—abandonment, capture, or accident. Any of these were viable scenarios. I searched the boat for signs of trouble. Pacing up and down deck, I whispered, "Pierre?"

No answer. In fact, there was no noise at all. The river was exceptionally quiet. I looked to shore but nothing gave me cause for concern. As I returned to the cabin door, I realized that the watchman's rifle was missing. I looked around cautiously and noticed the port side lantern was missing as well. It was clear to me that Pierre had jumped ship. Scanning the shadows along the banks of the Mississippi gave no clue as to which way Pierre was headed, if he was on land at all.

"Okay," I said to myself. "What now?"

Waking Captain Hennessy was my only option. I quietly stepped back inside and tapped on his door. I could hear grunts coming from inside his room followed by footsteps leading up to the door. The door creaked open halfway.

"What is it?" he said groggily

"Pierre is gone, sir. I've looked everywhere for him," I answered

"Are you sure?" Captain Hennessy was still fighting an unexpected rousting and let out a large yawn.

"There's more. The watchman's rifle and a lantern are also missing. He must have taken them and left sometime during his shift."

I was concerned with Pierre's motive for leaving. My initial thought was that he'd had enough and jumped when he saw his chance. On the other hand, was it impossible to believe that he was watching us from shore, waiting to fire upon all of us? He could have killed us in our sleep, but I don't think that would have satisfied him. He would want to see us scurry around deck to figure out what had happened. To see us sweat. Maybe even fire a few rounds off. Either way, we had to be ready. He had a gun and we were sitting ducks out here on the water. Pierre loved to manipulate and would relish the chance to back all of us into a corner.

"Wake Mac and meet me on deck," Captain Hennessy ordered.

He shut the door as I stood there. Looking down the short hall, I noticed the door leading outside swayed back and forth slightly.

I closed that, didn't I?

The hairs on the back of my neck stood up. Moonlight peeked in and out of the doorway, playing hide and seek with my imagination.

"Pull it together. Go get Mac and meet up with the Captain," I told myself.

A few minutes later we were on deck. Captain Hennessy walked to the stern and looked towards the nearest shoreline. Mac inspected the main ties anchoring our position and I scanned the banks upriver. We were busy securing the ship and looking for signs of Pierre when Captain Hennessy spoke up, "Mac, untie us. We're gonna move upriver a bit."

I manned the only remaining oar while Mac worked on the long pole. Captain Hennessy stood at the bow of Delilah, both hands on the railing. No one spoke a word. We moved extremely slowly as we made our way along the shallows. Traveling so close to shore at night was dangerous because of our limited visibility. Shadows easily hid large rocks, low branches, and made the possibility of ambush by river pirates a treacherous reality, but we dared not challenge the middle of the river on one oar and a long pole. I focused on keeping my side of the boat pointed and heading in the right direction. I took turns facing the stern and then the bow. *Keep a watchful eye* resonated in my mind. Captain Hennessy had made it through some harrowing situations, according to his stories, and I have experienced a tense time or two, but now I felt very uneasy and had a bad feeling.

We kept our slow course through the night. The sky that was

once riddled with stars was now retreating from the forthcoming day. Orange and red painted the horizon. A hazy mist appeared over the water as the cool of the night met the warming breezes that flowed down river. I was tired. We all were tired, but we pushed on.

Daylight allowed us to move further away from shore, as Captain Hennessy decided to put the paddlewheel into action. We took short breaks and rotated the duties. There was still no sign of Pierre, but I couldn't help but feel that we were being watched. I squinted as sweat dripped into my eyes, mixing with the bloodshot sting of sleep deprivation.

The cool morning quickly turned hot and sticky. Beads of sweat rolled off Mac's head. Captain Hennessy wiped his brow with a handkerchief.

"Men," he said, "Today is the day; a day in which we see what we are truly made of. We're down a man, our load is heavy, we're fightin' the current and the uncertainty of what may lie around the next bend in the river, but I'll tell you this…we will make it through. We will rid this boat of all its treasures, we will pocket the profits, and we will celebrate a triumphant return to our home port. This day, we make it through."

Captain Hennessy stood tall at the center of Delilah. A surge of energy welled up inside me, overtaking the fatigue that was setting in. I was ready for the day, but unprepared for what was going to happen.

CHAPTER 10

We churned our way upriver at a steady pace for most of the day, stopping briefly to eat a late lunch. It was then that Captain Hennessy announced we would continue through the night. This was not a shock, as it is usually the captain's plan not to stop so close to our destination port. The closer we came to St. Louis, the more we encountered other vessels, and more activity could be seen on shore. Our guard was up.

Just as the day had arrived, evening pushed its way back into the fold. The air cooled and felt comforting to my face. Fireflies danced in the air amidst the blackening backdrop of night. The flap, splash of the paddlewheel rhythmically echoed along. Darkness covered us like a blanket. The moon had not yet risen. We snuffed out every lantern except one hanging from the bow of the boat. Its glow reflected off the river, making it appear as if we were gliding through fire. A bird sang out, then another. Mac looked towards shore, first upriver, then behind us.

"Mac, what is it?" I whispered across deck.

He didn't answer. Captain Hennessy looked at Mac, then to me, and picked up his long rifle.

The birds stopped singing. The rush of their wings and the

thrash of the branches where they were perched scratched at the night as they flew from cover with the first gun blast. Another shot rang out, its bullet whizzing by. Captain Hennessy ran to the steering column and pointed the boat away from the gunfire. Mac ran to my post and took over the oar, pulling at the water ferociously.

"The light," Captain Hennessy yelled to me.

I scrambled to the front of the ship and reached out for the lantern hanging over the bow of the boat. My hands fumbled with the handle as I released the lantern from its hook. Another shot rang out. The steel ball blasted from its offender pierced the water just in front of me. River sprayed across my face. I dropped the lantern into the water but caught a glimpse of a heavily manned skiff quickly gliding right at us.

"Captain," I screamed, "In front of us!"

I dove from where I was and slid to the middle of the deck. Shots rang out from over the water. Captain Hennessy returned fire in their direction. I could hear yells and grunts closing in but understood none of it.

Mac strained as he pulled at the water. I crawled close to the cabin as I felt the thud of the skiff crash against Delilah. Immediately two men jumped aboard and closed in on the captain. Mac dropped the oar on deck and ran to the captain's aid. The moon had begun to rise, revealing what the darkness had concealed. Mac charged and landed a heavy blow to the first man's jaw, sending him flailing to the ground. The second man sidestepped Mac and grabbed him around the neck. Veins bulged from Mac's forehead. They wrestled to the side of the boat. A third man jumped on board, but Captain

Hennessy was ready. He fired his long rifle and hit the pirate in the chest. He screamed out in pain. Blood oozed from a smoldering hole now burrowed in the middle of his body. He fell to his knees and collapsed. Another shot rang out, but this time it wasn't the captain. Mac had just thrust his elbow into his attacker's stomach when the bullet found him. Mac was shot. Blood streamed from his side. As he fell to his knees, laughter arose from the man he was fighting. Mac looked me in the eyes. Wide eyed, I glared back and watched in horror as he was shoved overboard. His body hit the water with a loud splash.

"Mac!" I cried out.

What Are YOU? echoed from inside.

In an instant I relived the final moments when I saw my father being killed. Hiding under the house, a child, too scared to do anything. I wasn't a child anymore. I jumped to my feet and clenched my fists. Tight. Rage had overtaken me. I charged at the pirate Mac had been fighting with. Lowering my shoulder, I slammed into the man's ribs. I could hear bones pop. Rising quickly, I rammed the back of my head into the pirate's jaw. Dazed, the pirate stepped back, allowing me enough room to land a blow to the bridge of his nose. My fist landed with such force that it broke his nose, twisting it to one side of his face. Unconscious, the pirate fell to the deck in a bloody heap. Two more men jumped onboard, one headed for the captain, the other towards me. I wasn't quick enough to dodge my next attacker. The club he was holding connected with my stomach, doubling me over. He swung at me again, hitting the middle of my back. I collapsed to the deck.

Captain Hennessy reloaded quickly, but not in time to take aim. Another pirate charged at the captain, dodging his rifle blast. Wood splintered and flew as Hennessey's last bullet pierced the deck. Everything happened so quickly. Three pirates were now on board. The first pirate Mac had hit pulled himself up by the railing. The second kicked me in the side as I curled up beneath him, and the third wrestled with Captain Hennessy, pulling at his rifle with one hand and swinging a knife at him with the other.

"Move an' yer dead!" my attacker yelled at me.

Turning, he ran towards the captain. Once again, he used his club, striking Captain Hennessy between his neck and his shoulder blade. The captain grunted loudly and fell, landing on the deck with a thud.

Lying on the hard, wooden deck, I raised my head to see one of the pirates reaching into the skiff. He pulled out a long gun with one hand and a torch with the other. Laughter and howls of victory rang out from the remaining pirates onboard. As one pirate struck a match to light the torch, I could see that he was wearing a red bonnet on his head. Pierre? It couldn't be. I looked again. As sure as I was lying here, that was Pierre's bonnet. I looked to the gun. It was the watchman's rifle.

Where was Pierre? I thought.

"Pick 'eem up," the man in the bonnet said. "I wan' to look 'een dis man's eyes."

Two pirates lifted Captain Hennessy off the deck and held him by each of his arms. He sagged between them. Still groggy from the blow he had received, he mustered enough strength to raise his

47

head and glared at his assailant. The torch's flame cast shadows across the outer cabin walls, enlarging the images of the pirates on board. Captain Hennessy noticed the bonnet as well.

"That's not yer hat yer wearin'," he said.

"You be right, ol' man. You can tank de man I git eet from. Toll me all 'bout dis boat and what you be carrin'."

I raised my head a bit when I heard this. Anger welled up inside, but I had no move to release it.

"Beeen watchin' you all day. Too bad for de man dough. Tol us everting we needed to know. Even brought us dis nice gun. When he finish, I tank him, welcome him eento our camp, an den I cut his throat."

"Pierre! You idiot," I whispered to myself.

"Now, we are here, and we take dis boat," the pirate said.

Captain Hennessy was helpless, but his bravery was apparent in his words.

"Sir, you only think you're taking this boat. I'll be damned if you will."

Captain Hennessy struggled to get his footing, but the pirates holding him were too strong.

"You be damned den. Throw heem over!" the pirate wearing Pierre's bonnet said.

One pirate let go of Captain Hennessy and punched him in the stomach. All the breath seemed to leave his lungs. He coughed relentlessly. Doubled over, the other dragged the captain to the edge of the boat.

"No!" I mustered.

Laughter soiled the air around me. Captain Hennessy was forced to the edge of Delilah. She rocked back and forth in the water with the waves, trying herself to save him.

"Goodbye, ol' man," the main pirate said.

As Captain Hennessy was about to be thrown into the river, the pirate with him let out a scream and fearfully looked at his foot as blood sprayed from a hole in the top of his boot. It was Mac! Somehow, he had held onto Delilah, or she had held on to him. He pulled himself up from the water with one hand and, using his entire body weight, had thrust his boot knife into the pirate's foot. Letting go of the captain, the pirate clutched his foot. Mac grabbed ahold of the pirate's other leg and pulled him down to the deck and was dragging him to the edge.

Stunned, the two remaining pirates paused in disbelief. Charged by this surprise attack, I fought off my own pain and sprang to my feet. I rushed at the pirate wearing Pierre's bonnet as the other engaged Mac. I slammed into the back of the pirate, knocking the bonnet from his head, the torch from his one hand, and the rifle from his other as we tumbled to the deck. We scrambled for the gun. Reaching it first, I slammed the butt of the rifle against the pirate's forehead, splitting it open. He fell again and grabbed his head, yelling out in pain. Darkness oozed between his fingers and rolled off his hand. His scalp bled profusely.

I turned to look for Captain Hennessy. He had fallen to the deck but was able to grab ahold of the other pirate by the knees. Tackling him, he held tight as the pirate tried to free himself. The pirate was too strong. He broke free from the Captain's grasp and

49

stood up. He was about to kick at him when I flipped the gun back and took aim. Holding it firmly to my shoulder, I fired, hitting the pirate in the chest. He wavered for a moment, his eyes bulging as he looked down at the hole in his midsection. Spit drooled from his lips. The pirate staggered forward and fell down dead.

Mac still held tightly to Delilah with one arm and beat the pirate with all he had with the other. Captain Hennessy got to his feet to help him. With a solid punch to the head and a swift kick of the captain's boot, the pirate was sent flying into the water, knife and all.

I ran to the side of Delilah and reached out to Mac. With all my remaining strength, I pulled him out of the water. He looked up at me. He coughed. His hand grabbed at his side. Blood seeped between his fingers.

"You're gonna be okay, Mac," I said, not really knowing if he would be or not.

"Dat was my best knife," he said out of breath.

Still moaning, the last remaining pirate lay on the deck of Delilah. The torch I had knocked from his hands had landed against the cabin and ignited the wooden slats. Flames shot higher as the fire spread from the torch to the walls of the boat. Smoke billowed to the sky. Ash sparkled in the moonlight.

"The barrels! The gunpowder!" Captain Hennessy yelled.

I got to my feet and raced with the captain to try and put out the fire. Using a tarp, we beat at the flames, slowing them but not extinguishing them fully. Flames were approaching one of the barrels of gunpowder. I ran to the barrel. I reached for my knife, but it wasn't there. I quickly began pulling and tugging at the knots on the ropes that held the barrels safely in place. I could feel the blaze coming towards me. Captain Hennessy pulled at the barrel. My fingers pinched the rope. Letting up, Captain Hennessy released enough slack in the line allowing me to untie the main knot holding the barrel. My fingers hurt, and the knot was tight. Finally done, the other ties slipped quickly apart, freeing the barrel from the ship. We rolled it safely away from the flames.

Mac was still lying where we left him, but the pirate whose head I had split open had gotten to his feet and ran at us like a mad man, his mouth wide open yelling a fierce battle cry. Flames reflected in his eyes as he charged. It looked as if the devil himself had come to finish this fight. Bypassing the captain, the pirate lunged at me, knocking me into the fire weakened cabin walls. We crashed through. The walls collapsed around us, the roof gave way, leaned towards the edge of the boat, and then fell overboard. Most of the remaining fire was extinguished by the collapse. Neither of us moved.

"Rowdy!" the captain yelled.

The weight of the collapsed walls pressed down on my chest. It was hard to breathe. One of my arms was pinned behind me while the other disappeared beneath a wall stud. I could feel moist skin against my fingers. I could hardly flex my hand. I was trapped on my back, but thankful to be alive. I heard the Captain's yell. I could feel him digging his way to me. Throwing board after board aside, he searched ferociously. Pulling the last board that covered me from the open air, Captain Hennessy freed me. He pulled me out of the tangled mess of wood and ash and hugged me tight. Stepping back, he let go of me. He looked at me as though I had been lost to him. He didn't say a word, but his eyes told me everything. We looked down and saw the pirate's still feet sticking out from beneath the remaining wood pile. Blood trickled between the slats and spread across the deck.

"We'll clean that mess up later," Captain Hennessy said.

I smiled.

We returned to Mac. I collapsed next to him. With his free hand he reached out and grabbed mine.

"Rowdee," he whispered. "Tank you."

During the attack, the paddle wheel had continued to churn until the cabin collapsed on top of me. We left a snakelike trail in the water, but now were starting to retreat with the current. Captain Hennessy made his way to the steering column and guided our way towards shore. We ran aground, and Captain Hennessy tied us securely to an overhanging tree. He returned to us and assessed Mac's injury.

"Tis bad," Mac said, holding a hand over his wound.

"Don't you worry now, Mac. You'll be just fine."

Captain Hennessy looked at me.

"Rowdy, can you manage getting something to cover Mac with? I'm gonna find some bandages to help stop this bleeding."

Captain Hennessy gently lifted Mac's hand to examine his wound. I slowly got up, my muscles stiff and aching. I looked around the boat for a blanket or tarp, anything at this point to cover Mac. It was dark, but I knew my way around Delilah.

I returned with the tarp from the paddlewheel to find Captain Hennessy packing Mac's wound with an expensive fur that we were hauling for sale. We covered Mac and sat on deck beside him. Captain Hennessy leaned back and hummed to himself. I looked out over the water. The moon was mid-sky and reflected its elongated image on the ripples of the Mississippi. The three of us remained where we were until morning.

CHAPTER 11

The sun rose to reveal extensive damage to the cabin and deck of Delilah, but luck had not deserted us completely.

"The skiff! The pirates' skiff! It's still moored alongside," I shouted.

We walked over to see that it had not dislodged during the battle.

"It's an ill wind that don't blow somebody good," claimed the captain. "We can make use of them oars. Little shorter'n than ours; they'll serve."

I hopped down into the skiff and handed them up.

"Rowdy, you take the starboard and I'll pull away at the port side."

Slowly, but surely, we limped upriver. Each pull took its toll on my body, but I was strengthened with the need to get us to port.

"Mac's lucky," Captain Hennessy said softly.

I looked over at Mac. He was asleep where we had left him.

"Bullet passed all the way through. Seems like it didn't hit any vitals."

"He's strong," I replied.

"He'll pull though if infection don't set in," said Hennessy.

"We'll make him set quiet for a spell."

"He won't like that," I said with concern.

Mac would indeed need luck on his side. Too many chances for an infection to find him on the river. We had to keep moving.

We reached the outskirts of St. Louis by mid-day. Seeing our crippled state, a local river pilot and his crew agreed to help us the rest of the way in. Captain Hennessy gave them two crates of silk as trade for helping us. He never did mention the barrels of gunpowder or the furs we had stowed. Upon our arrival, we were met by Major Bristol of Fort Sheridan and Jack LeRoy, the dock master.

"We'll be needin' the town Marshal, Mr. Dock Master," Captain Hennessy called out, "and, Major, you'll be glad to know your gunpowder survived our little fracas downriver."

The Dock Master sent a runner for the Marshal. We cut the ties that secured the gunpowder and unloaded the barrels. The Major was happy and paid handsomely. The dock master's runner returned with the town Marshal who whistled through his teeth when we showed him the bodies of the two dead pirates. He listened carefully to Captain Hennessy's account and nodded approvingly at the fate of the other pirates who had been forced overboard during the fight.

"We're well rid of 'em all," he said. "I'll dispose of these two bodies."

He turned to Mac. "You'd best let me take you up to see Doc Horn."

He frowned and pointed at the crude bandage covering Mac's wound.

"I 'spec I stay wit Ole Delilah an Cap' Hennessy, sir,"

"Suit yourself," the Marshal said to Mac.

He tipped his hat and returned to town.

I never asked the captain why we hadn't dumped those dead pirates into the river. The furs and silks and leather were in high demand and quickly made their way off Delilah and into the hands of dealers and sellers ready to double their investments. Our pockets hung heavy with gold and silver coins. This take was the biggest to date. Captain Hennessy was right, we made it through.

Looking back, selling Delilah was the right thing to do. Captain Hennessy shared his paddlewheel design with the river pilot that had pulled us in. He was fascinated by it. Captain Hennessy had a way with people. He dealt a crippled, burned out boat with one good paddlewheel and a questionable boiler to the river pilot and in exchange received the deed to a house just upriver with five acres of land and the best view a retiring captain could ask for.

"Are you gonna miss her, Captain?" I asked as we walked away. The captain looked at me, smiled, looked straight ahead and, raising his right fist, sang out.

"Upriver men!
Our fortune awaits around the bend.
The current will fight, we'll push through the night,
To your posts! Upriver men!"

I looked at him and we both laughed.

CHAPTER 12

A few days later, I approached Captain Hennessy, knots twisting in my stomach.

"I'm headin' west, Captain." I paused, wondering what he'd say.

He looked at me. A slight smile curved from the corner of his mouth.

"Bought myself a train ticket this mornin'. Guess I'm about ready to find out what's out there," I continued.

Captain Hennessey looked at his boots and then back at me.

"You're ready," he said. "You've become yer own man, Rowdy. I half expected you might look to move on."

He chuckled.

"Can't say that I blame you. Hell, if I was as young an' strong as you, I'd go with ya."

Captain Hennessy stood tall in front of me. Although he wasn't my father, he helped me become the man I am today. I had a deep respect for him. Not many a man would have taken me in, let alone take the risk to save me from that storm so many years ago. Yes, Captain Hennessy wasn't my father, but I loved him just the same.

Mac stayed on with the captain. I guess he planned to help him with his land or his next venture. They were connected, and my guess was that would always be the case. I had grown up with these two men. I spent time sweating, working, and fighting beside them, yet, I couldn't stay.

My bag was packed, my pockets were full, and I was set to go. As I said my goodbyes, Captain Hennessy handed me the watchman's rifle.

"Carry this with ya," he said.

I held it in front of me remembering the first time he showed me how to use it. And still, more recently when I had to use it.

"Thank you, Captain Hennessey."

He placed a hand on my shoulder and squeezed.

"Take care of yerself, Rowdy."

A train whistle called to me in the station in town. I smiled at him, shook his hand, and walked away. I was headed west, away from the river and into a new wilderness.

"Past the water, following the moonlight sun,
Along the water and I'll soon be home."

I sang this tune to myself, unsure of what lay ahead. Even so, I was ready for a new day, a new beginning.

INTERLUDE 1

It was mid-afternoon. The sun had finally broken through the sky, building a steamy atmosphere around the Circle 'R' ranch. Dog followed Roberson to the stalls of the barn while Rowdy made a few final preparations before leaving on their hunting excursion. Water dripped, rippling in muddy puddles around the base of the porch. The storm that so fiercely pounded them had now turned its vengeance in a different direction. In the distance, lightning flashed in jagged fragments across the sky. Rowdy stepped off the porch and headed into the barn to join Roberson. Mud clung to his boots.

"It'll be sloppy, but at least we'll cover some ground before nightfall," Rowdy said, entering the barn.

"It's about time." Roberson snuffed. "Huntin' don't get much better this time of year and I ain't gonna miss it."

Still annoyed by the delay of the storm, Roberson double-checked his pack and tightened the lead lines to his horse. Dog looked up at him and then walked over to Rowdy.

"Not this time, Dog," Rowdy said.

He reached down and scratched Dog on the head between the ears. Dog retreated to a swatch of hay and lay down. Rowdy walked up to Delilah, placed his hand on her hind leg and, rubbing her as he walked, made his way in front of her. Placing his hands on either side of Delilah's head, Rowdy rubbed her checks.

"Are you ready ol' girl? We're goin' for a ride," he whispered.

Delilah bucked her head gently and grunted her approval, seeming to say, *Let's get on with it.*

"I'm figurin' we'll make Snake River by nightfall. Be a good place to set up camp for tonight," Roberson said. He put a foot in the stirrup and mounted his horse. "You comin'?"

Rowdy looked up at Roberson.

Roberson offered half a sneer, kicked his feet, and yelled, "Giddya!"

He galloped out of the barn leaving a fresh trail of soggy hoof prints in his wake.

Shaking his head, Rowdy led Delilah outside by the reins. Sunlight poured down on the Circle R. A warm breeze brushed across Rowdy's face as he surveyed his surroundings. Dog would be fine for a couple days. There was enough feed in the corral to satisfy the three heifers there. One was carrying a calf but wouldn't give birth for a couple months. Only Roberson's wife knew where they were going, and she wouldn't tell a soul if anyone asked. A deserted ranch could spell trouble if the wrong sort of people came across that information.

Rowdy placed one foot in the stirrup and swung his other leg up and over Delilah. His leather saddle squeaked and stretched as he took his seat. Roberson was already at the edge of the Circle R and continued riding. Firmly grasping the reins, Rowdy gave a whistle.

"Walk on, girl," he said.

As Delilah trotted ahead in the direction of Roberson, Rowdy patted her neck. Images of her as a sickly, malnourished horse waiting for death as she quietly stood in the shadows of the Byrne Ranch flooded his mind. *Patrick Byrne*. He was a powerful, cruel, unconscionable man. He was a man who always had his way and yet Rowdy had given him reason to pause. He had stood toe to toe with Byrne—no fear, no backing down—and talked his way off the Byrne Ranch with Delilah by his side. It wouldn't be long before he and Byrne crossed paths again. Byrne didn't like him. No one stood up to him. Ever. Byrne aimed to see Rowdy pay for outwitting him. And pay he did.

Almost a year had passed since Rowdy was confronted by men sent by Byrne. He didn't pay much mind to the past but always had a feeling his business with him wasn't finished. Regardless, one thing was certain, Delilah was his.

"Byrne," Rowdy whispered to himself.

Delilah snorted. Rowdy leaned down to her.

"You remember, don't you?" he said.

Trotting forward to meet up with Roberson, Rowdy remembered. How could he forget?

CHAPTER 13

"Faster!" I yelled over my shoulder, "Run faster!" Jeb was behind me by a few steps and was out of breath. "Come on! Move it!" I yelled again.

"I can't. I can't do it," Jeb cried back.

I could see the fort. Its high walls, wooden turrets on every corner, and an American flag flying high above stood before us. I waved my arms in the air as we headed for the main gate. Two soldiers standing guard saw us and raised their guns. As we ran closer, I could see they were taking aim, but I could not hear what they were saying.

"Rowdy!" Jeb yelled.

I stopped and turned to see Jeb. He had stepped in a prairie dog burrow, twisting his leg. He lay on the ground, grabbing at his leg.

"Get up," I said.

Two more soldiers appeared atop the fort wall on the western most post, guns raised. Jeb remained where he was. I lunged for him. Grabbing the seat of his pants, I hoisted him up. We half ran, half stumbled towards the fort. Shots rang out. The report of the soldiers' rifles echoed. You could hear the *whiz* of bullets as they tore through the air past us.

"Whoa!" I yelled, my right hand waving, my left hand supporting Jeb as we fled. We dared not stop. One soldier lowered his rifle and motioned us to run in his direction. Shots rang out again, intercepting the small band of Indians behind us.

"Almost there," I panted.

I could hear the *Yips* and *Hollers* more clearly. I could feel the pounding of horse hooves as they closed the distance between us. Three more shots were fired at the small band of Indians charging towards us, this time hitting one and knocking him from his horse. The band pulled up, turned, and began retreating. We reached the gate. Jeb collapsed on the ground at the feet of one of the soldiers.

"Hold your fire!" was ordered from somewhere above us.

I looked back from where we had run. The injured Indian remounted his horse, glaring at the fort and the soldiers. He circled his horse never losing sight of us. He looked fierce. Black hair flowed over his shoulders. Three feathers dangled on one side of his stern face. Blood covered his left arm as it rested across his horses back. Snorting with anticipation, the horse stomped its feet at the dirt. Raising his right fist, the Indian let out a loud scream, reared his horse, and galloped after the others. A hazy dust trail lifted behind his withdrawal. I turned and looked at the soldiers. They looked back, emotionless. I stepped over to an exhausted Jeb and helped him to his feet. Beads of sweat rolled down my cheeks. We were dirty and tired, but we were alive.

"Got yerself in a bit of trouble there, boy? Huh?" one soldier suggested. "Civilians never know when to—"

"Hold that tongue, soldier!"

Each soldier stood at attention as a man in officer's attire walked over to us. He wore a blue Cavalry uniform and holstered a Remington Army revolver on his right hip. He walked with a slight limp. A lingering battle injury perhaps? He stopped in front of us. The shadow from his hat covered his face.

"I'm Colonel Lewis Forsythe. You two okay?" he asked.

"Yessir," I answered.

Jeb was still shaken up and paid more attention to the hilltops on the horizon than to our meeting with the Colonel.

"Corporal, bring these two to my office," he ordered.

He turned and walked back through the gates of the fort and disappeared.

We entered through the gates of the fort. A corral and stable stood off center to the yard. One lone horse stood tied to a post. Its eyes were wild and seemed to say, *Stay back if you know what's good for you.* A tall flagpole rose just beyond the corral supporting Ol' Glory. This was the center staging point for muster and was the most open part of the fort. The walls that surrounded us stood at least 20 feet high. The ends of each pole had been shaven to a nasty point, stabbing at the sky. We were led through the yard to a series of small buildings. A bunkhouse, a mess hall, an infirmary, and what I thought to be an armory. The door leading in was ajar and adorned with heavy padlocks. A guard stood just inside the door. I could see his silhouette through a small window as we walked by.

Jeb and I were led into a larger building and proceeded down a narrow hallway. We passed an open door that led into a meeting room and approached the door at the end of the hall. Our escort motioned for us to stop. He lightly tapped on the door, opened it, and went inside. He reappeared as quickly as he had gone and motioned for us to enter the room. Colonel Forsythe was sitting at his desk, reading a slip of paper. He wore steel rimmed glasses that sat on the edge of his nose.

"So," he said inquisitively.

He was still looking at the parchment when I spoke up.

"Sir, we were on our way to the Byrne Ranch when we ran into that small band of Indians. They were headed south when we saw 'em."

"Yeah, and we hid," Jeb said nervously. "But they saw us. And... it... it was too late. I ran. We ran. Here... to the Fort. You know? For help."

Both Col. Forsythe and I looked at Jeb. He wasn't looking at either of us as he spouted off.

"Calm down, son," the Colonel finally said.

Jeb gulped.

"If you would go on." The Colonel motioned at me to continue.

"Yes. Well there just wasn't enough time. They came over a small rise just south of Bunker's crossing and were basically right on top of us. I think we were both caught off guard because they didn't charge us right away. They were spread out a bit and by the time they turned to chase us, I had grabbed Jeb and took off running. I led us down into the culvert by Samson's Point. We ran along the bottom. There are lots of rocks and boulders down there. I figured it

65

might give us a little cover. When the culvert started to widen near Gander's creek, we climbed the far side and ran as fast as we could."

The Colonel looked at Jeb and then turned his glance back to me.

"Let me get this straight. You were heading to the Byrne Ranch, stumbled onto these Indians, and outran them? Here? With this kid slowin' you down the whole way?"

I looked over at Jeb. He was still visibly shaken up by our Indian 'run-in'. He had not heard a word of what Col. Forsythe had said. I looked back at the Colonel.

"Yessir." I paused, "Are we in trouble?"

"No, son, you're not in trouble. Your story impresses me. Not many civilians would have made it, especially your age. They'd either tried to fight and would have gotten killed or ran like you and would have gotten killed or captured. You displayed courage today, young man. And quick thinking too. That's not a skill many boys your age are able to harness. You did the right thing by coming here."

Col. Forsythe took off his glasses and placed them on his desk. A small, wooden table stood against the wall. A half bottle of whiskey with two sipping cups and a picture of a lady's face sat on top of it. His saber hung from a hook to his left and a crude map of Fort Dodge and Dodge City was nailed to the wall.

"Who is in the picture?" I asked.

He didn't respond. Instead he posed his own round of questions. Where did I live? Who did I work for? Why was I smack dab in the middle of the flattest piece of country on earth?

"Son, why don't you join up with the Cavalry? Seems to me

you have a good head on your shoulders and no one to tie you down. You could do some good for your country."

I sat there and realized I was politely being backed into a corner.

"Not sure the Army suits me, sir. Plus, I don't know how long I'm stayin' round here anyway," I carefully answered.

Col. Forsythe seemed like the kind of man you kept close. I didn't want to burn any bridges today.

Col. Forsythe rocked back and forth. Jeb shifted in his seat and nearly fell out of his chair.

"We've got to get back to town before too long. Mr. Shepherd will need me to restock the stove wood," I said.

"That's right, you work for the Blacksmith."

He brought all four legs of his chair to the floor.

"See that saber over there? Shepard hand crafted that for me just over a year ago."

Col. Forsythe stood up and took the saber from its hook, unsheathed it, and swung it around. The sound the blade made cutting the air was entertaining. I could tell the Colonel was trying to impress.

"Wow! Can I try?" Jeb asked excitedly. He had finally come around and was now watching the Colonel.

Realizing I wasn't going to be persuaded by flashy swords or exciting maneuvers, Col. Forsythe slid his sword back into its scabbard and returned it to the hook on the wall. Jeb slouched in disappointment.

Sitting down again, I could tell he still wasn't convinced that I had no intention of joining the troops at Fort Dodge. Had I committed to the Army, I was sure to be shipped off with the next regiment heading east for training and then who knows where after that. Fort Dodge was guarded by a mostly black company of soldiers, as they were the first to reoccupy the Fort after its desertion many years before and provided protection to Dodge City and its surroundings. Troops would pass through heading for New Mexico, Colorado, or even over the mountains to California and brought news, supplies, and newly trained, but mostly acquired, troops. Fort Dodge was even a muster point for the Army during their pursuit of renegade Apaches who terrorized farmers, ranchers, and towns all the way south to Mexico. And now that Dodge City was growing with the new railroad, Fort Dodge, along with Col. Forsythe, assisted the town Marshal as necessary. The local Marshal had about all he could handle in a town as tough as Dodge City, and that's saying nothing about Patrick Byrne.

Byrne, I thought. *I still have to get out to the Byrne Ranch.*

Jeb and I sat across from Col. Forsythe. An awkward silence loomed in the room as the conversation had gone dry. Jeb looked around, tapping his feet on the ground. Col. Forsythe reached for his glasses and placed them back on his face. He looked at me.

"Well," Forsythe finally broke the silence. "I have a supply wagon heading to town in about an hour. You can hitch a ride with them."

He wrote something down on a piece of parchment.

"Give this to the supply officer and he'll see to it you get back safely."

Thanking Col. Forsythe for helping us and for providing a safe ride back to town, we stood up to walk out the door.

"Remember, Fort Dodge is here to protect you. Heck, everyone in and around Dodge City. Come back and see me when you change your mind. We could use a man like you."

Jeb looked up at me. I nodded to the Colonel and walked out the door.

We waited for the supply cart near the corral. Jeb watched two soldiers try to break in a horse. One would hold the bit while the other jumped on its back. They made several unsuccessful attempts. Neither was extremely skillful at their present job, but I guessed they had to learn as they went. Jeb was fascinated with the soldiers. When it was time, I tapped him on the shoulder and told him to come with me to the supply wagon.

Our ride back to town was uneventful. The sun was low in the sky, but the heat of the day still lingered. I kept an eye on the horizon as we traveled, watching for Indians and thinking about getting out to the Byrne Ranch before it was too late.

CHAPTER 14

When I first came to Dodge City, I arrived by train. I was told that this was the "Gateway to the West". The pack on my back, the watchman's rifle, and a pocket bag of silver was all I had besides the four gold dollars Captain Hennessy gave me when I left St. Louis. I had a hollowed-out portion of my belt where I kept two of the dollars. The other two were secured in my boots, one in each. I never liked keeping all my money in one place.

I found work with the local blacksmith, Barrett Shepard, and learned quickly how to shoe horses, melt and reshape raw and old metals, as well as make new horseshoes and numerous fittings for saddles and bits. It was hard work, but I was no stranger to that. I lived in a spare room adjacent to the Blacksmith shop and worked most of the time. Mr. Shepard occasionally had me over for supper, but mostly I was on my own. I saved as much money as I could, not really knowing what I was going to use it for. It didn't amount to much, but I was content.

After work I would walk up one side of Dodge City and down the other. Excitement was never very far away. It simply depended on what kind of excitement you might be looking for. Cowboys and ranch hands, trail drivers and railroad men could be seen coming and going from local saloons and bath houses, sometimes alone, sometimes in packs. They were always looking to blow off steam. There was hardly a night that you didn't hear gunshots echoing down Main Street, sometimes in celebration, other times in retaliation.

The Marshal's office was in the center of town and was also a place frequented by many a man. One night in the tank was the usual routine for drunkards. Gunfighters, bank robbers, cattle thieves—you could find them all here mixed in with everyone else who were trying to make an honest living.

Dodge City was growing… Fast. The railroad had opened a whole new opportunity for buying, selling, and trading. Cattle were driven from all directions to be sold at market and shipped. New people were coming in every day. Patrick Byrne, a local rancher, had been instrumental in the railroad coming through to Dodge City. He was a powerful man around here. He always had enough money to put behind an idea. He also had the muscle. Some say he even had ties with a renegade Apache Indian tribe in Texas but no one, not even the Marshal, was willing to confront him about that.

One evening after I had finished my work and said goodnight to Mr. Shepard, I took my usual walk around town. There was more activity than usual. I quickly learned that a large cattle drive had just come in from Texas. The saloons were packed, and the train yard was bustling with commotion. You could hear the "mooing" and moving of cattle halfway across town. I came to the edge of the wooden walkway in front of the Main Street hotel and the Dodge City bank. It was here that I first met Jeb.

People walked up and down the boardwalk, but it was his running and yell for help that rose above the normal hustle and bustle. Jeb was being chased by two cowboys, both yelling for him to "come back here". As I watched the scene unfold, I noticed that he was barefoot and headed in my direction.

"Mister. Help me, Mister. Those men are gonna kill me!"

He ran straight up to me pleading. He was out of breath.

"Whoa, boy! Go on now," I said.

It was one thing to finish my own fight, but was I willing to stick my nose into somebody else's business? That usually meant more trouble than it was worth. Jeb jumped behind me. The two cowboys saw Jeb had stopped running and that he was using me for a human shield. I turned to Jeb. The fear in his eyes yearned for help.

"Please," he whispered, his bottom lips quivering.

I turned back around and faced the two cowboys.

"Step aside. This ain't none of yer concern."

The taller of the two men spoke to me in a low, raspy voice. His eyes were dark and wrinkled. He wore a brown bandana around his neck and a tattered cowboy hat. His face was unshaven with patches of stubble growing unevenly from ear to his chin. He was sweating, and his odor reminded me of the cattle yards by the railroad depot. The other man was short and stocky and smelled just as bad. I stood my ground, blocking their path to Jeb. He stared at Jeb with angry eyes.

"Didn't ya hear? Move aside," he said.

Pick yer battles.

I spoke up.

"I can hear just fine, but I don't feel like moving much at the moment. What's a kid like this done to get you all riled up anyway?"

Both men looked like they were ready to tear Jeb to pieces, and although I had no idea why, I felt a growing need to stay between them.

"Boy, this is none of your business, but yer about to find yerself knee deep in it if yer not careful," the shorter of the two chided.

"Knee deep?" I said. "Still be twice as tall as the likes of you."

"Watch that tongue of yours, boy. This is your last chance," he replied.

A crowd had begun to gather around us. I turned and looked at Jeb. He cowered behind me near a water trough.

"You want to go with them, kid?" I asked. "Or would you like to come with me?"

Jeb looked at me, shocked by my invitation but was quick to accept.

"You," he said, "I wanna go with you."

I turned back to the two cowboys and slowly moved my right leg back.

"Seems like the boy is coming with me. You two can go about your business."

"Big mistake, boy." The short, stocky man stepped to my right. I was smack dab in the middle of this now, like it or not. He charged, swinging his left fist at my face. I ducked. He missed his mark and stumbled off balance just enough for me to shove him at the taller cowboy. They tumbled to the ground.

"Get off me, Shorty," the taller cowboy griped.

They gathered themselves and prepared to attack again.

"Shorty?" I said.

He sneered and stepped towards me, fists in the air. The taller cowboy moved to my right and engaged as well. The crowd surrounded us on the walkway leaving no room for retreat.

Use your head, Rowdy.

The two men shared a glance and then charged together. Shorty grabbed me around my waist and lifted me off my feet. The other cowboy raised his fist but before he was able to land his punch, I raised my feet and kicked at his face. The heel of my boot connected with the bridge of his nose, crunching on impact. He fell backward into the crowd, his nose ruined by the heel of my boot. I brought my feet down, and Shorty let go. He punched at my ribcage from behind landing two quick blows. A stinging pain shot from my back to my stomach. I stumbled forward and turned around just in time to catch the brunt of a third punch to my mid-section. I stumbled back a few steps and doubled over.

"Had enough?" he spat at me.

Having caught my breath, I looked back at him, squinted my eyes, and smiled. "I can go all day… Shorty."

I lunged back driving my shoulder into his chest. He tumbled backward as I continued to push ahead. We came to the edge of the walkway and rammed against the railing that ran from the hitching post to the water trough. Shorty grunted at impact. I stepped

74

back and punched him in the jaw. Briefly stunned, he wobbled from the blow. I wanted to end this quickly. I grabbed his shirt and bandana and in one hard jolt, sent him flying off the walkway and into the water trough Jeb was hiding behind. He splashed about, sending water in every direction. The taller cowboy ran up behind me, but I turned in time to defend his approach. Our eyes locked on one another, my fists held high and ready to strike. Shorty struggled to get out of the water trough. Drying blood spread across the tall cowboy's upper lip from his nose to his ear. His hat had fallen off in the fight and was lying just behind him on the ground.

"Are we finished?"

I glared at my opponent, ready to defend and attack. He looked at me with a 'what the hell just happened' look and stepped back a step. Behind us, Shorty had finally gotten out of the trough and was standing, staring at both of us, dripping. The two men shared a look.

"For now, boy, but you better watch yer back," Shorty said angrily.

The taller cowboy leaned over to pick up his hat. I lowered my fists a bit but stayed ready. He brushed the dust from his hat and placed it on his head. Shorty walked over to him, whispered something, and then looked back at me.

"See ya soon," he said.

I was sure I would. They walked away and disappeared into the crowd of onlookers. I looked out beyond the walkway and saw Jeb. He had watched our fracas amongst the crowd. He stood still and alone as the street cleared. I walked out to him.

"Come on. Let's go git a bite and have a talk," I offered.

He smiled but said nothing. From that day, Jeb came to see me all the time at the Blacksmiths. As it turned out, his pa had worked for the Byrne Ranch and was in Texas overseeing a cattle run which was scheduled to come to Dodge City later this month. He never made it out of Texas. Word got back to Byrne that his entire crew had been ambushed by Indians, no survivors. Jeb, only twelve-years-old, was alone, as was I. He was in need and I just happened to be there.

Doin' right for yerself is good. Doin' right by others makes all the difference.

Something else Dad was right about. Captain Hennessy, too. Jeb looked up to me and I would do my best to be his friend.

CHAPTER 15

Our run-in with the Indians postponed my trip to the Byrne Ranch, but I was determined to get out there. Jeb heard they were going to put one of their horses down. It was weak, and everyone knew that Patrick Byrne only kept the best horses. He sold off those that weren't up to his standard and would easily shoot one than waste time and money on if it were the least bit weak or lame. Jeb said the ranch hands called it 'Canijo', which is Spanish for puny and weak. It was just a matter of time.

Working with the Blacksmith, I had learned how to shoe horses and prepare them for riding but did not have one myself. I figured when the opportunity presented itself, I would look into getting a horse of my own. It seemed to me that at the very least I should go out and take a look at the ill-fated horse at the Byrne Ranch. How bad could it be?

We arrived at the general store after leaving Fort Dodge. Jeb jumped off the wagon, landed in the dirt, and sent a plume of dust swirling about. I thanked the supply officers we were sent with and stepped off the back of the wagon. Jeb came with me to the Blacksmiths and stayed around while I worked.

"Did ya see the look on that Injuns face, Rowdy?" Jeb asked.

He had been mostly quiet since we left the fort, but I could tell he was ready to relive each detail, needing an explanation or assurance for each part of his retold story.

"He looked angry, didn't he? And did you see all that blood on his arm. It looked like he was painting his horse with it. I hope I don't ever see him again."

I continued with my duties as Jeb went on and on about the Indian and the chase and how he fell, almost dying. His embellishments grew as the story continued, but I guess it was good for him to get it out. People have a way of working through things that they do or that happen to them and this was Jeb's way of saying 'I'll make it.' Mr. Shepard came through the front door as Jeb was finishing his story and looked over to me.

"You been out to the fort today? What business did we have out there?" he asked.

"None Mr. Shepard. We were—"

"We were chased by Indians!" Jeb interrupted. "We almost got killed, or worse! That's what Col. Forsythe said."

"Forsythe?" Shepard replied.

"Yup," Jeb answered. "He wore a funny hat and had a sword, too. Said you made it."

"Jeb! Why don't you run on and I'll come get you tomorrow on the way?"

I looked at Jeb, more ordering him to leave than asking. He looked back and hopped down from the stool he was on.

"To the ranch?" he said and looked at me longing to stay.

"Yes, now I'll see you first thing in the morning."

"Okay, Rowdy. Don't forget."

Jeb burst out the front door of the Blacksmith's full of energy and revitalized from the day's events. The hinges creaked as the rusty door slapped closed. I could hear him yippin' and hollering like the Indians from earlier today as he went. That would be an adventuresome memory for him. I don't think he realized how much trouble we had been in and how lucky we were to make it to the fort.

I finished my work quietly, trying not to think about the day. Mr. Shepard did not question me any further either. He was not one to meddle in somebody else's business unless he could see it coming back at him. He only offered a small bit of advice before leaving to go home that evening.

"Be careful of Patrick Byrne. He's not one to be trusted, Rowdy. You'd do good to steer clear of him."

With that, he put on his hat and left. The door to the shop swung back and clanged against the door frame.

I could hear music coming from the Brubaker Saloon and could smell the train yard stench blow in. I decided not to take my usual stroll around town. Instead, I headed home to prepare a small meal of beans and dried venison. It was by no means a feast but quenched my need for refueling and helped me settle down a bit. I ate alone and went to bed early.

Sleep did not come easily. I was comfortable enough, but my mind raced. Jeb, the Indian, Col. Forsythe, Byrne, Mr. Shepard, round and round their images raced in front of me, each tugging at a different emotion, but all of which continually roused my state of consciousness. I tried sitting up. No good. I paced around the room.

Nothing. I laid back down and stuffed my pillow over my head. Nothing helped.

It was halfway to morning when I put on my boots and headed outside. The streets were empty. The saloons were quiet, and all but one light was out in the Main Street hotel. Dodge City was at its most peaceful moment. I leaned against the edge of the walkway and looked up at the western sky. The stars consumed me and took me briefly back to the river. Not just to my time with the Captain, but earlier, back to my first night on the river, alone and unsure of my future. I looked for comfort. Was someone watching over me? My father perhaps? I was much younger and scared then, but the same feeling crept its way back into me. Was I affected that much by the chase today? Did Col. Forsythe see something in me I was missing? Why had Mr. Shepard warned me about Byrne? Would I come across those Indians again?

The sound of a horse whiny snapped me out of my stargazing state. A lone rider slowly made his way down the middle of Main Street. I stood still and watched from the shadows. The rider sat low in the saddle, moving with his horse as they passed by. Never wavering from their direction, they sauntered on, disappearing into the night.

"Who was that?" I whispered to myself.

I decided to go back inside, but first looked down the street in the direction of the mysterious rider. The road was empty. A faint sheen of fog started to build towards the edge of town where the rider had gone. Hairs on the back of my neck stood up and an unsuspecting chill electrified my spine. Everything was too quiet for my liking. I slipped back inside, took off my boots, and peered back out to the street though a crack in the window shade.

"You're gonna spook yerself, Rowdy," I said to myself.

I stepped back from the window and lay back down on my bunk and shut my eyes. My mind raced less, and I was able to cut out all the randomly placed images, except one. Patrick Byrne. I had never met the man, but I could see him plain as day. He looked at me and smiled, shaking his head. A forceful look replaced the smile and his dark eyes glared at me. His mustache twitched to one side as he talked, although I had no idea what he was saying. Over and over the same scene repeated itself in my head. Then from out of nowhere, the dark rider rode in between us. His horse reared up and kicked its feet. The rider looked at me and I back at him. His face was too dark to see, as if guarded by shadows in mid-day. He pointed at me and then reached out.

I woke with a start, realizing I had been dreaming. So vivid a dream in such a short amount of time made me feel uneasy as I pondered its meaning. The sun had started to rise but was still below the horizon. Morning was breaking over Dodge City. I dressed, pulled on my boots, and headed out into the street still empty of travelers. I looked to the dirt. The dusty passage leading through the heart of Dodge City was as it was the night before. I looked for hoof prints where the mysterious rider had passed but found none. I walked twenty paces in either direction from the Blacksmiths but could not locate a single fresh track.

"What the…" I whispered.

I stood still for a moment and gazed towards the edge of town.

"I might regret this," I said.

I turned and headed for the Byrne Ranch.

CHAPTER 16

I arrived at Jeb's to find him sitting on the front porch of Ms. Compton's house ready to go. His feet dangled over the edge and swung back and forth. He hadn't been back to the Byrne Ranch much since news of his father made its way to Dodge City. He stayed with Ms. Compton, a widower with two younger boys. She knew Jeb's father before he died. When Byrne took over his father's stead, claiming he needed it more and that it would almost cover the cost of his losses from the cattle drive that saw his father killed, Ms. Compton took him in. Jeb had nowhere else to go. He stood as I approached and waved, grinning all the while.

"Mornin,' Rowdy."

"You ready, Jeb?"

"You bet!"

Jeb jumped down from the porch and in two large leaps, was at my side.

"Are we goin' the same way as yesterday? You think those Indians will be back?"

"We'll be fine, Jeb," I reassured him.

Ms. Compton stood in the window of the house looking at us. She was an older woman, stronger than you might expect, but was gentle and kind. She gave a small wave. I tipped my hat to her and we were off.

It didn't take long for us to get to the Byrne Ranch. We moved quickly and purposefully, keeping an eye out in every direction for signs of trouble. We made our way to the edge of the Byrne property where we were met by two riders. Jeb recognized one of them instantly.

"Hey Boone." Jeb waved his arms. "Rowdy, that's Boone."

The riders stopped in front of us.

"You know this boy, Boone?"

The two riders sat tall in their saddles.

Boone looked at Jeb and said, "You Hank Anderson's boy, ain't ya?"

"Yessir."

"Well, who are you then?" he said, looking at me.

My opportunity to answer was cut short, as usual, by Jeb's interjection.

"He's with me," he said, proudly pointing his right thumb to his chest.

I looked up at the riders and could tell their annoyance level was on the rise.

"My name's Rowdy," I said. "Heard you may have a horse that's bein' put down. I've come to offer to take it off Mr. Byrne's hands if he'd allow it."

Boone looked at the other rider who spoke up now.

"He means Canijo I bet. What you want with a sorry sack of a horse anyway? It's good fer nothin'."

"Well, sir, that's a good question, but I'll keep my business between me and Mr. Byrne though, if you don't mind."

Boone laughed out loud.

"Shoot. We got a business man here. Come on businessman. I'll take you to see Byrne."

The other rider hunched over in his saddle and stared at me.

"You may regret this, boy," he chortled.

Let's hope not, I thought.

He pulled on the reins of his horse and led the way to the main house. Ranch hands were everywhere. Tending cattle, preparing to brand new acquisitions, mending a broken fence beam on the corral, everyone was busy. Jeb ran over to the corral. He still knew his way around and felt right at home, forgetting all the while that we were uninvited. Boone dismounted and tied his horse to the hitching post at the front of the house.

"Wait here," he said and walked up the steps and through the front door.

I turned and scanned the ranch again. It was immense. The corral was to the left of the main ranch house and was shaped like a circle. It had a swinging gate on either side. One opened out into the yard while the other, smaller gate opened into a chute that led to a holding area just outside the barn. The barn had two levels with a sliding door on the top. The front had two large sliding doors. One door was opened slightly while the other was closed. To the right of the ranch house were two buildings that looked like the workers quarters. They were small and plain. Beyond that was a larger building and then the fence line. I looked back to the barn again and noticed a horse tied to the back corner of the building. It stood there alone with its head down. I took a step closer but stopped when I heard the door to the ranch house creak open.

Boone walked onto the porch and stepped to one side. Two other men followed, stepped off the porch, and stood in front of me. Patrick Byrne was the last man out the door. He stopped at the top step of the porch and looked down at me.

"What's yer business here, boy?"

He had a harsh tone in his voice.

"Mr. Byrne, I heard you have a horse that's of no use to you, to anyone actually. And that you were gonna have yer men, uh, take care of it."

"Take care of it? Hardly, it's not worth the effort." He squinted his eyes at me.

"I'd like to take it off yer hands if yer willing."

"Yer wastin' yer time, boy." His answer spilled down on me with a stench of rotten beans. "A bullet'll be the best thing for it."

I looked at Patrick Byrne, the big, powerful rancher who could just say the word and make something happen. Not this time though. I wouldn't let him.

"Seems like a waste of a bullet if you ask me. At the very least it'll be off your ranch and out of your way. It'd be my wasted time and my bullet, I guess, if I happen to agree with you."

I stood there watching Byrnes reaction to my counter. His mustache twitched. I could tell I had gotten to him.

"If YOU agree with ME?" He sniggered. "You either got guts, kid, or yer just one stupid cuss."

He looked over to Boone.

"You kill that nag of a horse yet?"

Boone shook his head and looked over to me.

"She's tied up next to the barn. Was gonna do her first thing after making rounds, but ran into these two on the way back in."

Jeb walked into the scene as Boone talked with Byrne. For once, he didn't say a word.

Byrne looked at Jeb, trying to place him, and then seemed to realize who he was. He stepped down from the porch and walked up close to me. We stood eye to eye. I could feel his breath on my face as he talked.

"I'm gonna give you a chance to make a big mistake, son."

"Rowdy. My name is, Rowdy," I boldly interrupted. "If you're suggesting meeting with you was a mistake, then I guess I've already made it. Otherwise, I believe I can live with the consequences."

I could tell Byrne was a little taken back by my interlude, but I stood tall and confident. Anything less and I'm sure he'd have me forcefully removed from his ranch with a couple firm reminders not to return.

He squinted his eyes again, trying to read my face. An uneasy pause in our conversation remained. I did not speak. I believe his mind was made up, but he was waiting for me to change it for him. I wasn't going to make it that easy.

We stood there looking at each other when he finally broke.

"Boone! Get this boy outta my sight," he said. "And send ol' Canijo with him."

I held back a huge smile but shared a quick glance at Jeb. He smiled for the both of us. Byrne turned, walked up the steps to the door of the ranch house without saying another word. The two men who had led him out now followed him back inside. Boone stepped off the porch and walked over to me.

"You better git that horse and move on before he changes his mind. Yer a wildcat, Rowdy and Mr. Byrne don't like wildcats. Says they break the herd."

Boone was right about one thing, I was ready to go. The visit had been brief but intense. He walked over to the barn and untied the horse. It followed as he led it back over to us. Jeb patted its side as Boone handed me the rope.

"Not sure if she's the lucky one or you," he said.

Boone turned and walked towards the ranch house.

"Hey, Boone."

He stopped and turned his head to me.

"Thanks," I said.

With that, he silently turned back towards the house, climbed the steps, and went inside. The door closed with a clang.

I looked at my horse. She was so skinny that her ribs stuck out from her middle and the ridge of her back was outlined by her spine. The hair on her hind legs was thin and her tail was a tangled mess. I put my hands on both sides of her cheeks and looked into her large black eyes.

"Are ya ready, ol' girl? We're goin' home."

She nuzzled her nose against my hands as I stroked her cheek.

"Come on, Jeb."

We walked through the front entrance of the Byrne Ranch and headed for Dodge City. I wanted to look back. I wanted to see if we were being watched. I had won this round and I would not readily seek out another encounter with Patrick Byrne. Maybe I should have listened to Mr. Shepard and left good enough alone, but on the other hand…I was my own man, growing more by the day, and in this case, by the minute.

"Watcha gonna call her," Jeb questioned as we walked back to town.

I thought for a moment and then realized there was only one name that would suit her—a name on which I learned about trust and fellowship, hard work and loyalty. I smiled as I answered. "Delilah. I'll call her Delilah."

CHAPTER 17

The bond that forms between an animal and its keeper is amazing. How they seem to know what you're feeling and thinking, Delilah was truly one of a kind. Six months passed since I walked her home from the Byrne Ranch. I paid for a spot at the stable next door to the Blacksmith shop which allowed me to spend a lot of much needed time with her and keep up with my responsibilities at work. Each morning, I would brush and feed her. When I had time to eat lunch, I would sit with her, sometimes sharing what I ate. We both looked forward to the evenings though. At first, I walked her up and down Main Street, late at night, gaining strength and trust with each outing. She ate well and gained weight quickly. Obviously fond of our nightly routine, she always greeted me with a nod of her head and a gentle whinny.

When she was strong enough to ride, I began looking for a saddle. Jeb told me that Ms. Compton had one and would ask if it was for sale. I visited with her and we agreed on a fair price. It fit Delilah perfectly. She did not seem to mind wearing it, and it wasn't too uncomfortable to sit on. The leather was worn but soft and flexible.

"That fits Delilah just as good as it did on my Pa's horse," Jeb commented one day.

"Your Pa?" I said.

"Yep. It was his," Jeb said with a smile.

I tried to give it back when I learned it had been his father's, but Jeb was adamant, saying that he wanted Delilah to have it. He didn't have a horse anyway.

Delilah and I went for rides every day, mostly around town at first. As her strength grew, I could sense her desire to let loose, but we took it slow and easy walking and trotting as we went.

CHAPTER 18

It was early Spring and the last of the snow had melted away. A hint of spring began to show itself in the trees in town. Wildflowers sprouted coloring the prairie in spotty patches. I was finishing my duties for the evening when the door to the Blacksmiths opened. In walked Boone. I hadn't seen him since I left the ranch with Delilah. I walked over to greet him but could tell by his look that he was not here for a blacksmith. I offered my hand anyway. Reluctantly he obliged my handshake. He had a strong grip but did not aggressively squeeze. He was here to talk.

"Rowdy," Boone said quietly. "Word is going around the ranch that you got that horse of yer's healthier than ever. Seems to be a fairly good horse after all."

I looked at Boone, wondering what his real motive for coming to see me was.

"She's doin' alright, I guess. Likes to eat and sleep."

I felt the need to leave out the fact that she had gained a great deal of strength and was actually doing extremely well.

"Listen, Rowdy, you've been seen around town. Mr. Byrne has already mentioned he may come after his horse."

His horse? I thought.

"I'm simply here to remind you not to be a wildcat. Byrne hates wildcats and would like nothing more than to spend a bullet on one that disrupts his herd. Get my meaning?" Boone spoke clearly and quietly.

This was obviously a warning, but why had he felt the need to come to me? Why not let things play out?

"Byrne doesn't know you're here, does he?" I questioned.

Boone looked at me. His posture changed. He stepped closer to me and spoke in a rough whisper. "If you know what's good for ya, you'll be smart about this. You don't know this, but Byrne almost had you and that horse shot as you were leaving the ranch. Was gonna say you stole it. Not exactly sure why he didn't, but he's been stewin' on it off'n on since. It wasn't just that you talked him out of the horse, it was how you did it. No one stands up to Byrne the way you did. You might have thought being tough would be respectable to a man like him. You only poured fuel on the fire, Rowdy. Sooner or later those flames are gonna get hotter. Last thing you need, or that Jeb and poor Ms. Compton needs, let alone anyone close to ya, is to be burned."

Would Byrne go that far? What would stop him?

As he turned to leave, I spoke up.

"I respect you for comin' in, Boone. Yer a good man."

He continued out the door. The wind closed it abruptly behind him. I turned to finish what I was doing when I saw Mr. Shepard standing just out of sight.

"Mr. Shepard, I—"

He cut me off.

"Rowdy, not one person in town wants a man like Patrick Byrne gunnin' for'em, especially me. I warned you not to get tangled up with him. Now, it seems that you've gotten on the wrong side of the wrong man."

I tried to speak up, but Shepard interrupted me again.

"I like you, Rowdy. You've done a good job here and I trust you. Now, I trust you to do right by me."

I couldn't believe what I was hearing. I looked at him. His face was firm, but his eyes wavered with a different emotion. I looked at him, understanding exactly what he meant.

"Leave," I said. "That's what yer asking of me."

He looked at me in silence, still standing in the shadows of the room. His lack of response was all the answer I needed. I took off the apron I was wearing, wadded it up, and placed it on the table next to me. My frustration began to grow, not so much with Mr. Shepard, but with Byrne. It was clear I was in his sights. What bothered me most was he had taken away any place I would turn to and did it solely with words and reputation. Now I had nowhere to go. I watched as the apron unraveled and fell to the floor. Delilah was mine, and no one, not even Patrick Byrne was going to change that. I would not unravel or be spooked into doing something I didn't want to. I bent down to pick up the apron again and spoke as I rose with it.

"Mr. Shepard, I understand. You do what you think is best. As for me, I refuse to lay down to any man that tries to tell me the ways things are. I'll pack and be on my way at first light."

"Rowdy, Patrick Byrne has this whole region under his belt.

If he wants something, he's not going to ask." With that, Shepard retreated out the back door.

"Maybe not," I said to myself. "But then again, no one ever told him he had to."

I left and went to the stables to see Delilah. She had grown from a horse condemned to die to apparently the most sought-after horse in Dodge City. She grunted and stomped her front feet gently with anticipation of our nightly ride. I reached out to rub her face. Her nose brushed against my palm as I raised my hand to her. Her large, dark eyes looked into mine.

"Things are changin', Delilah. Tomorrow we're gonna look for a new place to stay."

Delilah grunted again.

"Easy, girl, everything's alright."

Was it? My tough guy attitude spawned from the comments Shepard had made and the warning Boone had provide now yielded to a calmer and more collected side of me.

Be smart, Rowdy, resounded from within me. It was suddenly very clear to me where I had to go. If I wasn't going to leave Dodge City, I needed a place where Byrne couldn't touch us. Although he may try to track me down, even Patrick Byrne, self-proclaimed king of the Kansas ranchers, wouldn't step toe to toe with the U.S. government. I looked at Delilah again and whispered to her, "Tomorrow morning, we are going to see Col. Forsythe."

CHAPTER 19

It was a long night. My senses were wary of every sound, no matter how slight. Was I letting Byrne get to me? He did a good job of disrupting my current way of life, but was he getting to me? I decided to leave the one room shack of a bunk house I called home for the stables and Delilah. I packed what things I had, loaded my rifle, and prepared for the coming day. I wanted to get to the fort just as the sun was coming up. I was mentally prepared to handle trouble but was cautious none the less.

Always looking upriver.

I gathered my things and carried them out the door, kicking it closed with the heel of my boot as I left. I entered the stables quietly from the rear of the building. I was about to round the corner to Delilah's stall when I heard voices. There were two, maybe three men, slowly walking in my direction, but still halfway down the chutes.

"Which one is it," one raspy voice whispered.

"She-ut up and come on," the other man said, "It's just up here on the right."

Delilah's stall was the only one at this end of the stables and from their direction would have made hers the one on the right. And that voice? I recognized the voice but couldn't place it. I slowly set my things down on the ground and grasped my rifle. The men walked closer, finally stopping right in front of Delilah's stall

"Here she is, Buck," said the shorter of the two.

I know that voice, but from where? I raised my stance a bit to gain a better view. Looking between the slats of the wall I clearly saw two men. I didn't know the man called Buck but recognized the other instantly. It was Shorty. I hadn't seen him since I threw him in a watering trough the day I met Jeb.

"Get the rope ready," Shorty said to Buck.

This was my cue. I rounded the corner, rifle pulled firmly into my shoulder and pointing directly at the head of Shorty as I advanced on the two men.

"Are you sure you want to do that?" I said, now only a foot behind them.

Both men whirled around, caught off guard by my advancement. They stood in front of me, sizing me up.

"Here's what we're gonna do. Yer gonna drop the rope and step away from the stall real slow. Keep yer hands where I can see 'em."

I eyed each man like a hawk eyes it prey, the barrel of my rifle following their movements to the center of the stables.

"Do you know who yer messin' with?" Shorty said.

I stepped a bit closer giving him a clearer view of me.

"I know exactly who I'm messin' with. Do you?"

My hands were steady as was my aim.

"You," Shorty said. "I knewed you was dumb, kid, but now

97

you've dug yer own grave. Ain't no goin' back now."

Calmly, I changed my aim from the both of them to just Shorty again and stepped closer.

"There's only one of us that should be worrin' about their grave, and that's the man that steps one foot closer to that stall."

I looked at both men.

"Buck, is it?" I asked, my aim never wavering from Shorty.

"Piss off," he answered.

I let out a quiet laugh.

"Well, it's good to know I'm not dealin' with an educated man."

Buck was not amused by my comment.

"Why you—"

Shorty interrupted him, "Listen here, boy—"

"No! You listen. The last person that called me boy didn't end up so right, so I suggest you keep your mouth shut. Yer not runnin' the show here," I countered at Shorty.

"He ain't gonna shoot no one," Buck said, leaning closer to Shorty. "I got this."

With that, he reached for Shorty's holster and pulled his gun free. Things started moving in slow motion. Shorty's eyes bulged as he yelled, "NO!"

At the same time, Buck growled and raised Shorty's pistol. He wasn't fast enough. The click of the firing pin connecting with the firing mechanism in my rifle brought everything back to real time.

BLAM!

Buck was thrown backward, landing in the dusty walkway

of the stables. Shorty's pistol flew into a hay pile and disappeared beneath the straw. His arms sprawled out to either side, blood oozed from Buck's chest and dripped from the corners of his mouth. His left leg kicked out at the air. The boot from his right foot remained where he had been standing. Buck gasped for air, gurgling out to Shorty for help. A horse at the opposite end of the stables was spooked by the blast and kicked at its stall wildly. Smoke had barely escaped from the end of my barrel when my aim turned back to Shorty.

"Ain't no goin' back now," I said smoothly to Shorty.

He looked at me in disbelief. "Yer dead, kid," he stuttered. "Byrne is gonna chew you up and—"

BLAM!

Shorty grabbed at his head as the hat he had been wearing flew off, ripping to shreds in mid-air.

"JESUS!" he yelled.

"Yer gonna need more than Him to save you if I ever catch ya tryin' to get yer hands on my horse again. You tell Byrne that he needs to let this one go."

I stared at Shorty, wanting to shoot again. I felt myself start to squeeze the trigger. The hammer of my rifle began to slowly rear backwards into a ready position. Shorty's eyes opened wider and he put his hands in front of his body.

"Wait a minute," he said, almost pleading at this point.

"Would you?" I answered back.

I quickly advanced the short distance between the two of us, barrel raised and ready. I yelled, "AHHHH!"

Shorty flinched and cried, "Please!"

Releasing the trigger, I firmly grasp my weapon and struck Shorty on the side of the head with the metal barrel, sending him careening over. He landed with a portly thud and rolled over. He was out cold.

Looking around to see if our confrontation had roused anyone, I quickly made my way to Delilah, grabbing my pack on the way. She looked at me as I entered her stall and stamped her feet.

"Easy, girl," I said. "Are you ready to run?"

I gently stroked her cheek. Quickly, I readied her saddle and tightened the strap.

"There, all done."

Approving, she snorted as I climbed onto her back.

"Let's go, Delilah," I said.

We bolted from the stables and headed through Dodge City. The night was cool and still. A harvest moon illuminated Main Street, casting shadows from buildings throughout town. A light was on in the Marshal's office up ahead and I could see movement behind the windows. I pulled on the reins, stopping Delilah. I looked back to the west, past the stables and decided to ride in that direction. The fort was east of town, but I wasn't ready to go anywhere near the Marshal's office yet. I galloped westward, passing the Main Street Hotel, the bank and the Blacksmith. I looked through the still open door of the stables as I passed. My brief view gave me a heightened sense of caution. Lifeless, Buck remained, but Shorty had apparently recovered and was nowhere to be seen.

"Come, Delilah, let's pick it up a bit."

I nudged her ribs with my boot. We accelerated to the edge of town and proceeded off the main road and into the rough. The wind in my face felt exhilarating. Delilah's rhythmic gallop reminded me of a chugging steam engine making its way into port. We came to a rise just beyond the outskirts of town and slowed to a stop. Behind me I could see Dodge City. It slept dark and quiet, but I knew things would start to get riled up soon. Leave it to Shorty to get that rolling. In front of me lay the plains of Kansas with the mountains further beyond. For a moment I wanted to keep heading west, to make a run for it.

"No. Not yet," I said to myself.

I needed to get east of town before the sun came up. Surveying my position, I led Delilah north. We quietly made our way through the grasses and brush, startling a group of jackrabbits out for an early morning bite. We kept our distance from town but remained close enough to watch for anything out of the ordinary. As we approached the north rim and headed east, morning began to make its appearance. The sky in front of me changed colors as the sun announced its arrival. The dark, black of night faded to a purple haze, and then to an orange glow on the horizon. The stars overhead fled the brightening sky. I was hypnotized by my surroundings. This beautiful sunrise would soon shed light on a darkened stable. Delilah must have felt me easing up in the saddle and bucked her head up and down, snorting as she went. I snapped back to the moment, remembering my destination and resurfacing the urgency that I had so carelessly placed aside. I gave Delilah a pat on her shoulder.

"Thanks."

We rode hard. Delilah sped on as I guided her along. We approached the railroad where the line came into town and jumped the tracks in one leap. The stockyards near the train station were empty in anticipation of the next cattle drive. I could see the far edge of town more clearly now and was close to making the final turn towards the fort. I pulled back on Delilah, realizing that if I could see town, someone in town could see me too and might wonder why a rider would be high tailin' it on like I was. We slowed to a trot. The sunrise faced me as we rode on. The mesh of colors that had been was now gone and rays of sunlight shone across the prairie. A hawk glided above us as we made our way. It gave no indication that it was hunting, but merely out for an early flight, meeting the day head on as we were.

We made it to the main trail just east of town that led to Fort Dodge. I looked over my shoulder towards Dodge City one last time before bringing Delilah to a gallop. Her long strides made good time and left a hazy trail of dust looming in her wake behind us. The last time I ran to the fort I was being chased by a small band of Indians. Now I was running from something much bigger. Col. Forsythe was the only one I felt I could turn to. I just hoped he accepted my explanation of what happened as truth. I had no reason to be anything but truthful, although I knew for a fact that Shorty wouldn't hesitate to conjure up an alternate ending to our ordeal. My guess was that he had either run to the Marshal's office or was just about to get to the Byrne Ranch. Either way it would end up with Byrne. He had this town in his pocket, no doubt. Everyone…except me.

CHAPTER 20

"Halt! Who goes there?"

I slowly approached the front gates of Fort Dodge and raised both my hands to the soldier guarding the front gate. Delilah moved on without my guidance.

"My name is Rowdy. I'm here to speak with Col. Forsythe."

"What's yer business with the Colonel?" the guard asked.

With my hands still raised above my head I answered, "If you will, my business is with the Colonel. I can tell you that I was invited by him to come to the fort when I was ready."

"New recruit, huh?" The guard sized me up, raised an eyebrow as if he were deciding my place among the soldiers.

Not exactly, I thought to myself. "Is there a place inside to tie up my horse?"

"Wait here," the soldier said.

He walked through a small door at the front of the fort that was part of the main gate, disappearing. I lowered my hands and patted Delilah.

"What do you think?" I asked her.

The soldier returned with another, seemingly higher-ranking officer. He approached me, asked me to dismount, and follow him.

The main gate was opened for us. I led Delilah inside and was instructed to tie her up by the coral and that I was to remain there until he returned for me. The guard at the gate was relieved by another and was ordered to stay with me while I waited. The corral was as I remembered it, but empty. I tied Delilah up and scratched the bridge of her nose. She nuzzled up to me looking for a treat.

"Got nothin' for you right now, girl. Be patient."

The fort was slowly starting to stir with activity. Soldiers moved about, tending to horses in the stalls across the yard while others relieved those on night shift. The solider with me yawned.

"Long night?" I asked, trying to spark some conversation. He did not reply at first. He looked at me warily and finally answered me with a question of his own.

"Yer up kinda early, ain't ya?"

"A man can get a good deal done before breakfast if he's up early enough, don't you think?" I replied, knowing that I had already done plenty.

He paused. "Yep, guess so."

The soldier yawned again.

"That's a fine horse you got there."

I started to answer when I noticed Col. Forsythe across the yard. He was talking to the man that had led me through the gates. Their conversation paused as they both looked over at me. Col. Forsythe grinned. He turned and walked away as the soldier he talked with walked in my direction. The soldier watching me had continued to talk about Delilah, but I had not heard a word. *Here it comes,* I thought. I'm either good to go or I'll be escorted out the front gates and on my own, again.

"Sir, my name is Captain Loring. Col. Forsythe asked that I bring you to his office. Follow me."

Captain Loring was polite enough, but firm and to the point. He began to lead me away from the corral.

"My horse?" I asked.

He looked at me and then to Delilah.

"Corporal, see to it that his horse is watered and placed in a stall until he returns to collect it," he ordered.

"Yes, sir."

I untied Delilah and handed him the reins. As the soldier led her away from me, she snorted and pulled against him.

"Go on," I said to her. "It'll be alright."

Reluctantly she followed, but not before she gave one final buck of her head, showing her discontent.

I followed Captain Loring to Col. Forsythe's office. I sat down in an empty chair inside and waited for the Colonel to arrive. His saber hung quietly on a hook behind his desk. I surveyed the room remembering my first visit to the office. Something I hadn't remembered was displayed on the wall over the door. It was an arrow, adorned with feathers. Its tip made of sharpened stone. Beneath it was a plaque with the words, *Wild and mean, sharp and keen*. I stood up and walked over to it, admiring the craftsmanship taken to make it. I had the urge to reach out and feel the feathers, to touch the carved tip, but resisted. I returned to my chair as Col. Forsythe entered. His boots scuffed across the floor. Standing behind his desk, he took off his hat and placed it on some books in front of him. He looked at me.

"Good morning, Col. Forsythe. Thank you for seeing me."

Col. Forsythe put both hands on his desk and leaned over closer to me.

"You finally decide the Army suits you now, son, or are you here on civilian business?"

He was blunt and to the point.

"It's busy times around here these days and I don't have time to waste. What can I do for you?"

I took in a shallow breath and spoke. "Colonel. Sir. I'm in a bit of trouble. I wasn't sure who else I could turn to, so I came here. I need your advice."

Col. Forsythe straightened up, reached for his hat, and placed it on his head. "The town Marshal will hear you out. You should take your problems to him."

"You don't understand, Colonel, I need to talk to you. I don't think the Marshal would help me even if he could. Please, give me a few minutes to explain."

"If you're not here to volunteer I really must bid you good day." Col. Forsythe started walking towards the door.

"I killed one of Patrick Byrne's men this morning."

I stood as I spoke, my voice cracking. Col. Forsythe stopped in his tracks. He turned and looked at me with a serious stare. I wasn't sure what he was thinking, but it was obvious I had seized his attention.

"Sit down," he said in a low, even voice.

I sat down, wondering what was going to happen next. Would I be arrested? Turned over to the Marshal's office? Col.

Forsythe stepped slowly to the door. He reached out for handle, stopped, and then turned the lock, securing us inside the room. I could hear the latch catch as the locking mechanism engaged. He walked back to his desk, sitting down this time. Folding his hands on top of his desk, he leaned forward and looked me dead in the eyes.

"Tell me what happened, exactly," he said.

His tone was no longer welcoming or even authoritative, just plain serious. I looked across the desk at him and explained everything that had happened. Boone's warning at the Blacksmith, parting ways with Mr. Shepard, and most importantly the altercation between me and Byrne's men, Shorty and Buck. Col. Forsythe never interrupted, never wavered from attention. It felt for a moment like I was talking to Captain Hennessy.

I was in deep now and needed a plan to confront this head on. Byrne would be ready to come at me, guns blazing, and would argue that he had every right to reclaim Delilah and that I should be locked up, or worse. Shooting a man is one thing but killing him was another. And horse thieves? He'd never admit to it. Add to the fact that Buck was one of Byrne's men and you'll have one heck of a storm brewing across Dodge City. This situation needed to be dealt with and then put to bed, hopefully with me on the free side of a jail cell and still breathing.

When I finished, I sat still, quietly waiting for a response. Col. Forsythe leaned back in his chair and folded his arms across his chest. He looked at me with an emotionless stare. I looked squarely back at him, wanting an answer, any answer. Finally, he unfolded his arms, leaned forward, and spoke to me.

"You know that regardless of how this turns out, Byrne won't be satisfied until he's gotten his way. Justice to a man like him doesn't come easy."

"What should I do?" I asked. "I don't think runnin' would help me. Byrne is too connected. I'd fight this in town, but again, he seems to have the entire place in his pocket. That's why I came to you."

Col. Forsythe stood and walked around his desk and over to the door. He looked up.

"You were looking at this before I walked into the room." He pointed to the arrow. "Why?"

I stood and walked over next to him. "I was admiring its craftsmanship."

"Did you read the slogan beneath?" He read it and then turned to look at me. "Wild and mean, sharp and keen."

"Yes, I read it."

Wild and Mean, Sharp and Keen.

"Mean anything to you?" he asked

"I guess it's describing how crafty and unforgiving an Indian can be."

"Let me tell you, it's not a description, it's a reminder, and it's meant for all men. You must be sharp as an arrow with the ability to outthink your adversaries. You must recognize that when someone is backed into a corner, or taken out of their element, their actions tend to be rash, wilder, and more careless, less thought provoked and meaningful. The arrow itself reminds me to be wary of others. Will they use it as a tool to hunt and provide or as a weapon to kill and take?"

I looked at the arrow wondering how this was going to help me. I looked at Col. Forsythe. He was still looking at the arrow when he started to speak.

"In just a minute, I am going to give an order for two of my men to ride to town and find the Marshal. They will inform him that he needs to collect Byrne and meet me at the fort this afternoon for a meeting. You are going to stay here while the message is delivered. Tend to your horse, grab some chow, and stay out of the way. When they arrive, I will meet with them to discuss this morning's situation and see where they stand on things. You will continue to lay low. I will call for you when I see fit."

"Sir, I'd like a chance to—"

Col. Forsythe interrupted, "You let me lay the groundwork. Then you can have your say."

"Yes sir," I answered.

I came to him for help and now was the time to put my total trust in him. This was my only rational move and hopefully my instincts about the Colonel would hold true.

"You go on now, Rowdy. I'll send for you later today."

I turned to open the door. Col. Forsythe returned to his desk, removed a piece of parchment from a drawer, and searched for a pen atop his desk. As I turned the latch to unlock the door, I asked him one final question.

"Col. Forsythe? Do you think I was wrong?"

He stopped, looked up at me. "Do you?" he said.

Shaking my head, I answered, "No."

"Alright then." He gave a nod and refocused on what he was doing.

I closed the door behind me and walked into the yard. Soldiers moved about seeing to their morning duties. The sun was barely in the sky, but the heat was already radiating, causing my neck to break out with sweat. I wiped my brow with the back of my hand. This was going to be a long day.

CHAPTER 21

It was well past noon and I was sitting in the stables with Delilah when the arrival of Patrick Byrne shook up the fort. He rode through the gates alongside Marshal Sam Trite, stopping in the middle of the yard.

"Okay," he yelled out as he dismounted his horse. "Someone want to tell me what in the sam-hell I'm doin' here?"

I peered through the beams in the stable and had a clear view of the scene Byrne was creating. Marshal Trite dismounted as well and walked over next to Byrne. The buzz of the fort had come to a halt as soldiers looked on at Byrne.

"Where is Col. Forsythe? Somebody git him out here right now," Byrne demanded.

His rant was impatient and foul. He paced from the front of his horse to the back looking in all directions as he went. Marshal Trite stayed where he was, silent as ever. On the opposite side of the fort, I could see Captain Loring. He had just left the building where Col. Forsythe's office was located. He approached Byrne and the Marshal with no apparent sense of urgency. Byrne also caught notice of Captain Loring and turned to glare in his direction. He spit on the ground between himself and the Captain.

"Afternoon gentleman, I'm Captain Loring."

He offered his hand to Marshal Trite who accepted his greeting with a sturdy handshake. Byrne ignored the Captain's welcome when offered and instead began to send a barrage of condescending remarks at him.

"Well! Captain, I don't suppose you know where the Colonel is? I've got serious matters back in town and don't want to waste another minute of daylight."

Captain Loring looked at Byrne, solid in his stance and steady with words.

"Marshal Trite, Mr. Byrne. Col. Forsythe is waiting for you in his office. If you would, please follow me."

He turned to lead them on, giving an order to a nearby soldier. "Corporal, see to these men's horses."

Byrne and Marshal Trite followed behind Captain Loring as they made their way across the yard. Their horses were led away to the stables where I was watching every move they made. Their talk, the way they walked across the yard, Byrne was exceptionally put off by being here. His impatient stomping sent dust flying with every step. His body language spoke volumes. Conversely, Marshal Trite calmly followed. I could tell right from the start who was in charge of this miniature posse. I imagined the scene Byrne must have made when the Marshal went to get him. I'm sure it wasn't an easy task for the Marshal, but that was the idea.

As things were set in motion, I decided that Col. Forsythe did believe me and was backing me up as much as he could. There was no way the Marshal or Byrne could ignore a summons by the fort. The Marshal was the law of the town, keeping the peace while the fort oversaw the region. Kansas was a young state and the U.S. government did not have direct authority over town matters, but in the case of Dodge City and the reputation it had for attracting the wrong sort of people, the Colonel in charge could impose direct authority over town matters as he deemed necessary. Fort Dodge was in place to protect the region from Indian attacks but was also a main support line for the town Marshal and a gateway for news and information to get to Washington if an urgent matter where to arise.

Wild and Mean, Sharp and Keen.

Just how would Byrne react? He's got no one to bolster his ego here. No one to stand behind him with a tough, intimidating demeanor. Even the Marshal had to play his cards carefully. He would juggle his responsibility for the town and concern for his good standing with Byrne all while keeping a calm, by the book approach when meeting with Col. Forsythe.

As they approached the door outside the Colonel's office, it swung open. Col. Forsythe stepped out and addressed Captain Loring. I was unable to hear what was said, but by Byrne's reaction, I could tell it must have put more imposition on him than he'd like. Col. Forsythe briefly greeted Marshal Trite and Byrne and then walked away from them as quickly as he met them. Captain Loring motioned for the men to follow him through the door. The Marshal obliged, but Byrne turned and shouted at the Colonel as he walked across the yard.

"You think you can just order us around like one of yer soldiers here, Colonel? If I were you—"

Hearing that, Col. Forsythe stopped and turned towards Byrne. "Watch your step, Mr. Byrne. You are a guest here at the fort, and I will treat you as such if I feel you are acting as one. Hostility will not be tolerated here."

He focused on Byrne as a hawk would its prey.

"Captain, if you please," he said, gesturing to Byrne.

Captain Loring approached and quietly said something to him. Byrne raised his right arm chest high and brushed by the Captain, tripping over the door stop as he entered the building. A slew of obscenities echoed through the fort walls as Captain Loring followed him inside and closed the door. Col. Forsythe continued walking across the yard towards the stables. I could see his business first attitude as he closed the distance between the two of us. I hunkered down back into the stall Delilah was in. He entered the doorway and summoned the soldier who was tending to Byrne's horse. I couldn't hear exactly what was said, but the soldier walked straight into Delilah's stall as the Colonel returned to the yard and headed towards his office. The soldier looked at me.

"What'd he say?" I asked.

"I'm Private Smoot. You need to follow me to Captain Loring's quarters. It is directly off the Colonel's office. He said to wait there and listen carefully. The walls are thin, and you should be able to follow what is said in the Colonel's office. He wants you close by and said you should come in when called."

"What's he going to say?"

"You'll know when he does. Just be ready."

I stepped next to Delilah and reached out to stroke her mane.

I looked into her eyes, large and black. She looked back at me. She could sense that I was feeling a bit nervous. She nuzzled my chest with her nose and snorted.

"This is it, girl. Be ready for me if I need you," I whispered into her ear. She nudged me again and whinnied gently, almost answering me.

"We have to go," Smoot said.

He stepped out into the open first, surveyed the yard, and motioned for me to follow. We moved with purpose, swiftly covering the ground from the stables to the perimeter wall. We approached the front gate, walked past the guards, and made our way across the entrance of the fort. I stopped at the opening and looked back towards town. The sun shone directly overhead. Waves of heat rose from the ground distorting objects in the distance. One guard was leaning up against the edge of the gate, the stock of his rifle resting on the ground. Another soldier was just beyond the gate talking to someone. I figured it was another soldier. I squinted my eyes to get a better look outside the fort. I was wrong. The soldier, who had been talking, turned to walk back to the gate. When he moved there was Boone, his hands still holding the reins from his horse. He took a step towards the gate and stopped. I moved quickly to catch up to Private Smoot.

Did he see me? I wondered.

Smoot, now past the gate, turned and motioned for me to hurry.

"Come on, don't fall behind."

We continued along the perimeter to the housing deck. The

soldiers bunk house was the first building, followed by the supply room and armory. The boards under our feet creaked as we walked. We passed through a doorway that led to a meeting room. The room was relatively empty, except for a few chairs, a table in the middle, a map on the wall, and a framed parchment hanging near the doorway on the far side of the room. Our walk slowed inside. I felt as if we were sneaking up on someone. We reached the doorway across the room. Private Smoot stopped and raised his hand silently, making a fist above his right shoulder. I stopped behind him. He turned to me and spoke in a much quieter voice than before.

"Captain Loring's quarters are through this door and down the hall to the right. Stay here while I make sure all is clear."

"Okay," I said.

He disappeared through the door and down the hall. I could hear his footsteps clearly as he walked. Following orders, I stayed put. I looked around the empty room and imagined all that may have taken place. Battle plans formed, strategies discussed, valor awarded, and dishonor dealt with, all possibilities within the confines of this room. I scanned my surroundings again. My eyes zeroed in on the framed parchment hanging on the wall. It was tattered and old, torn from an old fold down the middle, but still legible. I walked over for a closer look. Written with fanciful writing it said,

> *"...From this day to the ending of the world,*
> *But we in it shall be remember'd;*
> *We few, we happy few, we band of brothers;*
> *For he to-day that sheds his blood with me*
> *Shall be my brother..."*

I read this over and over, intrigued by its poetic tone. As I stood alone waiting, this group of words spoke to me. Its meaning fueled the fire I had inside to take a stand against Byrne. Against the odds, I was alone against the world. Yet I wasn't truly alone. Col. Forsythe had laid out the battle plan, brought the opposition to me, and was paving the way for my arrival. He was with me. One way or the other, a resolution needed to be made. Today! I could hear footsteps coming closer from down the hall. I stood still, my back flat against the wall. Private Smoot leaned through the doorway and motioned for me to follow. Quietly, I went with him. As I passed through the doorway, I glanced once more at the parchment.

"For he today that sheds his blood with me shall be my brother..." I whispered.

My battle had already begun. It was time though to end the war.

I walked softly behind Smoot. The door to the Captain's quarters was ajar. Smoot opened the door and stepped aside so I could enter. He pointed at a desk across the room. On the desk was a piece of paper. I walked to the desk and reached out to pick it up. It had only one thing written on it, *Wild and Mean, Sharp and Keen*.

A smile crept across my face. I looked back towards the door, but Private Smoot had already gone. Turning back, I could see that Captain Loring's room was well kept. There was the desk, a cot in the corner with a bible resting on his pillow and a chair in the opposite corner of the room. There were no windows and the only entrance/exit was the door I came through.

Stepping closer to the wall, I could hear men talking. I recognized one voice right away. Byrne was actively looking for answers as to why exactly he was "summoned" and that he would "get to the bottom of this!" The harshness in his voice mixed with his arrogance made me angry. I wanted to charge into the Colonel's office and confront him right then.

Use yer head, Rowdy. An old familiar voice seemingly whispered in my ear, although he wasn't there at all. *It's time to take a stand.*

I looked down at the paper in my hands again, folded it, and placed it in my pocket. While I could hear the men in the other room, it was hard to understand everything. I leaned against the wall pressing my ear to the wood slates. This was a small improvement and turned out to be the best I was going to get. I listened to Col. Forsythe talk with Byrne and Marshal Trite.

"It seems to me, Mr. Byrne, that there is a situation going on in town and I wonder if you'd be so kind as to fill me in on the details." Col. Forsythe spoke eloquently with a touch of authority.

"Forsythe—" Byrne started.

"Col. Forsythe, Mr. Byrne. I would appreciate you to address me as such as I will return the courtesies to you and Marshal Trite here. We are men of leadership and have earned our place in society."

Byrne paused. I could tell he was fuming on the inside and it probably wouldn't take much to send him over the edge. My walking in on the meeting might just do it. I listened with anticipation, waiting for my signal, though not knowing exactly what to expect.

"You may continue," Col. Forsythe said.

"Col. Forsythe," Byrne spoke with apparent irritation. "I appreciate your interest, but I don't believe town matters are your concern. You've got much more to worry about, especially with the growing Indian population. You never know when a savage band might step out of line and test your …defenses."

Col. Forsythe directed his attention to Marshal Trite.

"Marshal Trite, we both know that the authority imposed on your office to keep the peace in Dodge City is one of great importance. But we also can agree that from time to time, as directed from the Governor of Kansas himself, Fort Dodge may assist and direct law and order not only in the region, but within the limits of the town as well. Now, if you will Marshal, fill me in before my walls get overrun by a band of rouge Indians."

The room was silent.

"Marshal?" Forsythe questioned again.

Marshal Trite finally answered. His voice cracked and seemed hoarse. "One of Byrne's men was shot and killed this morning tending to some horses. According to one witness, the shooter was the Blacksmith's apprentice."

"Does the accused have a name?" Col. Forsythe asked.

Byrne spoke up. "I believe he's called Rowdy. Right now, Col. Forsythe, we need to be getting along. We need to locate the Blacksmith and see if he knows where the little murderer is hiding."

"All in good time, Mr. Byrne. I'd like to hear some more of the facts, so I can look further into this as well. And let's use the boy's name instead of murderer. I hate hangin' anyone without finding out the whole truth."

Col. Forsythe paused. Noise reverberated from the room as a chair was being pushed out of place. Footsteps paced across the floor. It was Col. Forsythe. He continued to ask more questions. "Marshal, what time did the shooting take place?"

Byrne spoke up, "Just before sunrise."

"Mr. Byrne, I do believe I directed that question towards the Marshal, but don't worry, I have a question or two for you as well."

"It's like he said. One of Byrne's men ran into my office this mornin', woke me up hollerin', sayin' there had been a killing."

Col. Forsythe's paces headed in the other direction.

"So, before sunup. Okay. And where exactly did the shooting occur?"

"Happened in the stables just outside the ranch. Now, we must be going." Byrne interrupted again, stood up, and from the sounds of it was heading for the door.

"Mr. Byrne. I am a patient man and as you will see, I will remain patient. However, if you speak out of turn again, I will hold you as long as I see fit and will continue this meeting with Marshal Trite in a private location. Now, if you will, please take your seat."

I have spoken to Col. Forsythe only twice before and each time I felt comfortable. The tone in his voice now had changed. He spoke with authority and power yet had enough wherewithal to make his point without raising his voice or fumbling his words.

"Marshal Trite? You just said that one of Byrne's men ran into your office. Before sunup? How far is the Byrne Ranch from town?"

"It's a ways, but not too far," the Marshal replied after clearing his throat.

"And the stables? Just outside the ranch? According to Mr. Byrne anyway."

Col. Forsythe's paces had stopped.

"Now see here, Colonel. I know my ranch and I know my town and I know I've got a killer to find," Byrne spouted out.

"Your town? Mr. Byrne, I hardly think that is what you meant to say. Marshal Trite, where were their horses tied when Byrne's man came to alert you?"

"Beg your pardon, Colonel. Their horses? I can't say that I remember. Colonel, I must agree with Mr. Byrne here. I've got to see to this back in town and don't feel like we are getting anywhere."

Marshal Trite finally spoke with a more confident tongue, but I knew he was stretching himself thin—both with Col. Forsythe and with Byrne.

"Oh? Well, we are just about done. There's just one thing I just don't understand. How is it that Byrne's man comes straight to you all the way from the Byrne Ranch, without a horse to be seen? I figure it would have taken most of the morning to walk to town. Also, if one of my men has any trouble what-so-ever, I am the first to be informed. It would only seem right that Mr. Byrne has the same authority over his own men. And then why, Mr. Byrne, didn't you ride into town yourself to report this incident?"

"Col. Forsythe," Byrne spoke up in a furious, accusatory tone. "Don't think for one minute I don't see what's going on here."

Col. Forsythe replied, "What's going on here, Mr. Byrne, is that I don't think I'm getting the whole story. I look at you two men, upstanding citizens of Dodge City. A businessman and a peace keeper and not a shred of truth between you. Can anyone around here tell me what really happened?"

That was it! That was my cue. I swiftly walked to the door, opened it, and in two steps I was standing outside Col. Forsythe's office. Captain Loring stood to the right of the door as I approached and nodded as I reached for the door handle. Brewing on the other side of this door was the biggest

storm I had ever faced up to now.

"Sharp and Keen," I whispered.

I turned the knob and stepped into Col. Forsythe's office.

"I know exactly what happened," I said.

CHAPTER 22

When I was younger, before my father and brother were killed, I learned to hunt and shoot. Deer mainly, but occasionally I was included on a bird hunt. We would track turkey, pheasants, quail, and sometimes duck. While deer hunting required patience and quiet, bird hunting also tested our accuracy and reflexes. Each of us would carry our own weapon and had a responsibility to look out for the other person, especially when preparing to fire upon something.

Seniority also played a role during these excursions. The eldest, father, would get the first shot followed by my brother. Finally, if a target was still available, I'd get a chance. I rarely fired my weapon during those hunts, but the first time I did would be the one I will never forget.

It was early morning. Cool air brushed against my face, chilling my ears and drying my lips. My father, brother, and I—along with Scout, our hunting dog—were coming to a field at the edge of a wooded thicket near our farm. The golden glaze of morning swept across the meadow in front of us turning the overgrown grasses a light bronze that swayed gently in the breeze. I watched as my father breathed deeply through his nose, taking in the early morning aromas around us. My brother was indifferent to the morning and was ready to shoot if given the opportunity. Scout, on the other hand, had already picked up a scent.

Father raised his arm, motioning for us to stop in our tracks. Scout's right leg was tucked under his belly and his eyes were focused just to the left of where we were standing. His nostrils twitched as he awaited the command to run and roust the fowl in front of us. Father leaned down towards Scout, brought his right hand close to his head, and snapped his fingers. At this, Scout shot out of his stance and bolted into the grasses ahead. It didn't take long for him to locate the small covey of quail, flushing them out of hiding and into the air to escape.

BLAM!

My father's gun blasted, and one quail spiraled to the ground.

BLAM!

My brother fired just after my father but missed his mark.

BLAM!

I fired…

I never saw if I hit one or not. All I remember seeing is my brother's hat disintegrating in mid-air after being blown from the top of his head by my shot. I dropped my gun, not knowing what to do, but scared for what had just happened.

And there it was. The look on my father's face. Shock. Disbelief. Disappointment. Anger. My brother dropped to the ground, stunned but unharmed. My father walked over to me, bent down, and picked up my gun. The three of us remained still, recovering from a near disastrous situation. I cried. My brother sat up and glared at me. Scout returned from the brush with a quail in his mouth. He stopped just in front of us, dropped the quail to the ground, and looked at each of us probably wondering what the hell had just happened.

Without saying a word my father picked up the dead bird, placed it in a burlap sack he carried, and walked back in the direction of the farm. My brother stood, his face as white as a snowy morning, and followed.

I stood alone and cried. Scout walked over to me, put his paws on my chest, and licked my tears. I don't know how long I stood there, but to this day I will never forget the look on my father's face. And now, I was seeing it again. Patrick Byrne and Marshal Trite both stood as I made my entrance and declaration. Byrne's face said it all.

CHAPTER 23

"You!" Byrne yelled. He started to move towards me.

"Captain!" Col. Forsythe said.

Captain Loring had followed me into the room and positioned himself between me and Byrne. Byrne tried to push by him, but Captain Loring never budged. He held his ground and restrained Byrne, keeping him a safe distance from me. The Marshal never moved. He only looked to the Colonel, a questioning expression upon his face.

"What is he doing here, Forsythe?" Byrne pointed and shouted at me.

"Mr. Byrne return to your seat," Col. Forsythe said, but Byrne remained engaged with Captain Loring.

I looked back at Byrne, firm in my stance, emotionless in my glare. Byrne snarled as would a dog guarding his bone. He lunged towards me, placing his hands on Captain Loring's chest, pushing him as he tried to get by. It was immediately apparent that Captain Loring was not only trained and skilled in diplomacy as an officer should be but was equally skilled in hand to hand combat. Upon being pushed, Loring grabbed Byrnes right wrist, stepped back one step and twisted. He swiftly placed his free hand on Byrne's right shoulder, forcing him to double over. Loring stepped back into Byrne applying just the right amount of pressure on his arm and shoulder to incapacitate him. Byrne was pinned before he knew what happened. Loring held fast as Byrne yelled for him to let go. Col. Forsythe calmly walked from behind his desk and approached Byrne. He leaned over to speak to him face to face.

"Mr. Byrne, do you know the penalty for striking an officer?"

"Go spit!" was Byrne's reply. "Trite!"

Looking at Col. Forsythe and then at Captain Loring, Marshal Trite finally spoke up. "Colonel Forsythe, I must insist that Mr. Byrne be let go."

Straightening up, Col. Forsythe turned to face the Marshal.

"Marshal Trite, I think I am coming to understand your position more clearly now. Have a seat please."

He turned back to Byrne.

"And you, sir, if you wish to remain free of any military charges and be allowed to leave Fort Dodge on your own accord, I strongly suggest you take your seat and remain there until this meeting is over."

Col. Forsythe now looked at me. "Rowdy, have a seat in my chair. I believe we are just about ready to hear your side of the story."

"Yes, sir."

I promptly moved behind the Colonel's desk and sat down. The entire office seemed bigger from this vantage point.

Veins bulged from Byrne's forehead, reddening his face. Sweat dripped from his nose. Marshal Trite looked at me and then looked away.

"Captain Loring, I do believe we have this gentleman's full attention. At ease if you will."

Loring nodded at the Colonel and released his grip on Byrne who stood up huffing and rubbed his shoulder.

"Now, let's get down to business, shall we?"

Col. Forsythe positioned himself at the edge of the desk, while Captain Loring posted himself near the door behind Byrne and Marshal Trite.

"Rowdy, if you will, please tell us what happened this morning."

I looked across the table. Byrne sat back in his chair and sneered. Marshal Trite sat upright and looked back at me, seemingly waiting for my testimony. The room was quiet, and for a moment I felt uneasy.

Use yer head and tell 'em like it is. A voice from the past awakened my sense of purpose and reminded me I had nothing to hide.

"It's tragically simple," I said. "Last night Mr. Shepard and I had a discussion that ultimately ended my apprenticeship with him. When all was said, I returned to my bunk and packed my things. Unable to sleep, I decided to get an early start, so I headed to the stables to prepare my horse and ready my gear. When I entered the stables, I heard voices. As they came closer, it was clear to me that their conversation suggested that they were going to steal my horse."

"That's a lie," Byrne spouted out. "Are we really going to sit here and listen to this boy conjure up a tale like this knowing fair well that he is wanted for murder?"

Col. Forsythe was about to interject when I stood up.

"Murder?" My voice rose, and an angry tone protruded from deep inside me. "Mr. Byrne, your men were there to steal my horse, were caught in the act by me, and disregarded my warnings to stand down. Shorty seemed to have enough sense to stop, but your man Buck drew down on me. I fired at him in self-defense."

I was starting to sweat and realized I was beginning to shout. I looked down at the table to collect myself, took a breath, and looked up again. My eyes caught the plaque on the wall. It was Byrne that was out of his element right now. My emotions were trying to take over, which was only paving the way for him to gain ground in this debate. I looked to Col. Forsythe. He stood firm, unwavering. I sat down again and continued.

"I protected my property, my life, and would do it again as I am sure any man in this room would if they were presented with the same situation. Would I take it back if I could?"

Marshal Trite shifted in his chair and glanced at Byrne.

"I would. No man deserves to die an unnatural death. But that same man does not have a right to take from others, whether it is for himself or for another man's benefit."

I looked directly at Byrne. He flinched just enough for me to notice. Col. Forsythe seemed to notice as well. The room was quiet for once. I looked across the table at Byrne and then spoke to Marshal Trite.

"Marshal, do you have any questions for me?"

I got the feeling Marshal Trite was caught a little off guard by this. He shifted in his chair, looked to Byrne and Col. Forsythe. Finally, he stood and walked around behind the chair.

"Why were you leaving so early in the morning, Rowdy?" he asked.

"It's like I said, I couldn't sleep and since I was no longer employed or obligated to anyone in Dodge City, I decided to head out before sun-up."

"So, if you were living in town, why was your horse stabled on Byrne's property?"

It became obvious that the Marshal didn't have all the facts and that once again Byrne had thrown his weight around in order to get his way.

"Marshal Trite, sir, my horse is stabled right next to the Blacksmith's. You know, McCrary's stables, in town."

I noticed Col. Forsythe watching our conversation and saw the smallest glimpse of a smile emerge from his lips. Byrne, on the other hand, was starting to get fed up again. I pulled a slip of paper from my pocket and held it out to the Marshal.

"I have Mr. McCrary's signature right here proving that I paid for a stall."

Byrne looked at my hand. Marshal Trite looked at my hand. Col. Forsythe looked at me. Neither Byrne nor Marshal Trite reached out to inspect my piece of paper. I returned it to my pocket and sat back in my seat.

Col. Forsythe spoke up.

"Gentleman. It seems clear to me that what we have here is a clear case of self-defense on the part of Rowdy. I would, however, question whether to investigate Mr. Byrne's men's motives this morning, and why it seems there was some 'misinformation' as to where exactly this incident took place. Marshal Trite, I will pass that responsibility on to you. Rowdy—"

"Hold on a minute, Col. Forsythe," Byrne said with a sneer. "I'm out a man because of this vagrant."

"The only vagrancy that has been seemingly proven is on the part of your men. Drunk perhaps? Following instructions? Maybe. Whatever the case may be, Rowdy is clear of any charges in the state of Kansas. I will be forwarding a report of this incident to the Governor's office citing self-defense, or would you prefer defense of personal safety and property from horse thieves, Mr. Byrne? The later may find you down a second man."

He turned his attention to the Marshal.

"Do you have anything to add, Marshal Trite?"

Col. Forsythe was smooth. I fought back a victory smile as I listened and awaited the direction my future was about to take.

Marshal Trite, still standing, looked over at me and said, "I think…Yes, I believe you have said it all, Col. Forsythe."

Byrne stood up, placed his hands on the table, and looked me dead in the eyes. Bloodshot with anger, they seared the air between us. Defeated yet again by me, Byrne was not about to go quietly.

"Rowdy. You had better ride. Ride like you have never ridden before. Is that horse of yours worth the risk?"

Col. Forsythe put a hand on Byrne's shoulder and pulled

him away from the desk. Byrne squared up to the Colonel, puffing his chest out like a rooster would its feathers just before a fight.

"There will be no retaliation. No eye for an eye, Mr. Byrne. No man is good enough to govern another man without the other's consent. Fort Dodge will be watching."

Looking past Byrne now, Col. Forsythe addressed Loring.

"Captain, if you please, see to it that these men retrieve their horses and are safely on their way."

"Yes, sir."

Captain Loring opened the door. "Marshal Trite, Mr. Byrne. Please come with me."

Marshal Trite headed out the door. Byrne stepped backwards, slowly disengaging from the Colonel. His eyes spoke of discontent; his body language portrayed bitter defeat. He stepped again, breaking his stare from Col. Forsythe and turned towards me once more. Our eyes locked.

"Good day, sir," Col. Forsythe said to Byrne.

With that, Byrne turned and stormed out. Col. Forsythe walked to the door, closed it, and turned to me. I stood up, vacating his seat behind the desk.

"Thank you, Col. Forsythe."

I offered him my hand and he accepted with a firm, gripping shake.

"What are your plans now, Rowdy?"

I had no idea, but one thing was clear. I was done with Dodge City.

"I imagine I'll move on. West, I guess. I've heard stories about the vast mountain ranges and how beautiful the land is. I'm sure there will be something for me there. For now, I'm looking at making it one day at a time."

"Rowdy, you know that when you leave the safety of Fort Dodge, it will only be a matter of time before Byrne starts looking for you. It'll be hard going but knowing you as I have briefly come to know you, I have all the confidence that you will be fine. Stay here at the fort tonight, and I'll see you off in the morning."

Col. Forsythe gave me a pat on my shoulders. It was a tempting offer, but I wasn't sure staying would be the best move for me.

"Col. Forsythe, I appreciate your offer to stay, but the way things are going, I think it might be best if I headed out tonight. You're right about Byrne. He'll want to settle things with me his way. The sooner I go, the more distance I can put between us."

I paused, looking at the Colonel.

"If it's okay with you, I'd like to see to my horse now."

Col. Forsythe nodded his head, understanding my urgency. I turned and headed for the door. Col. Forsythe spoke up as I opened it to leave.

"There is one thing I'd' like to know, Rowdy. You said you had McCrary's signature on that piece of paper in your pocket?"

I smiled at Col. Forsythe as I pulled the paper out, unfolded it, and showed it to him. He chuckled when he saw it.

"Wild and Mean?" he said.

"Sharp and Keen," I replied.

I walked out the door and returned to Delilah where I waited for nightfall.

CHAPTER 24

The glow of lantern light dissipated as Delilah and I traveled away from Fort Dodge. The moon was bright. The evening air was fresh. The heat of the day had diminished and a breeze with an occasional wisp of coolness flowed by. The trail from the fort was smooth and easy. There were a few trees that cast shadows across my path, but for the most part, all was clear. I had originally decided to swing by Ms. Compton's to tell Jeb I was leaving, but the way things went today, a stop in town could be a mistake and that thought was now about to be confirmed.

Ahead, standing next to his horse, was Boone. I could see him in the moonlight as he stepped away from his horse and raised both hands shoulder high. For a moment I considered bolting past, but strangely I felt obligated to talk with him. I rode up to him but stayed mounted on Delilah in case I needed to make a break for it. Boone had warned me before, but what was he doing here now? Like it or not, he was still one of Byrne's men.

"Boone," I said, my hands still grasping the reins.

"Rowdy," he replied, lowering his hands.

"Do I need to be wary of you, Boone? I got a very real feeling that Byrne was not through with me when he stormed out of the fort today."

Boone looked at me, then turned and walked to his horse. He reached into his saddlebag.

"Boone?" I said.

His back was to me. Slowly, I reached back into my pack and slid my rifle out. Laying it across my legs and in the direction of Boone, I called out to him again.

"Boone, I've respected you from the start. You do right by your employer, but more so, you've just done what's right. The one thing I don't understand is why Byrne?"

Boone pulled something from his pack and turned around.

"Rowdy, I've been around these parts a long time and I've seen lots of things. Hell, I've done lots of things, some of which I'm not proud of."

He stepped closer to me. My left hand tightened on the reins while my right hand raised the rifle from my lap. Boone stopped where he was.

"There's no need for that, Rowdy," he said.

"You'll have to excuse my sense of caution, Boone. I'd be a fool if I trusted anyone connected with Byrne which basically means anyone in or near Dodge City. The man is dangerous."

I focused on Boone, watching his movements carefully.

"Rowdy. The man you killed, Buck, was a hired gun. Turns out he was a wanted man north of here. Dakota Territory. He was runnin' with a gang of murderers and thieves. Word has it they would raid a spread, kill the workers and families, and steal everything. What they couldn't sell, they'd burn. He's not much of a loss but it gives Byrne an easy reason to come after you."

My head spun with questions, none of which Boone could possibly answer, and with each moment I spent here I was wasting time.

"Buck wasn't only after that horse of yours, Rowdy."

"Boone…"

"Byrne hired him to kill you, Rowdy."

Boone stepped closer.

"You're young, but you ain't dumb. I knew that from the start. The problem is that since you got to town you've crossed hairs with Byrne on more than one occasion. People 'round here know you don't go toe to toe with him."

I looked directly into Boone's eyes. "You aim to kill me, Boone?"

"Rowdy, you listen real good now. You ride. Ride west as fast as you can go. Here." He lifted his hand up to me and handed me a slip of paper.

I opened and read it aloud. "Sam McAlister? Lincoln, New Mexico? What's this?" I asked.

"It could be a new start for you. McAlister is always looking for a good hand. The way I see it, he'd be better off with someone who can stand on their own two feet. Yer young and smart. Go or don't go, but if anything, it could help you start over. Things have gone from bad to worse for you here and we both know yer not staying."

I looked at the name again.

"What's his connection to Byrne?"

My suspicion had not subsided.

"No connection. Not anymore," he said.

I gave Boone a puzzled look.

"Sam McAlister is my father. I'm on my way now to see about taking Ms. Compton and Jeb to Colorado. She's been widowed a while now and Jeb's a growing boy. I've mentioned it to her before, but never had a good reason to act on it. Now seems as good a time as any. I'm done with Byrne," he said.

I lowered my rifle and loosened my grip on the reins. Boone went out on a limb for me before and was risking a lot now. He didn't owe me a thing and yet was essentially standing up to Byrne in a bigger way than I ever did. Sometimes a man has got to stand up for what's right, no matter what the consequences might be. Doing right by others was a code I could understand and was a staple in the way I lived my life. I offered my hand to Boone. He reciprocated firmly.

"Thank you, Boone."

"You get a move on, Rowdy. Night's early and bright and Byrne will be watching if he isn't already."

I let go and gave Boone a final glance.

"Good luck to you."

He didn't answer. He walked to his horse, put his foot in the stirrup, and hoisted himself into his saddle. I patted Delilah on the neck.

"Let's go, girl," I whispered, and we were off.

Boone headed towards town casting a long shadow in the moonlight.

CHAPTER 25

Delilah and I hadn't traveled five minutes when a single gunshot echoed across the plains. I stopped her and turned in the direction of the blast. I could hear a galloping horse coming closer. I pulled my rifle from its sheath and took aim. Riding towards me at a full gallop was Boone.

"Ride!" he yelled.

I hesitated, trying to see past Boone.

"Go!" He yelled at me again. I pulled at the reins and gave Delilah a kick. She reared slightly and then shot off like a canon. Boone was behind me, following my lead and direction. Concealed by darkness, our pursuers charged on. I could hear the rhythmic gallop of horses behind us. I slowed a bit, allowing Boone to pull alongside me. I looked at him as we raced into the night. He led his horse with right arm. His left hung at his side, dangling as he rode.

Protruding from his shoulder on either side was the shaft and broken tip of an arrow. I could see blood dripping from his hand, spattering the side of his horse's belly as we went.

We continued furiously on riding past bush and bramble. The band of Indians behind us kept up their pace. Neither Boone nor I said a word, though we could hear the yips and hollers echoing out of the moonlit shadows behind us. Delilah's stride was strong, but Boone's horse was starting to noticeably tire, as was Boone. He had lost a lot of blood. We had to find a place to hide, to take a stand. A place where I could at the very least try to stop the blood oozing from Boone's wounded shoulder. The terrain changed slightly as we went. The flattened grasses became bumpy and somewhat rocky. I quickly realized we were about to come to a dead end.

The river, I thought.

Sure enough, about a hundred yards from where we were, lay the banks of the Arkansas river. Jeb and I had fished here once a long time ago, but I hadn't been back since. A small coppice threw a shadow into view. Boone was now starting to sag in the saddle, and we were slowing even more.

"Boone!" I yelled.

His head bobbed back and forth as we rode.

"Head for cover!"

I nudged Delilah gently and quickened our pace to take the lead. Boone was weak but understood and followed. We sped into the shadows of the small tree grove, stopping as quickly as we entered. I hopped off Delilah and quickly wrapped her reins around a low-lying branch. Boone tried to dismount but fell to the ground with a thud.

"Umph!" he groaned.

I grabbed the reins of his horse and wrapped them as I had Delilah's.

"Stay down, Boone. They're getting close."

I looked between the branches back in the direction from

which we came. No more yips and hollers. No pounding hooves, only quiet night. The moon was nearing the horizon and the light was starting to wane. Shadows grew longer. I scanned the area from left to right but did not see anything.

"They're on foot," I said.

The stark realization that at any moment we could be ambushed from any direction stirred what remaining adrenaline I had inside me. I crouched down next to Boone. He was still bleeding.

"You got a plan?" he said.

"Yeah," I said. "Try not to get killed."

I looked more closely at Boone's wound.

"We gotta get that out and try to stop the bleeding."

The broken tip of the arrow dangled behind Boone's left shoulder. I reached around behind him and snapped the remaining bits from its shaft, leaving a rough but manageable end. Not knowing how much time we had, I grasp the opposite end of the arrow that was protruding from Boone's front side.

"This is gonna hurt," I said.

Boone looked at me, his eyes bloodshot, his face pale, but his resolve steady and strong. He placed his right hand on my shoulder for balance.

"Do it," he said, gritting his teeth.

I firmly pulled on the broken shaft, sliding it quickly through and out of Boone's body. Blood bubbled from the hole where the arrow had been. I tore a strip of cloth from my shirt, wadded it up, and pressed it to the wound. Boone never made a sound.

"Hold this," I told him.

I glanced around again. The small grove of trees we were in provided enough cover but was an obvious hiding place. What were they waiting for? I checked my rifle for ammunition.

The river churned on behind us. It wouldn't wait for action. It wouldn't slow down. It gave no concern except that its purpose was to move on, regardless of what was going on around it. Its flow was smooth and quiet, yet anything in its path was conquered. If we were to have any chance at survival, I was going to have to take the fight to them. We were both hampered by the darkening night, but the numbers played greatly in their favor.

"Boone. Lay low. I'll be back," I said.

Boone didn't answer but gave me a *don't do anything stupid* look. I slowly crept to the edge of the coppice and looked out towards the river. I picked up a large stone and hurled it towards the water's edge as far from me as I could. The rock connected with the surface of the river. The splash that accompanied the rock's penetration did not make nearly the splash I had hoped for, but it was enough. Directly in front of me the stars lowest in the horizon disappeared and then reappeared. I followed the shadow with my eyes as it moved towards the banks of the river. I picked up a second stone, this one not much bigger than my hand and moved swiftly in the direction of the shadow. I closed the distance between us quickly. My eyes, now accustomed to the dark, sighted my first target. I picked up speed, moving my feet quickly, and ran at my attacker from behind. I threw the rock mid run into the water downstream from where I was headed. The splash was quick and direct, causing the Indian crouching in front of me to scan the water in that direction.

I charged, ramming him with the butt of my rifle between his shoulders. He fell forward, his face plowing the dirt in front of him. I leapt on top of him and rolled with him towards the river. He did not put up a fight. His limp body sprawled out beneath me as our final roll brought us to the water's edge. Quickly, I pushed his body into the current and watched him drift downstream.

I turned back towards shore in time to see two shadows heading straight for me. I raised my rifle and pulled the trigger.

BLAM!

The report of my rifle echoed across the plains while the bullet trailed off into the blackness. I quickly reloaded and took aim again. My attackers were bearing down on me. I fired again, this time hitting the mark. A scream erupted from one would be attacker, followed by words I couldn't understand as he toppled to the ground. The second charged and let out a holler as he jumped at me. I had no time to reload again. I raised my rifle holding the barrel in one hand and the stock in the other. Wielding a knife, the Indian collided with me, knocking me to the ground. He stabbed at my face, missing barely. I pushed my rifle into his chest, knocking him off me, but he was fast to recover. He came at me again. I rolled as he thrust his knife at me. He continued to holler. He stabbed once more. This time I let go of my rifle and caught his arm as he swung at me. Still on the ground, I pulled at him, sending him hurling over me and onto the ground as well. I could hear the blast of a pistol in Boone's direction. Another blast closely followed the first. I had no time to discern whether it was Boone taking the shot or becoming their first kill but the thought of losing him intensified my will to fight.

I wrestled the Indian, clenching his wrist tightly with one hand to avert any use of his knife while holding firmly to his other arm. He hollered out as we rolled around.

"I I I Ya!" he yelled.

I gained a small amount of leverage and rolled on top of him.

"Ahhhhh! Yourself!" I yelled back.

Looking into his black eyes, I saw my chance. I rammed my forehead into the bridge of his nose. I could hear the crackle underneath me as his nose splintered, contorting into a bloody mass of mangled face.

Dazed and in pain, the Indian released his grip on the knife and clutched at his face. I didn't stop my attack. I couldn't. I punched at him again and again, landing blow after blow to his check, his hands, his jaw, as he tried to roll away. With a final strike and a painful crack, the Indian ceased to move.

Slowly I stood up, still wary of what might be coming next, but weary from consecutive battles. I tried to catch my breath. The cool night air rushed in and out of my lungs. My right hand throbbed to the tips of my fingers. I tried to make a fist but stopped as a sharp stabbing pain shot from my hand and up my arm. I doubled over, almost throwing up. My adrenaline started to subside, and I was becoming overrun with exhaustion. I scanned the ground for my rifle. I could hear the Indian I shot nearby. He was not screaming or hollering, but merely talking, chanting perhaps. It was rhythmic and sounded like prayer, although I had no idea what he was saying. I found the Indian's knife that had come so close to carving a new smile into my face laying only a few steps away. I picked it up, tucked it into my belt, and continued to look for my rifle. Someone was coming. I heard steps behind me.

Where is it? I thought, frantically scanning the ground.

The blackness of night was consuming, but the stars gave me just enough glow to see. Lying in the sandy loam, the barrel of my rifle silhouetted the earth beneath it. I crouched down and reached out with my good hand. I pulled it to me, but it was useless. I was out of bullets. I stood to face the oncoming steps that were slowly closing the gap between us. I reached to my belt and grasp the hilt of the Indian's knife I had found.

"Rowdy?"

It was Boone.

"You dead?" he called out.

"Not hardly," I replied as I to walked over to him. "I heard the shots and feared the worst for you though."

"Well, the other guy had it comin'. While I laid 'neath those trees dead like, he crept by, untied the horses and then caught sight of me. His guard was down sure enough. He walked right up to me, kicked my boot, turned, and walked the other way. Imagine his surprise when I told him, 'Don't do that again!' He thought I was dead 'til I showed him otherwise. Never had a chance neither. One shot was probably enough, but two? Well, you just never can tell."

Boone chuckled. I laughed, too.

"Come on," he said, turning to walk back towards the trees where we hid.

"My shoulder is killin' me and you best round up the…"

He never had the chance to say *horses*. Boone fell backward mid step, the handle of a tomahawk sticking out of his chest, its blade embedded deep within his body. He crashed to the ground with a thud, his arms and legs twitching. A low gurgle slurred from his throat.

"No!" I yelled out.

Boone, only an arms-reach away, was gone.

CHAPTER 26

Out of the shadows Boone's killer appeared. Our eyes met. His, blackened by night, furious with anticipation, bore into me. I did not succumb to fear but became filled with rage. I couldn't feel the pain in my hand. I couldn't hear the flow of the river or the slowing whisper of the dying Indian laying nearby. I centered in on him. He was all I saw.

I stepped to my left and reached for the knife in my belt. I placed my rifle on the ground next to Boone's body and then stepped to my left again. We moved in circular pattern, watching each other, waiting to make a move. Another step, and then another. I was now on the opposite side of Boone, the Indian's back to the river and still I patiently waited to make a move.

From the dark, beyond both of us came the pounding of hooves. Delilah leapt between us, hurdling Boone's body and landing just out of our circle of vengeance. Her disruption gave me the window I needed to attack. Everything seemed to move forward in slow motion. My eyes opened wide as I yelled out, "BOOOOONE!"

I lunged forward and jumped across his body. Mid-air, I grabbed the hilt of the tomahawk that had slain him. Twisting my body and using all my force, I pulled it from Boone's body and hurled it at the Indian. It cut through the air just as before, hilt over blade, slicing through the gap between us. The Indian let out a scream as the tomahawk's blade lodged in his body. He stumbled backward, retreating into the shadows. His figure wrestled in the blackness. I watched his resurgence but was bumped from behind.

I turned swiftly, ready to fight, only to see Delilah standing directly in front of me. She whinnied loudly and shook her head vigorously.

"What is it, girl?"

CHAPTER 27

The sky was still black, but a hint of morning trickled in on the horizon. My surroundings slowly recaptured me; my senses regained some normalcy. A night hawk called out somewhere above. The flow of the river filled my ears. The night breeze chilled my skin. My hand throbbed. And then I felt the ground start to vibrate under my feet. I squinted my eyes trying to see through the blackness. The starlight that had guided me through battle was an ally when my enemies were close but gave me no hint of what was to come. The wounded Indian continued his retreat, but now was not quiet at all.

"YIP, YIP, He RAAAAW," he called out.

"What the…" I said to myself.

The hairs on my neck began to stand on end and a cold chill of adrenaline pulsed into my body. Starting in my chest, it filtered to my arms and legs as I heard the Indian's cries being answered. First one, then two, possible three high pitched replies echoed directly at our location. The starlight on the horizon blinked irregularly as shadows of riders galloped forth, gaining ground. The 'Yips' and 'Hollers' became louder, more distinct. There was to be no surprise attack, no quiet advance, and no opportunity to hold my ground or formulate a defense. I was going to be overrun if I didn't move out.

To the west the land was still dark, barren just beyond the river and flat. The eastern sky slowly turned from black to a dark shade of purple, creeping in as my attacker's reinforcements made their charge of rescue and revenge. I turned to Delilah, grabbed the reins and began to step into the stirrup when I stopped. Boone lay still on the ground behind me. I stepped down and knelt beside him having only a few moments to spare. I placed his hands on his chest just over his wound. It still leaked of blood and fluid. He was cool to the touch.

"Boone... I..."

I had no idea what to say. I had no time to care for him, to bury him, to tell anyone what happened to him. He had been there from the beginning, covering my tracks one way or another and for no other reason than in his mind it was the right thing to do. It didn't matter that he worked for Byrne. He was his own man, tending to his responsibilities, but standing firm for his beliefs, no matter the outcome. In the end, he had been there for me and made the ultimate sacrifice a man can make for another. I reached for his hat to cover his face.

"For he today that sheds his blood with me shall be my brother," I said as I knelt next to him.

I paused. Delilah stomped at the dirt. I placed his hat across his face, stood up, and mounted Delilah. I looked down on my friend.

"Good-bye, my brother."

I turned my attention to the river. The band of Indians continued their advance. Nudging Delilah with my boot, we made our way into the cool, dark waters of the Arkansas River. The current pulled at us, but Delilah trudged onward. Her hooves barely touched the bottom. Swimming at times, the current fought us all the while. Finally, Delilah made it across the river and climbed the muddy banks to the dry grasses just beyond. We were soaked through.

Safely on dry land, we set off at a gallop following the retreating dark of night. As we went, I turned in the saddle to look back. The sun cracked the horizon. The cries of the Indian raid ceased as morning broke ground beyond Dodge City. By now they had discovered the battleground. Did they find Boone? Would they locate Delilah's tracks leading into the river? Were they looking for me? Would they resume their pursuit or return with their dead and wounded? I patted Delilah's neck and whistled at her, keeping pace to an inexorable escape. It would be a hard day of riding.

CHAPTER 28

The growing distance between me and Dodge City lengthened, but I knew this would not be the last time I would see its shadow on the horizon. As long as Byrne lived, that shadow would follow me. I was sure our paths would cross again.

Injured, exhausted, and torn by the troubles left behind me, I forced myself to look forward. The rising sun lit the way. Storm clouds slowly formed in the distance, reaching upward and outward across our path.

Dawn had presented an opportunity to start anew. As the sun rose in the sky, Delilah and I pressed forth. Westward, beyond the clouds were the mountains and Lincoln, New Mexico. I had to find Samuel McAlister, Boone's father.

Somewhere a riverboat captain watched the water, soaking in its morning reflections, yearning to reach the next bend in the river. A rancher, powerful and nasty, paced sleeplessly, waiting for news of a successful raid and the prize that would accompany it. A wounded warrior is carried back to his people, the vision of an unfinished battle haunting his dreams. And then there was me. My father's voice surfaced from deep inside.

A man acts like one because he has to. A boy acts like one when he wants to. What are you?

What had I become? I was my own man and I knew what I had to do. I tightened my grip on Delilah and galloped westward.

INTERLUDE 2

Dog walked back to the porch, reclaiming his spot at the base of Rowdy's empty chair. He watched as the images of Rowdy and Roberson became silhouettes in the distance. Closing his eyes, he slept.

INTERLUDE 3

The heat of mid-day turned as evening approached. The sun, low in the sky, cast long shadows behind Rowdy and Roberson as they approached Snake River. Traveling side by side, Rowdy pointed out a suitable place to make camp. Roberson nodded in agreement.

"Looks like the same spot we used last spring with Hatchem," Roberson commented.

"Pretty close," replied Rowdy.

They rode in and dismounted next to a large boulder leaning its way towards the river. A large Rio Grande Cottonwood stood directly across from the boulder, its branches reaching out as if to catch itself before tumbling into the river. A natural barrier of water, tree, and rock provided a secure place to spend the night.

Rowdy and Roberson made camp and settled in for the evening. A campfire lit the night between them. A pan of water rested in the glowing coals, bubbling. Roberson sat near the fire. His outstretched body sprawled lazily in front of him. He propped his bootless feet up near the flames and leaned back on the boulder for support. Rowdy sat across from him.

"We should make Potter's Ridge by mid-day tomorrow. Be passin' by Brubaker's too," Rowdy said.

Brubaker's was on the way, but not a necessary stop. The general store always had lots of stock, but the saloon and card room were a trap for any man if they weren't careful.

"Nah," Roberson replied. "Last time I stopped there I almost lost my horse and saddle to a trader headin' for Californy. It's a good thing he was caught cheatin'. You can still see his beaver hat hangin' over the bar in the saloon."

Rowdy laughed.

"You never were good at cards anyway."

Roberson shot Rowdy a glare that would offend any other man, but Rowdy smiled back knowing he'd had some fun at Roberson's expense. Roberson leaned over and spit in the fire. The hot coals sizzled. A trail of smoke puffed its way into the air, disappearing through the branches that covered their camp.

"Eh!" Roberson grunted as he leaned back against the boulder once more, sliding his hat over his face.

Rowdy followed the trail of smoke through the trees, eyeing its path as it rose. He lay back on the ground, watching the light of the fire dance above him. His eyes became increasingly heavy. Entranced by the sporadic flicker, Rowdy closed his eyes. He could still smell the campfire, even as he drifted off to sleep.

The rippling water lulled him, the fire warmed him, and the smoke... The smoke rose. Blackening the night, the smoke encircled him, filling his nose, filling his lungs. He couldn't breathe. Ash fell onto his lips. He couldn't move. Sweat dripped from his brow. His forehead was hot. The buttons on his shirt burned his chest.

Somewhere in the distance, an Indian warrior let out a victory yell. "Yip Yip He-Yaw!"

Not in the distance. He was right there. Standing over Rowdy, he raised his tomahawk. Blood dripped from the Indian's arm. The whites of his eyes turned bloodshot. He clenched his teeth and swung the tomahawk down at Rowdy.

"AHHH!" Rowdy yelled out.

Snake River flowed calmly nearby. Fireflies littered the shoreline. Rowdy's scream exited the night as quickly as it had entered. He scrambled to his feet, reaching blindly for his rifle, his knife, something to fend off his attacker. Quiet darkness was all that was there.

"A dream?"

Rowdy rubbed his eyes. It felt much more than that. His head spun, and his eyes pounded. Rowdy walked barefoot to the river's edge. A night bird sang out in the distance. Squatting down, he dipped his hand into the cool current and splashed his face. He rubbed his eyes firmly. Water dripped from his forehead as he looked out over the river. Rowdy stood up and wiped his hands on his legs. He returned to his spot near the fire where he lay down. Coals were all that remained, but glowed orange, red, and yellow. Charred wood poked out unevenly from the hot ash around the fire.

"That was no dream," he whispered to himself. "Just the past paying me an unwelcomed visit."

Rowdy picked up a small stone and tossed it into the ash and coals and lay down again. Sleep eventually found him, but with it brought visions of a past he'd never forget.

CHAPTER 29

Delilah and I rode furiously to escape Byrne, Dodge City, and a life that had taken a sudden sour turn. The sun beat us down during the day and the night chilled us near through to the bone. Unsure if we were being followed, we stopped only for water. My hand, less swollen, still throbbed and was probably broken as it was difficult to close firmly. Delilah showed signs of exhaustion and needed a well-deserved rest, but rest would have to wait. We couldn't afford to let up. I had never been this far west. After two days, we changed to a more southerly route. Learning to navigate by starlight with Captain Hennessy all those years on the river was paying off.

By mid-afternoon on the fifth day, we came to an unscheduled halt. We were somewhere in Texas when I noticed a dark haze forming in front of us. As we came closer, it thickened and what I thought was haze turned out to be smoke. Black as night, it billowed upward and was carried off by westerly winds. I slowed Delilah, and then stopped completely. She stomped her hooves at the ground and snorted nervously.

"What is it, girl?"

I looked in each direction to see if I could see what might have spooked her but saw nothing. We were too far away to spot what was burning so we slowly crept forward, following the smoke trail.

Keep a watchful eye, I thought.

The terrain was rocky. Bluffs and plateaus were scattered about. Dried shrubs and tall grasses swayed in patches on the prairie floor. Instead of heading dead on to the smoke, we worked our way closer in a circular direction, flanking its position to the northeast and then north. We came to a small rise and I dismounted. I led Delilah by the reins, carefully scanning my surroundings.

"Look there, Delilah. Wagons. Four of 'em. Ain't no way that was an accident. We better hold up here and watch a bit."

I tied Delilah's reins to a small cedar tree nearby. It was easier to see from our somewhat raised position. I offered water to Delilah, and then sat beneath the cedar tree. Leaning back against its trunk, I sighed a bit of relief. I was beat and not ready to fall into the middle of another scrape if I could help it. Delilah drank while I watched the fire burn through the wagon train below in the distance. Not much I could do but sit. We both needed the rest and rather than throw caution to the wind and head straight on, we took this chance to regroup.

I dozed off for a bit. No telling how long though. The sun was lower in the sky and I had awoken to see that the billowing smoke below showed signs of letting up. The wagons were charred and crumbling, and still no signs of activity in or around the area.

"Come on, Delilah. Let's get a closer look before night falls on us completely."

I stood up, untied Delilah, and saddled up. We slowly made

our way from the ridge where we had been. The ground was hard. Careful not to fall prey to large cracks in our path, we maneuvered closer to the smoldering mass.

We slid down a short embankment and made it to a flat area just to the north of the wagons. The sun was skimming tops of the plateaus to my right. I hadn't much daylight left as I approached the ghostly caravan. I pulled my rifle from its sheath and held it across my body.

Guiding Delilah with my injured hand, we rode parallel to each wagon. We stayed about thirty feet away on our first pass. Coming to the lead wagon, we turned to walk down the opposite side.

"Damn!" I said and pulled Delilah to a stop.

Lying on the ground in front of me were the bodies of eight people. Four men, four women, and each one sprawled in a different position.

"Who did this?"

I hopped down from Delilah and knelt next to the closest body. It was a younger man. His face was rough and unshaven. I put my hand to his forehead. It was cool to the touch. His shirt was stained with sweat and blood and torn where he had been shot. His boots were missing as was any weapon he might have had.

"You never had a chance, did ya?"

I stood up and looked at the other victims. I walked the length of the scene, observing each person in their morbid spot. The three other males had similar wounds and were spread apart, stationed nearest what I assumed to be their wagon. The women however lay together, one next to the other. They were closest to the middle wagon and had tried to barricade themselves behind two splintered barrels. They had been shot as well. A single rifle lay on the ground at the feet of one woman, empty of ammunition and stained with battle.

Each wagon was smoldering and smelled of wood and cloth, hot metal and overcooked supplies.

"Come nightfall, every animal in the area is gonna be scavenging around this mess," I said to myself.

I whistled for Delilah.

"Come on, ol' girl. We've got some work to do."

I spent the next hour digging shallow graves, sorting through what I could of their supplies, and watching out for anything or anyone that might head my way. The ground was soft at first dig, but then became hard and dry. My hand hurt, my back ached, but these people needed closure; a spot at least where the animals wouldn't get at them. There was no bringing them to town because there wasn't one nearby. The last place I saw any activity or came close to western civilization was two days north east of here just outside the Oklahoma Territory. I placed as many rocks and stones on and around each of their sites as I could find. It was just at dark when I finished with the last body. This would not be an experience I would want to remember but was burned into my memory for a lifetime.

I built a small fire close to the first wagon and cooked a few cups of beans that I found in one of the supply chests near the back of the caravan. Most everything had been either burned, taken, or was just unusable. I was lucky to find what I did. Besides a small bag of beans, I recovered a leather canteen of water, a small burlap tarp, and a tiny pillow. It was crudely made and looked to be a work in progress, but it kept my head off the ground none-the-less. I took the cooking pot I'd gotten at Fort Dodge from the fire and offered a spoonful of beans to Delilah.

"Come now, these here are the finest beans you'll ever eat. Cooked 'em myself."

Delilah snorted, but gladly took as much as she could lap up. I stroked her nose and scratched at her ears. Her large, brown eyes reflected the firelight and for once I felt some peace. I sat down near her and helped myself to a spoonful. She bit at my hat and knocked it from my head.

"Hey!" I laughed.

Delilah looked straight at me and snorted once again.

"You want some more, huh? Told you these were the best."

I took one more bite and then fed the rest to Delilah. We each had a helping of water and I laid out the burlap tarp near the fire. I checked my rifle for ammunition and slid it next to me as I lay down. It was uncomfortable, but sleep found me quickly. It found me quicker than I had thought, and I slept more soundly than I should have. It took Delilah's loud whinny and hoof stomps to rouse me from my slumber.

CHAPTER 30

Startled awake, my head was still foggy, and my eyes fought to adjust to the darkness around camp. I reached for my rifle and stood up trying to figure out what was going on. The fire had died down. It exuded an orange glow but was too dim and didn't provide ample light by which to see. The sky was riddled with stars, but the moon had apparently decided to sit this one out. I stepped towards Delilah.

"Calm down, girl. What's got you in a fuss?"

As if on cue, yips and howls sailed through the night, echoing in the distance. I could hear a low growl, and then another. Delilah snuffed and stomped nervously at the ground. Using my boot as a poker, I stoked at the embers in my fire, trying to rekindle a flame. Coal charred the bottom of my boot, but a small flicker of hope sparked to life. Flames engulfed an untouched portion of wood and was just enough for me to work with. I quickly tore a strip of burlap from the tarp I had been sleeping on and wrapped it around the end of the shovel I had used earlier that evening, making a small torch.

The yips, howls, and growls were getting closer. I threw my remaining firewood onto the fire and walked over to Delilah. She was tied to the wagon remains behind us and was safely behind the fire, but out of reach of any wild flames.

The fire grew. Wood crackled, and sparks jumped at the sky, disappearing just overhead. I walked a few paces in front of the fire and wedged the shovel into the ground. The burlap still burned but was slowly diminishing. I returned to my spot near the fire and waited.

Delilah had calmed down a bit but was on high alert. Her ears twitched, and her eyes were wide with anticipation. I stepped close to her, put my arm around her muzzle.

"Whoa, girl," I whispered. "We'll be okay as long as that fire stays lit."

I stepped back to the fire. The fresh wood was at full blaze and lit a wide area around our camp. I looked at the flames.

"You better last."

The first set of eyes I caught sight of approached us from the front of the wagon, but stopped in the shadows, just short of the firelight. The eyes glowed white with the reflection of my fire. The animal didn't make a move. It stood still and watched. A second pair of eyes joined the first and then a third. I checked my rifle once more. Delilah's ears twitched again, leading her to look in a different direction. I followed her gaze to see two more pairs of eyes coming in from our right.

"This could get ugly," I whispered to Delilah.

The group of three began a low, vibrating growl. The middle pair of eyes took a few steps forward in advance of the others. Breaching from its shadowy cover, I could clearly see a large gray wolf standing only 20 feet from me. As if in a standoff, the wolf stared at our camp. I took a step to one side trying to break its gaze, but when it did not follow me it became clear what they were here for.

The two wolves, who had sat in the shadows to my right now stood and moved forward two steps, then a third. Baring their teeth and rolling a low guttural growl made the hairs on my neck stand straight up. Delilah pawed nervously. I was worried that she'd panic and break her ties trying to make a run for it. Our only hope was to end this before it began. I raised my rifle, took aim, and fired at the two wolves. A piercing yelp filled the air as my bullet connected with one of the wolves. The other fled into the night. The wounded wolf fell to the ground and wriggled about, whimpering as it struggled in pain.

I turned back to the main pack that had come directly on to us. Only the alpha wolf remained. Though poised and ready to leap, it remained still. It showed no teeth, but its stare bore into me.

"Where'd yer buddies go, fella?"

I raised my rifle again preparing to fire.

"Sorry pal. It's you or me, and I ain't going yet."

I pulled on the trigger but was stopped short. Delilah reared up behind me and whinnied loudly as two wolves had leapt into camp from behind. Both wielding deadly jaws, they advanced on Delilah. I turned but couldn't get a clear shot. Delilah reared again, kicking her front legs at her attackers. I raced into the scene, rifle raised and ready.

"Ahhhhhh!" I yelled.

The hungry wolves didn't flinch, but moved quickly, trying

to avoid Delilah's stomps and kicks. I charged at the wolf closest to me. Its attention and action fully engaged with Delilah. The second wolf attempted to circle behind her and mistimed its jump. As it lunged in at Delilah, she brought her rear hooves up and kicked out at the wolf. She solidly connected with it, sending it yelping and flying onto the charred wagon she was tied to. The remaining wolf retreated a few steps before regaining momentum. It was just enough time for me to pull the rifle to my shoulder and squeeze off a lethal shot. The blast rang through the night and entered the wolf's neck, exiting through its jaw. It never had time to yip or yowl. It died instantly. I looked to Delilah and raised my arm.

"Easy, girl. It's all right now."

But it wasn't. Looking straight at me, Delilah reared again. It was in that instant I remembered the alpha wolf. I turned but had no time to take a shot. The alpha wolf was mid leap when I turned to face it. Its large body tackled me to the ground, its teeth snapping at my face. Using my rifle as a brace, I shoved at the wolf. It was no use. It clawed at me, tearing my sleeves to shreds and leaving deep scratches in my forearms and shoulders. Delilah whinnied loudly, helpless in her position. If just one wolf returned to our camp, she'd be in serious trouble. Not able to free myself and feeling the ache in my injured hand, I struggled with this vicious animal. I had no time to think, no last remembrances. There was only time to survive and my time was running out.

Turning my cheek to avoid one of multiple snaps of teeth, I saw a new pair of eyes charging at me. Using my last bit of strength, I pushed as hard as I could. My broken hand lost grip of my rifle during my lunge and shot up into the air over my head. The wolf targeted my arm and bit securely into me. Its teeth sank into my arm just above the wrist. Blood dripped from the wolf's mouth, spattering my face and the ground around me as he thrashed his head about.

"Ahhhhh!" I screamed in pain.

I felt a sudden jolt above me and was twisted as my arm was being pulled away from me. My body followed, and my arm was set free. I rolled sideways, coming to rest on my stomach, my face in the dirt. I raised my head to see the wolf entangled with another animal. Its black fur camouflaged it as they wrestled in and out of the shadows. I couldn't tell if it was another wolf, but it was smaller than the alpha that had attacked me. They fought viciously.

I pulled myself to one knee and looked down at my arm. It was messy. Puncture wounds seeped blood. The flesh from my wrist to the middle of my forearm was badly bitten. Grasping my rifle, I stood slowly. Feeling woozy, my only thought was to get back to Delilah and don't pass out. I stumbled back towards the fire.

The snarling and growling continued at the edge of the lighted part of camp. Shadows danced and rolled, distorted behind the remaining fire light. There was a definitive yelp, and then all was briefly quiet. The Alpha wolf gingerly limped into view followed slowly by the dark creature. As the wolf turned to make another stand, I mustered the strength to raise my rifle with one hand, holding it as if it were a pistol. I took as careful aim as I could, though my arm wavered a bit. The dark animal lowered its head, preparing to engage once more. I pulled the trigger and never gave it the chance. I would remember this shot not because of its difficulty or the pain it caused my entire body with the jolt it gave me, but for the luck in the bullet finding its way and landing a perfect deadly strike to the wolf's head.

The echo of the report sounded off through the night. The dark animal, which had for all practical purposes saved me, disappeared into the dark terrain ahead of me. I sat down next to the fire and looked at my arm again. I would need help soon or this wound would be the end of me. I reached for my canteen and poured some water over my arm trying to wash away the grit and slime from my struggle. I had nothing to clean it with. Most of the punctures had stopped bleeding freely and were just seeping blood and fluid, but one was still flowing and gave me cause for greater concern. I applied pressure but was feeling dizzy again and felt like I might pass out. For fear of bleeding to death if I did black out, I reached into the fire pit and grabbed the unburned portion of wood that was sticking into the glowing coals. I pulled the wood from the fire to see the opposite end glowing deep orange. It pulsated as it smoldered in front of me.

"You stay put, Delilah."

I looked at her over my shoulder. She had calmed down, but I could tell she was still agitated. She looked at me, and then out to the dark, seemingly asking for reassurance that everything was okay now.

I set the glowing tinder down and pulled my knife from its sheath. Looking at my arm once more, I took a deep breath.

"This is gonna hurt," I said.

I placed the hilt of the knife between my teeth and bit down. Without taking another moment to consider my options, I reached for the fire stick and jammed the burning portion onto my arm where I was continuing to bleed. My skin sizzled, hot blood dripped from me. I could smell the hairs on my arms burn as they curled up beneath the heat from the scorching fire stick. My teeth sank into my knife handle creating divots in the leather strap surrounding it. My head lurched backwards as I let out a loud, muffled, pain-filled groan. For a moment, I could see the stars above me. They seemed brighter than before, but slowly became hazy, blending into each other as one massive white blur. I fell backwards away from the fire and all went black.

CHAPTER 31

Daybreak cracked the horizon, pouring light onto the charred remains of the wagons, the fresh shallow graves, and carnivorous aftermath that surrounded me. I hadn't moved all night. The sun shone on me, warming my body and waking me gently. I strained to open my eyes to the brightness of daytime. I started to get up. The slightest movement triggered pains in my arms to my shoulders. Dried blood and dirt crusted my shirt and arms.

"Come on...Get up!" I told myself.

My lips were as dry as my throat. I rolled slowly attempting to find a position in which I could prop myself up. Painful or not, I had to move, to stand. Once I was on my feet all I needed was to mount Delilah and then let her do the rest but getting to her was going to be a challenge.

I took a deep breath, positioned my good arm beneath my chest, and pressed at the ground. My body lifted from the ground and I was able to raise one leg to a kneeling position. Using my thigh as leverage, I placed my hand on my leg and pushed myself up. Stabbing pain shot up my arm to my shoulder. I stumbled back a step or two but remained standing. Blood rushed to my head, hitting me with a wave of dizziness. My arm throbbed, my shoulders itched and ached from the claw marks, and my stomach filled with nausea. I hadn't much to eat or drink, but what was there exited quickly followed by violent dry heaves. I doubled over and almost lost my balance.

When the last of my stomach convulsions subsided, I wiped my mouth with my shirt sleeve, torn as it was. My rifle was on the ground to my right, my knife sticking blade first in the dirt to my left. I decided to leave them there while I prepared Delilah for the days ride. I turned to face her. She looked right at me and half snorted half whinnied.

"I know, I know. I look how I feel. You gotta git us into town. Somewhere."

I wasn't exactly sure which direction was the best route.

"Let's see where these wagons were goin'. That'll at least give us a start."

I slowly walked up to her and stroked her nose. Her right side had a long scratch from her hind leg to her belly. It wasn't deep and looked like her only battle scar.

"You put up a good fight, Delilah."

I went to untie her from the wagon and noticed that she'd broken free of the knot, probably during the night, most likely while fighting off the wolves.

"Look there. You are one loyal friend. Glad you stuck around."

I scratched her ears and she bumped me with her snout.

"Ouch. Still beat up, girl. Go easy on me."

I checked her straps and lines. Everything looked good to go. I turned to look at my camp, a battle ground that had seen two fights by different foes in just one day. I stepped forward to retrieve my knife and rifle and then stopped in my tracks. Sitting on the edge of camp, not 20 feet from me, was a medium sized dog. It had a long snout and shaggy but straight black fur. Its ears stood triangular above its head and its tail curled around its hind legs as it sat. It watched me. I looked back at it.

"So, dog, you come to finish the job or look for a reward?"

The dog remained still. I didn't feel threatened and had good reason to believe that this was the animal that intervened last night.

I slowly stepped forward and gingerly knelt to pick up my knife and rifle. Before trying to stand, I slid over to the leftover burlap tarp and cut a strip from it with my knife. Tying a knot one handed was tricky, but I managed to get it done. I slipped the looped burlap over my head and around my neck.

This should help some, I thought.

I used the stock of the rifle as leverage to help me stand upright and walked back to Delilah. I looked at the dog and wondered if it had been part of this wagon train. Unless there was a ranch or town nearby, this dog would have had to be a part of the doomed caravan.

I placed my rifle in its sheath on Delilah's pack and slipped my knife back into my belt. I stepped one foot into the stirrup on Delilah's left side and grabbed the saddle horn with my good hand. My other arm dangled next to me, tingling, burning, pulsating. I pulled and stepped hard and fast. I had only enough strength to give myself one good hoist but made the most of it. I swung my right leg over and sat down in the saddle. I gently placed my injured arm into my makeshift sling. I was relieved to find that this helped with the pain some.

"Let's go, girl. Take me anywhere there are people. I gotta get this arm looked at."

We headed out in the direction the wagons would have gone. As we exited camp, we passed by the dog, still sitting in the same spot. He followed us with his eyes as we headed out.

"What do you think, Delilah? Could we use another travelin' buddy?"

As we walked on, I looked over my shoulder and called to the dog.

"You comin?"

It was nowhere to be seen.

Delilah and I traveled in the same direction most of the morning and into the afternoon. The sky was filled with patches of white clouds. In between was the bluest sky. Rays of sunlight poked through and landed on the prairie floor in front of us. Beads of sweat rolled down my cheeks. My arm was warm. It itched. It throbbed. As the day progressed, I felt myself becoming heavier in the saddle and I started to become concerned. Waves of cold chilled my body and were becoming more frequent. Flashes of heat followed. I was nauseous. My mouth was dry. I reached for my canteen and sipped some water. That didn't help. I was certain I had a fever but was too drained to fight it. Delilah kept us on our way. I strained to keep my eyes open. Squinting was all I could muster.

We traveled onward. A hawk soaring somewhere above us screeched, startling me. I had been in a daze, but for how long?

"Keep it up, girl. I need you more than ever."

For a moment I thought I saw something ahead of us on the next rise. A horse maybe? First it was there, and then it was gone. I slumped over in the saddle and whispered to Delilah.

"Tis a bad ting, girl,"

I spoke as Mac did when facing danger on the river.

Slowly, I sat upright and looked onward. My eyes burned, drowning in salted sweat. My head pounded and felt dizzy. I noticed our path going in and out of focus. A hazy view was all I had. I let go of the reins and slumped over again. I reached for Delilah's neck, trying to gain a little support, but it was no use. I slowly slid off Delilah and crashed to the ground in a heap.

I let out an angry scream of pain as I landed on my mangled arm. I reached out, grasping for anything, wishing for an end of the agony. My breath was hot and labored. I coughed as I inhaled dust from the settling earth beneath me.

Delilah stopped where I had fallen and stood next to me. Sunlight shone down through a break in the clouds. I slowly rolled to my side, my eyes closed but succumbing to the brilliance of the sun's illuminations. Dazzling sparks and streaks of light shot across my eyes as if I were watching a swarm of fireflies swoop and dive over the river on a moonless night. Vulnerable and helpless, I lay in a heap. Sweat rolled down my cheeks and plopped in the dirt.

Gradually, the unyielding ground pounded beneath my battered body. Rhythmically, it became more noticeable. Was someone coming? The pounding ceased, and all was quiet. Delilah bellowed a cautious whinny that seemed far off. I strained to open my eyes. Something. Someone was near. I heard whispers as I lay on the ground but didn't understand. The shadow moved over me, blocking the sun. I had no strength, no means of protection. I was at my most vulnerable point.

A callused hand pressed against my forehead. Faintly, more whispers trickled over me. I was gently shaken, and then rolled onto my back. My eyes fluttered. Sunlight, shadow, whispers, and then finally my eyes slowly squinted open, focusing just enough to see the blade of a knife being slowly lowered towards me. I tried to move, but the shock of exhaustion and fever crashed over me. As I faded into blackness, I felt the blade touch my skin and heard a whisper I did understand.

"Shhh…"

CHAPTER 32

Embers from an exhausting fire crackled and snapped as I awakened. Stars blanketed the sky above me as I lay on the ground. My eyes opened to the blackness of night, slowly adjusting to the darkness around me. I tilted my head towards the fire. Its yellowish glow illuminated my face, causing me to close and reopen my eyes again. I tried to sit up but was unable to.

"You shol stay put, Señor. No try to geet up."

This strange, new voice spoke to me from the other side of the fire. I twisted my head to see who was speaking, but I was too stiff, and he was just out of sight. My muscles ached; my hand throbbed, as did my arm. My arm! I tried to lift it, but it was secured to something on the ground and I couldn't move it.

"My arm. Why can't I move my arm?" I said to the dark.

"Shhh, Señor. Rest. In the morning ju will see."

I hadn't the strength to argue, though I was concerned with my restraint. A horse snorted close by. Delilah! Was that her? I made a clicking noise with my tongue on the side of my mouth and waited. Could she hear me? Another snort and a huff whinnied from just beyond my feet.

"Your horse. She is okay, but you are not. I tell you when it is light."

I tried again to lift my arm. I pulled as hard as I could, but pain seared through my forearm and shot through my fingers in one direction and to my shoulder in the other. I felt dizzy again. I lay my head down again to see a blanket of stars shining above me. A bright light appeared overhead and streaked across my field of vision but was gone before I knew it. I closed my eyes and drifted into a hazy, restless sleep.

CHAPTER 33

A tingling sensation from my injured forearm roused me from sleep. I opened my eyes to grey skies. Wind blew through camp in short bursts and was cooler than the night before. I looked at my arm to see that my sling had been removed and my shirt sleeve had been cut. My arm was wrapped with cotton clothes and was strapped to a log next to me. It was as long as my body, thick, and very heavy. I gently lifted my head to see that my left leg was also bound to this log. I was stuck. A dark substance seeped from the edges of the wrap but seemed to help alleviate some of the pain and itching in my arm.

"Hey," I said aloud.

No answer. I turned my head in different directions, taking in my immediate surroundings as best I could. I needed to know where I was and who the stranger was. Friend? Foe? His help, not withstanding, I remained cautious.

To my right was a burned-out campfire surrounded by a circle of stones. A larger boulder sat just beyond the fire pit, blocking my view of what lay beyond. Past my feet was open country. To my left was the log that immobilized my arm and body, which I couldn't see over very well. I tilted my head backwards to see what was behind me, but I was too stiff and sore to move much at all.

Who had helped me and why? And where was he now? Had I been abandoned? This wasn't exactly a friendly part of the country. Most wouldn't chance helping an injured stranger, especially out in the middle of nowhere.

I clicked my teeth and whistled out for Delilah. Last night I thought I had gotten a response, but this morning received none. I lay looking up at the sky, listening. Near the boulder I heard a rustling sound, too small for a horse, but possibly a person. I leaned my head to the right to look. Peeking around the edge of the massive rock, I saw the dark hair and head of a small child.

"Hey," I said.

The head of hair disappeared behind the rock.

"Can you help me?"

Slowly, from the same spot, the child peeked out once more, this time bringing a finger to his lips, motioning for me to be quiet. It was a small boy. He pointed in the direction across the log where I couldn't see.

"What is it?" I whispered.

The boy placed his finger to his lips once again.

"Shhh," he whispered, his eyes pleading for me to be quiet. I had no choice but to trust him.

Without speaking or making any other gestures, the boy crept out from behind the rock and slowly stepped in my direction. He was dressed in a raggedy white shirt and scuffed pants. There was a hole in one pant leg just below the knee. On his feet were tattered sandals that needed repair. One flopped as he stepped closer to me. He wore a red bandana around his neck. As he got closer, he raised his finger to his mouth again. He crouched down about ten feet away from me, squatting on both feet and looked over the log.

"What do you see?" I whispered.

"Vamos! No te dije estes listo? Quieres que el Hombre se suelte y nos mate?"[1]

The boy sprang to his feet and ran back behind the boulder. Speaking from behind the log and out of sight was the voice that I had heard last night.

"How you geet so banged up, Señor? Looks like you got chewded by a dog or wolf or somsing."

I heard footsteps as the stranger circled around into view. His step was not in sync. He was somewhat dragging a leg, limping his way around.

"Where am I?" I asked. "What did you do to my arm?"

"Ju are at my camp. I foun you yus over there, pass the ridge."

He pointed beyond the log, again where I couldn't see. I tried to sit up but was unable to move my arm or leg within my bindings.

"Will you untie me?"

"Not jus yet, Señor. You are badly hurt, and I don't know you. Maybe you kill me and my boy and run?"

"No no. I'm not that guy. What's your name?"

"Maybe you are an' maybe you not. We will see."

He looked at me with cautious eyes.

"My name is Santiago Hidalgo."

Santiago called out to the boy.

"Traé agua y bendajes."[2]

He turned back to me.

"We should make a new wrap for your arm, Señor. Eet is time."

He limped towards me, pulling at his right leg and dragging his boot in the dirt. His clothes were also old and dirty. He wore a sash around his waist and his pants were tucked into his boots. There was a tear in his right leg and a stain surrounding the opening. I assumed it was dried blood, but I hesitated to ask. He stood next to my waist and looked down at me. His face was dark and weathered. Wrinkles fanned out from his eyes and matching scars on either cheek stretched from under his eyes to just above his lip, disappearing into his mustache. His face was dirty. He reached behind his back with his right hand and pulled out a large knife.

"Try nothing, Señor. I would hate to have wasted my time."

Bending over, he lowered the knife towards my arm and carefully cut the bindings holding me to the log.

"Do no move. The medicine on your arm will work, but you mus stay still so eet does no fall. I have no more to give."

The boy arrived with a canteen and fresh cloth. He placed the small canteen on the ground and began tearing strips of cloth. Santiago cut the old cloth and unwrapped it from my arm. A green, pasty, mud like mixture clung to my entire forearm. I could not see my injury, but I could still feel the pain, although it was not as fierce as before.

"Poner agua?"[3] the boy asked.

"Solo un poco."[4]

Santiago watched as the boy gently dripped fresh water onto my arm, moistening the poultice that covered my injury.

"Sufficiente,"[5] Santiago said.

The boy placed the canteen back on the ground and sat down. Santiago wrapped my arm and tied the cloth near my wrist so it wouldn't slip. He sat back and looked me in the eyes. I could tell he was still very wary of me. He lifted his knife and pointed it at my nose.

"No trouble? I no tie you back. Comprende?"

I raised my free arm and bent it at my elbow.

"No trouble."

Silence separated us until the boy spoke out and pointed into the distance. Dust rose from beyond the rise where Santiago had found me.

"The wind, she is peeking up."

Santiago motioned to the boy. "Cuida los caballos."[6]

The boy stood up and jumped over the log I had been tied to. I followed him with my eyes and saw that he was running toward a small patch of brambly trees. Tied in the shade were two horses, presumably Santiago's. And then I saw her. Delilah. A bucket stood on the ground in front of them. My saddle and supplies had been removed and placed against the trunk of one of the trees. When the boy reached the horses, they greeted him with head bobs. Delilah turned her head to look at the boy as well. He stroked the first two with both hands. Reaching into a sack that lay just out of reach, he pulled some dried grasses and offered them to each horse. They each took a handful and chewed. The boy then went back to the bag and pulled one more handful from it. He slowly approached Delilah, reaching his hand out to her. Delilah stood watching and gave a small snort. The boy did not flinch but stayed attuned to his task. Reluctant, but seemingly grateful, Delilah received the handful of grass and chewed until it was gone. I turned to speak to Santiago.

"How long have I been here?"

"You sleep for almost two days. Wheen you wake lass night, eet was the first time you say somsing. You had fever. Your arm was bad an' your blood was sick. That horse, she did no want me to take you from by her. She stood over you all that first night. After, Juan Diego finally got her to stay with the others."

"Juan Diego?"

"The boy. He is my brother's son, but he is with me now. Hee's family was attacked by Comancheros in the south near Chihuahua. My brother, he was keeled. Only Juan Diego survived. He hide in a water barrel when they come. He sees everything. His mother, his father, his brother, all shot. He stay in the barrel for two days. Everyone thought he was taken to the Commanche."

I looked back at Juan Diego as he worked near the horses. Young and alone, he had my sympathy. I knew how he must have felt, how he must feel. He was lucky Santiago took him in, lucky that he had family close by. Family close by, but only Santiago? I turned back to him. He was very cautious around me from the start, but should I return the feeling? Why did he help me? I quickly decided to go along with everything he had said and would say, but with restraint. I had an uneasy feeling, but I couldn't quite put my finger on why.

183

"Do you know how far we are from the nearest town?" I asked.

"Where you want to go, my friend?"

Santiago leaned back and looked at me curiously.

"I have work in Lincoln. Hopin' it's not too far off. Those wolves did a number on me, but thanks to you, I'm feeling much better."

Santiago stood up and turned his back to me. I watched as he took a dragging step away from me and then turn around again. He looked to the horses and then to me again.

"Señor, it is not a good time. You mus rest."

He called out to Juan Diego. "Trae comida. Estamos ambrientos. Apurate!"[7]

His call startled Juan Diego causing him to drop a bucket of water he had collected for the horses. The water splashed from its brim and spattered on his clothing. Running with his arms outstretched at his side, Juan Diego disappeared behind the boulder. Santiago watched with a crooked smirk, content that his order had been followed quickly. Juan Diego reappeared and ran towards us. He carried a small burlap bag in one hand and a jug in the other. He placed the jug by the fire pit and approached Santiago with the bag. Santiago took the bag and looked inside.

"Señor, I hope you hungry. We will eat good." He reached into the bag a pulled out a dead snake.

"Rattlesnake?" I had heard you could eat snake, but never thought I'd have the stomach to do so.

"Si. Ees very good. We make the fire and cook now."

I sat where I was and watched as Juan Diego gathered kindling to restart the fire, bring the logs, and follow the instructions given to him. Santiago sat back, pulled a knife from his belt and skinned the snake, looking my way all the while. My arm was sore, but the throbbing had gone away. My hand was discolored, but I was able to wiggle my fingers. My shoulders were stiff as was my back, probably from lying on the ground for so long.

Santiago cooked while Juan Diego assisted in the chore. As they worked the fire and cooked the dead snake, I stretched my legs in front of me. I slowly wiggled my toes and flexed my leg muscles. It felt good. My legs felt tight but were loosening as I moved about. By the time the meal was ready, I was able to comfortably sit up and hoisted myself onto the log I had been strapped to. I was more capable than I thought and was given a surprised glance by Santiago as I sat in front of him. I needed to move around, if not only to loosen up, but to investigate my surroundings.

"Be careful, Señor. You do no want to strain yourself."

Santiago watched me closely, paying less attention to the fire. Juan Diego pulled the snake from the fire and cut it into bite sized pieces. He placed a fair amount on two dusty metal plates, and the rest in a coffee mug. He placed one plate near Santiago and the other he brought to me.

"Thank you," I said to Juan Diego.

He smiled a toothy smile, but quickly wiped it from his face as Santiago caught sight of it.

We ate quietly. The afternoon passed, and the gray clouds broke apart, spilling blue patches of sky overhead as we finished our meal. Eating snake is not something I will rush to do again, but under the circumstances it was filling. It had little taste, but its texture was not as savory as I would have liked. It was more like eating the fatty gristle from a good steak without tasting any of the meat. Luckily, there was plenty of water to wash it down. As Juan Diego took the empty plates, cleaned them and put them away, I decided to try standing. Bracing myself with my good arm, I pushed up on the log and made it to my feet. I was a bit wobbly, but not too bad. Santiago stood up. Before he could say anything, I spoke.

"I'm gonna check on my horse."

"Señor, as you can see, she is there. Ees alright. You no need to worry," he said, smiling.

Really? I thought.

"Not worried. Just want to give her a rub."

I started towards her slowly. I clicked my tongue on my cheek. Delilah's ears perked up and she turned her head towards me. The horses she was standing with also looked. I did not look back to Santiago though I could sense that he wanted to say something more. I approached Delilah and reached out to her. Her nose met my outstretching hand. She let out a soft whinny. I glanced around and found my duffle and saddle on the ground under the tree she was tied to. It looked undisturbed, except that it had been removed from her. I looked up to the tree where Delilah's reins were tied. Ordinarily a rider would only wrap and loosely tie the reins around a hitching post or branch. A good horse would stay as Delilah did. Strangely though, Delilah was securely tied with a double knot. She wasn't going anywhere, and I was starting to guess I wasn't going anywhere either.

I stroked Delilah's nose and saw her eyes grow larger as she looked past me. I turned to find Santiago walking towards me. Step, drag, step, his legs moved rhythmically as he went.

"Señor. Ees geeting late. Juan Diego will make a spot for you by the fire."

"Thank you for your hospitality." I looked around. "I am still wondering which direction will get me to Lincoln."

"Si." He raised his hand and pointed. "Lincoln. She is that way. Two days, maybe three. Rest tonight, and tomorrow I weel take you."

Santiago looked at me with curiosity.

"That sounds good," I answered cautiously.

Santiago raised his chin and squinted. The scars on his cheeks wrinkled.

"Do you have any coffee?" I asked.

I didn't really want any, but I wanted to break the silence that was growing between us. I imagined things were taking a turn for the worse. It was just a matter of time. My trust in Santiago was quickly fading.

Slowly, we both returned to the campfire. Once again, Juan Diego fetched the cups, pot, and coffee. As the water steamed, I looked out towards open land. Was Lincoln truly in the direction Santiago had pointed? One way or another, I was leaving in the morning. Dust rose on the horizon as it had earlier in the day. The wind was slight, not powerful enough to kick up such a cloud, at least near our camp. I guessed it was the same further off because the dust cloud I was watching seemed isolated to one area on the plains. What would cause such a disturbance? Riders? If it was, they weren't getting any closer. Yet.

I looked at Juan Diego.

"What do you think, Juan Diego, buffalo?"

I pointed at the cloud. He looked in that direction and without saying a word, stood up and walked over to the horses. He sat down by the tree they were tied to and remained there until dusk.

I ate plenty and was regaining some energy. I could stand up quicker and easier than I had early in the day. The wrap on my arm held fast and the poultice that surrounded my bite was doing a good job. I was sore, but the pain was manageable.

As the sun began to set, the colors on the western prairie painted a beautiful picture in front of me. I remembered the evenings on the river. As quiet and peaceful as they were, they didn't hold a stick to the picturesque scene that I was watching this night. The sun melted onto the horizon. Orange and yellow rays of light blended together and stretched out in every direction across the sky. A light shade of purple rose and met the soft, warm colors of the sunset. The strands of yellow and orange seemed to pull night over us. Pinks and reds flared up on the few remaining puffs of clouds as the final crest of sunlight disappeared. Slowly, light faded and night marched in. One by one, stars blinked overhead. The purple blanket of dusk changed to black as night fully engulfed the plains.

Santiago poked at the fire. Juan Diego remained alone by the horses. I heard movement just outside of camp. Santiago must have heard it too because he dropped the stick that he had and quickly stood up. The noise stopped as quickly as it was heard.

"Probably some animal gettin' a whiff of camp. You think?"

I watched Santiago. I wanted to see his face as he answered. It wouldn't really matter what he said, but how he said it.

"Si, Señor."

He looked at me. Turning back again he raised his arms, clenched his fists, and yelled out, "Aiiiiii Yaaahh!"

His yell disappeared into the dark without so much as an echo to give report. He sat back down, picked up his poking stick, and began stirring the fire again.

"That shoul scare heem away."

He talked directly to the flames as they bounced between us, never looking up at me. Light flickered in the black of his eyes as he stirred and poked at the burning wood. The scars on his cheeks were blackened by shadow as the rest of his face glowed orange and red, changing as the fire stirred. My trust for this man had all but vanished. Something wasn't right.

CHAPTER 34

"Wake up, Señor, wake up!" Juan Diego shook my shoulder as he spoke.

My eyes opened wide to see him kneeling next to me.

"What is it, Juan Diego?"

"Shhh, you mus go!" He spoke in a whisper, but his tone sounded urgent. "They come soon."

"Who's coming?"

"Men. Bad men to take you."

I sat up next to him.

"Santiago trick you. When he no looking, I ready your horse. Go! You mus go now!"

I could hear heavy breathing from across camp where Santiago slept.

"Okay," I said.

Slowly, I got to my feet. Juan Diego stood next to me. We quietly walked to Delilah. She was loosely tied to a tree and was saddled, ready as Juan Diego had said. I stroked her muzzle. It felt good to be close to her again. She nodded her head, ready to go. Juan Diego untied her and held the reins. I started to mount up and then stopped. I turned to look at Juan Diego. In the dark, the silhouette of a small child stood before me. He reached out with the lead line. I took the ropes from his small hand.

"Vaya con Dios," Juan Diego said.

I started to say something but lost my chance. He turned and ran into the blackness of camp, disappearing.

"Juan Diego?" I spoke in a raised whisper.

No answer.

"Juan Diego?" I called again, louder this time.

Again, no answer. How could I leave him?

Go…

This word whispered into my ear, from nowhere really, but was clear as a bell. Reluctantly, I climbed onto Delilah. The horses tied nearby became restless as they sensed our movement. We needed to go before they caused too much ruckus. The last thing I needed was for Santiago to wake up.

My boots gently tapped Delilah's haunches and we stole away from camp quietly. I looked over my shoulder as the camp blended with the nighttime landscape, becoming one blurry, darkened mass. No signs of Juan Diego. No reason to think Santiago was awakened by my escape. I looked forward into nothingness. Slowly we sauntered over the barren terrain, gaining more distance from danger with each rhythmic step. Under the cover of night, we made our way beneath a starless, overcast sky.

We pushed onward, stopping briefly at a stream that bubbled across our path. I led Delilah to the water where she drank. Light sparkled around the ripples in the slow-moving current. I dismounted and knelt in the soft mud, feeling its coolness spread across my palm.

My reflection bobbed below me. A worn, ragged face looked back. I was tired. My body was healing, but still ached. I dipped my hands into the water and splashed my face. Water dripped from my nose and chin. I rubbed my eyes. Reaching down, I splashed at my face again. I rubbed the back of my neck. I felt somewhat refreshed as I stood. Stretching skyward, I yawned and turned to Delilah. She had finished drinking and stood still near me.

I reached my hand out to pat her side but stopped mid-way. Just beyond Delilah, in the direction from which we came, I saw movement in the shadows. Morning was beginning to take shape and, although I was drowsy, my eyes caught the image as sharp as if it were midday. Slowly it crept towards us, low to the ground. Cautious. Instead of patting Delilah, I reached for my rifle and slowly removed it from its sheath, keeping my eyes on our darkened pursuer's approach. Delilah's ears perked up. She too now sensed something.

"Shhh, Delilah. I got this, girl."

I raised the rifle to my shoulder. Its weight, although not considerable, pulled on my healing arm.

Squinting, I took careful aim. My fingers rested just off the trigger. I took a shallow breath and moved my finger to a firing position. I started to squeeze gently, exhaling as I did. The animal slipped from the shadows, emerging into plain sight. The early morning provided enough light to halt my pull of the trigger. I lowered my rifle.

"You again? Thought you'd left us for good," I said.

I placed my rifle back in its sheath. The same black-haired dog that fought off my wolf attacker days before now stood in front of me. Its black eyes sunk into its long snout. Its fur carried a coat of dust but was still as black as the river on a starless night. Its pink tongue hung to one side as it stood, looking at me. I felt no alarm but took care in my movements. I stepped one step towards the dog. Its pointy ears twitched. I bent down on one knee to show I meant it no harm.

"Been followin' me?"

The dog tilted its head and dangled its tongue to the opposite side of its mouth.

I laughed.

"Can't remember the last time I did that," I said to myself. "Ya thirsty?"

I stood up and backed away slowly. When I reached Delilah, I patted her gently, reassuring her that the dog wasn't a problem. The dog circled around us and headed towards the water's edge. It lapped a good amount from the stream. I watched it the whole time wondering how long she'd been following us. Was she the 'noise' we heard outside camp early last night? Didn't matter, I guess. The dog was here now. Delilah was impartial. I stepped back down to the water and soaked my hands once more in its coolness. Dawn had broken, and day was emerging across the plains. Traveling would be easier, but also for trackers who might be looking for me. It was time to get moving. I wiped my hands on my pants as I stood up and walked to Delilah.

"Let's go, girl," I whispered to her as I rose to the saddle.

I pulled the reins to one side, signaling Delilah it was time to go. The dog looked up from where it stood. Its eyes connected with mine. Its nose sniffed at the air. Its tongue now rested just inside its mouth. She looked at me with curiosity.

"You comin'?" I asked.

The dog licked its lips and focused its ears. I gave Delilah a nudge and set off. Pressing my tongue to my teeth, I let out a quick, sharp whistle and looked back at the dog. It bolted from its standing position and caught up, walking next to us as we headed for town.

CHAPTER 35

It was nearing mid-day. The cloud cover from the night before had all but vanished. Small wisps of white traced through portions of the sky. It was hot, but tolerable. Sweat slid down my back. I brushed the bandage on my arm against my forehead, soaking up the wetness and dust that had accumulated over the course of the day. Where was Lincoln? By now Santiago was aware of my disappearance. Would he pursue me? Was Juan Diego okay? These thoughts bounced around my head as we moved onward. We came to a rise in terrain, a hilly area that I had seen coming for some time now. The dog kept up as we made our way, its tongue dangling from its mouth. I looked at it and somehow knew she was here to stay.

We reached the top of the rise and a smile crept across my face.

"Look there, Delilah. You too, Dog. Seems like we are headed in the right direction after all."

Luck was on our side. In the distance, buildings spread across the changing prairie. It was a long and narrow stretch. I could see there was plenty of activity going on, but it was hard to make out details. Was it Lincoln? I nudged Delilah with my heel and we set off to find out.

As we approached the outskirts, we came across a worn pathway. Wagon wheels had scarred the ground leaving tiny dirt canyons running side by side forming a trail to and from the town. I led Delilah alongside, and with Dog keeping pace next to us, we headed in.

As we approached the edge of town, a wagon driven by an older man slowly bounced towards us. It was led by a single horse. It looked tired and old but was still able to pull its weight. It was definitely not a horse ol' Byrne would've kept around. A young boy, maybe ten years old, sat next to the man. I tipped my hat at them. The man nodded as they passed. His wagon was loaded down with supply bags, a wooden barrel which I presumed held water, and two metal boxes. I turned my head to glance at them as they went on. The boy had turned and was looking at me. I gave him a small wave. He waved back and then plopped back in his seat. I wondered if that was his father. Didn't matter really, I guess I was just curious.

I entered town on the main road, stopping at a sign posted near the first building. A small corral stretched out and then behind the building. Two horses stood together to one side of the corral. They looked up as I stopped to read the sign.

"Lincoln's Livery," I said aloud

"Only one in town." An unfamiliar voice spoke out to me from the landing just outside the livery's front door. I looked over to see a short man wearing jeans, a white shirt, and leather suspenders. He stepped out onto the porch closer to us. He was bald on top but had shaggy hair that wrapped ear to ear around the back of his head. A round belly protruded in front of him and scraggly sideburns grew from his cheeks. He looked harmless, but if I've learned anything, you don't take things for chance.

Dog, having been watching the horses in the corral looked toward the man and rumbled a low "Gggrruffff!"

"Easy, Dog," I whispered. I looked back at the man again. "That so?" I said.

"A-yuh. Best one too, but then again, it's the only one." The man chuckled and curled his thumbs under his suspenders. "The names Jameis. Jameis Duncan. Don't suppose you'd be needin' a place for yer horse there? Or are you just passin' through?"

I'm sure it was an honest and as equally harmless a question, but I wasn't ready to share anything with anybody, yet. His offer was tempting, and I could use a decent night's rest.

"Could keep an eye on yer dog too, if yer wantin'." Jameis smiled a toothy smile, surely hoping to gain my business.

"Tell you what, I'm just getting into town. I'll be back later this afternoon and will take you up on yer offer if ya still have a spot."

Jameis' smile collapsed a bit. He'd probably heard that before, but it was obvious he wanted my business.

"Alright then. Be lookin' fer ya this afternoon. The Waterin' Hole Saloon is just up a bit if you need some chow. They have a pretty comfy bunkhouse too if that suits you."

I tipped my hat at him, thanked him, and pulled on the reins to lead Delilah away from the corral fence. I whistled for Dog to follow and headed further into town.

We clomped into the heart of Lincoln. People were busy on either side of us. Two younger boys were packing a wagon, a chubby man sat getting a haircut on the front porch of the barber shop, two ladies walked briskly up the way past a group of men hanging about watching them as they went. One of them whistled at the girls while the other men stood laughing. To my right just past that grungy group of eye gropers was the Waterin' Hole Saloon. On the opposite side of the street, and probably strategically placed, was the town Sheriff's office and city jail.

I led Delilah up to the hitching post outside the saloon and stepped out of the saddle. I caught a glance from one of the girls as they walked past. She had long brown hair, the smoothest skin I could remember, and eyes as blue as the sky over Kansas. She wore a long dress with ruffles and a hat. The other girl was dressed similar and carried an umbrella. Watching them go reminded me that even in the most desolate of places you could still find a gentleness and beauty.

Looking away, I tied Delilah's lead line to the hitching post and surveyed my surroundings once more. The group of men that had been watching the ladies now had turned their attention to me. I glanced past them, taking caution to not look directly at any of them. The last thing I wanted was to give them a reason to get in my business. My gut told me though that I'd be dealing with them soon enough. Dog stood near Delilah and looked at me, his dark eyes giving me full attention. I put my palm up facing the dog.

"Dog," I said. "Hang here with Delilah."

Dog licked his lips and took a small step forward, then sat back on his haunches. He watched as I stepped onto the walkway and entered the swinging doors of the Waterin' Hole.

The smell of stale beer filled my nose as I walked in. Someone clanged on a piano in one corner, its music noteworthy, but by no means good. The player didn't seem to care as he was enjoying an early afternoon stooper and entertaining a lady dressed in a very peculiar fashion. They both laughed and sang, and while they stood out like a sore thumb to me, no one else seemed to mind. A card game was being played in the front of the saloon near the windows. The players each wore a very stern face, their eyes focusing on every bet and movement of the opposition. A lone cowboy slept in a chair in front of me, his head resting on a support post that ran from floor to ceiling, his drink slowly dripping out of his glass and onto his pant leg. I stepped around him as I made my way through. The floor creaked as I walked. A long-paneled bar stretched along the length of the back wall and was polished to a spit shine. Beneath, a polished brass footrest ran along its base and several spittoons sat spaced out across the floor. The bartender saw me approach and came over to greet me.

"What can I get for you, stranger?"

He spoke to me as he leaned forward on the counter. His mustache twitched as he waited for my answer.

"Actually, I'm lookin' for someone. Samuel McAlister. Heard of him?"

The bartender stood up and wiped the space he'd leaned on with a towel. He seemed suddenly disinterested in my presence, especially since I wasn't looking for a drink. I quickly reached into my pocket and pulled out a small silver coin and tossed it into a glass in front of him. He looked at the glass and then at me.

"Friend, what's your business with 'ol Sam? He's half crazier than an unarmed man at a gunfight. Been that way for a while to boot."

He chuckled through his split front teeth and leaned back with a pompous grin on his face.

"My business is of a personal nature. Not one I'd wish to share, but I'd appreciate it if you told me how to find him."

The bartender crossed his arms and stroked his chin with his right hand.

"Now let me see," he said, humming as if he was searching for an answer.

My guess was he was waiting for another coin to plop into the glass between us, but it wasn't going to happen. I grew irritated with him and had to reach deep inside to find some patience. I might have leaned over the bar and grabbed him by his mustache, yanking him around, explaining that after all I'd been through to get here, I wasn't in the mood to play games with a half-baked bartender from little town Lincoln, New Mexico. Good sense won over the urge to rearrange the marbles in his head, and with a forced smile I stepped away from the bar and turned to walk out.

"Heeye, heeye, heeye," laughed a portly older man at a table close by. "I knowed old Sam McAlister."

He stood and wobbled over to me from the table. He walked like one leg was shorter than the other, stopping only a step from me. His breath was fresh with foulness and he smelled like the railroad yards in Dodge City. He wore the tallest cowboy hat I had ever seen and smiled as he spoke, as if he had the bulge on all the knowledge in the territory. Either way I felt compelled to hear what he had to say. I stepped back to cushion the distance between us.

"Can you tell me how to find him?" I asked.

"Tell you? Shoot, I'll take you to him. I will, I will. Foller me."

He stumbled off towards the door and I must have paused longer than I realized. Watching him rumble off, I wondered if I was being had. Noticing my hesitation, he turned to me with a questioning furrow in his brow.

"Well are ya comin' or ain't ya?"

"Yep. Let's go," I answered.

This was my only lead and probably the most harmless of guides, at least for now. I followed him to the doors and watched him push through like he was leaving his favorite place in the world.

CHAPTER 36

I followed him through and onto the front porch. The sunlight stung my eyes, but they quickly adjusted. Delilah was at the hitching post where I had tied her, and Dog had remained by her the entire time. Dog panted as he looked at me, drool dribbling off the front of his tongue. He was thirsty, but I didn't have time to give him anything now. I stepped down to the hitching post to untie and mount up.

"Hey, Cappy! You old coot. A little early for ya to be comin' out, dontcha think?"

I looked up and instantly remembered the gang of men I had seen on my way into the saloon. They were still milling in the same place as before, but upon our exit, had slowly moved in our direction. I looked over at my elderly guide, realizing I never got his name. He didn't respond and kept limping on his way. He headed for a beat-up wagon across from the saloon. A shabby black and grey horse stood in wait for its portly owner. The wagon reminded me of one of the charred wagons I came across on my way here, only this one didn't have any dead bodies slowly rotting underneath. The horse looked old and had a brand on its rear haunches that looked familiar, but I couldn't remember where I had seen it before. The man who had called out Cappy spoke up again.

"I say Cappy! What, are you deaf in the head?"

"Come on, old timer, give us a looksee," another chortled.

I watched as the men walked into the street towards him. I slowly untied Delilah and clenched the reins in my good hand. This time Cappy turned around and squinted in the direction of the group of men.

"That you, Percy?" He smiled a wrinkled, curvy grin.

"Has ta be. Only feller I knowed with hat that's uglier than mine."

Cappy stood near his wagon. His belly stuck out in front of him and his arms dangled to his side, not straight down to his hips, but like he was trying to balance himself.

"Shoot, Cappy, you gettin' braver or dumber?"

The group of men stopped about two horse lengths from him and continued their insult barrage.

"Whewee! One things fer sure, you get stankier and stankier ever' time I see ya."

"Yeah, bath time for Cappy."

Everyone laughed.

The man who said this stepped to a nearby water trough and filled a bucket full of water. It sloshed as he walked in front of his buddies, spilling slurps of water onto the dusty road with each step. Their full attention directed at Cappy allowed me to mount Delilah unnoticed. As the bucket wielder got closer, I had a decision to make.

Stay out or get involved. Voices from the past echoed through my head.

There comes a time when a man will find it necessary to take a stand, either for himself or for someone else. Pick yer battles, don't let 'em pick you.

I knew what I had to do. I nudged Delilah in her side and headed for Cappy.

Three long gallops and I was in-between the gang of men and my newfound friend. The man holding the bucket closest to Cappy was startled by my intervention, so much so that he dropped the bucket of water in front of him. Water sloshed out of the top, drenching his pants and spilling into muddy puddles around him. The men behind him sneered at me, but all I heard was a high shrilled laugh sounding off from Cappy.

"Heeye, heeye, heeye! Yer bout all washed up at ya?" Cappy laughed again.

He looked at me and smiled, either unaware of the dangerous situation we were in, or not caring. One way or another I had to get him moving to his wagon so we could get out of there.

"Cappy, why don't you show—"

"Hey, Hoss! You owe my friend here an apology!"

I turned to see one of the men pointing at me, angry fist in the air. He was just as ornery looking as the rest. Scraggly beard, chubby gut, dirty clothes, boots and hat the same. I glanced at him and then looked back to Cappy. I was about to repeat myself when I heard another voice grind out of the pack of men.

"Why don't you get down of yer mule and clean these boots, boy."

The man who dropped the bucket was speaking now. He kicked a muddy boot towards me, flinging spatterings of mud and dirt on Delilah. He smiled, showing his rotten teeth, probably feeling as though he was getting to me. I'd been through a lot before meeting this bunch, and between river pirates and renegade Indians, this bunch was more like a group of angry Sunday school teachers whose bibles had gone missing. They looked tough enough, but I could see what they really were, and they didn't scare me, probably why Cappy showed a noticeable lack of concern in the first place. I ignored his banter and led Delilah another step away from them. I stopped her next to Cappy and leaned over to him.

"Come on ol' timer. Show me the way, will ya?"

Cappy looked up at me. "Alright, but this was just gittin' good."

I shook my head and smiled at him, wondering what he thought was going to happen. I straightened in the saddle and that was when I felt a sudden sting in my back. A sharp pain radiated just below my shoulder and down my left side. I reached with my right hand but couldn't reach the stinging spot. I turned sharply to see the men were on the move again. This time spreading out in a semi-circle and advancing slowly on us.

"How'd that feel, coward?"

I looked but couldn't make out who had said that. My back throbbed. I couldn't have been shot. No sound of gun fire.

"Good one, Jed. Sling'em again!" the chubby one provoked.

205

An echo of hoots and hollers started to erupt from the group. I scanned the street from one side to another. We were the only activity. Everyone else seemed to have gone in doors. I thought I saw someone peek from a window across the way, but it didn't matter. Trouble was brewing in Lincoln, and not having even been here an hour, I was knee deep in it. Cappy stared aimlessly at the group, watching to see what would happen next. A hopeful look for action flashed in his eyes.

"Think that'd teach 'em, Percy?"

A tall, lanky man reached to his pocket and pulled something out. In his right hand he held what looked like a leather strap with a small stick tied to one end. He brought his hands together and was fidgeting with the strap. Beneath me I could hear Dog start to gurgle a low growl, anticipating the ensuing confrontation. I looked directly at the man they called Jed. He didn't blink while staring me down. I pushed my feet into the stirrups readying to jump down. Our eyes connected, daring the other to make a move. Through the hoots and hollers, I saw him flinch. I had just enough time to jump to the ground in front of Dog as Jed wound his arm and released his sling at me. A whiz of air sped past me as the object he'd thrown missed its mark. A window shattered behind me, its glass crashing to the ground and splintering into a thousand shards on the porch beneath it.

I'd fought two men at once before, but the numbers here were not in my favor.

"Keep my wits! Use your head!" I said to myself.

The scene seemed to freeze the moment the window shattered. I don't think they'd see me react as I did, let alone get away unscathed. Dog growled behind me. Without taking my eyes off the men I showed Dog an open hand.

"Quiet now, Dog," I said calmly. "Everythin's just fine."

The air in the street grew thick, as if a sweltering cloud of heat blew in from the desert and hovered around us. My throat tightened. We were in a definite showdown. People began to emerge from their hiding places nearby. The quiet and lack of carnage may have piqued their curiosity. The barkeep with the fancy mustache looked out over the swinging doors at the entrance of the saloon. Two men appeared near the general store about fifty feet away. Even Jameis down at the Livery stood watching from afar. Cappy looked around. I was in no position to enter a street brawl and had no choice but to turn the other cheek to these men. I stepped to the front of Delilah, holding the reins as I went. Cappy limped up to me.

"Ain'tcha gonna do nothing?" he quietly asked.

The look on his faced longed for a day's entertainment. As rough as this part of the country was, I had to be smarter.

"Cappy, load up and show me the way to McAlister's, will ya?"

My tone was direct, and the look I gave him must have broken his insistence on watching a good fight. He turned and hobbled towards his wagon without saying a word. I turned back to the men in time to see Jed and Percy stepping toward me. Jed had returned the sling to his pocket, his hands at his side, fists clenched tightly. Percy walked to my left. I moved to put my foot in the stirrups when Jed reached out and gave me a shove. I fell into Delilah. She moved slightly, cushioning my momentum. Percy was now directly behind her to my left.

"I don't think I like you, boy!"

Jed spit.

"Hear me?"

I stood motionless, waiting cautiously.

"I don't think he did, Jed. Tell 'im again." Percy laughed.

Jed clenched his fists and made a move to shove me again.

Here we go… I thought.

Jed lunged forward towards me again, fists raised and aiming, but I was ready. I moved to my right towards Delilah's head causing Jed to miss me all together. He bounced into Delilah. She snorted angrily when he made contact and bucked once, not only sending Jed tumbling to the ground, but her hooves connected with Percy's fat gut and sent him failing backwards. He landed on the ground with a loud grunt, holding his stomach and moaning. The rest of the men surrounding us looked at each other and then to Jed.

"Git 'em!" Jed yelled.

I raised my fists and prepared for the fight I had tried to avoid. Dog growled louder and this time there was no quieting him down. The group of men converged on us when… BLAM!

The echo of a shotgun blast filled the streets and caught everyone's attention immediately. I turned in the direction of the blast to see three men standing near Cappy. They all wore dark clothes and hats. One man had his pants tucked into his boots. The man holding the shotgun wore a brown vest and had the fullest mustache I had ever seen. The third man was older. There were grey streaks of hair near his ears where his hat rested. He wore a black leather vest with a large silver star attached over his heart. The Sheriff. No doubt about it.

Seeing that he had everyone's full attention, he stepped into the street and over to the scene. The other two men followed, shotgun raised in the air, but surly ready to fire, if needed. The Sheriff stepped between Jed and me and looked us both over. Seeing that Jed was still on the ground he pointed at him.

"Stand up, Jed Dooley! Care to tell me what all the fuss is about?"

Jed stood up, looked at me, then at the Sheriff.

I spoke up before Jed had a chance. "I was just gitten a nice welcome to Lincoln is all Sheriff. Guess'n you know these guys."

The Sheriff turned to look at me, a surly look upon his face.

"Who are you, and what's yer business in Lincoln?" he asked.

I decided to tell him exactly why I was here. It would do me no good to stretch the truth or leave out my purpose for being here, especially if I needed his backup one day... Like now.

"I just got to town. Met Mr. Duncan down at the Livery. Stopped in the saloon to ask if anyone knew Samuel McAlister. That's where I found Cappy. I'm lookin' for work and heard he might need an extra hand. Ol' Cappy was takin me to meet him when Jed and his *welcoming* committee decided to pay us a visit."

The Sheriff looked at me, searching for anything suspicious about my story.

"That so?" was all he said. He turned to look at Jed.

He was noticeably worked up but dared not go against my story or take a chance of seeing the inside of the town jail, a place I'm sure he was well familiar with. Jed didn't seem the killin' type but was definitely the town 'push around'.

"Sure Sheriff. It's just like he said," Jed answered sarcastically then spit in the dirt. A string of drool caught his lip and dangled until he wiped it with his hand and then on the seat of his pants. His toothy grin and stubbly face had 'liar' written all over it, but the Sheriff let it go.

"Anyone know how that window got smashed in? Miss Molly's gonna have a hard time replacin' it anytime soon."

He pointed to the porch beyond us. Glass lay strewn about. A little old lady swept at the shards, cleaning the mess. I felt sorry that had happened, even though it wasn't directly my fault. The lady continued to sweep when another, much younger girl appeared on the porch to help. A closer look revealed that it was one of the girls that had passed by me earlier before going into the saloon. She looked out at the mob in the street with a sour frown. Without a word she got to work helping the older lady clean up the mess.

"Jed, get your boys outta here. You've had enough fun fir one day, I reckon."

"You're the boss, Sheriff. Law and order every time."

He looked at me as he said the latter, spit again, and then turned and announced that they'd be headin' off to the saloon for little "peace and quiet". I huffed a small laugh knowing his game and realizing that I'd probably cross hairs with them again. Percy, still on the ground, but seemingly recovered, held his hand out.

"Little help here, Jed?"

Jed turned to look at Percy.

"Git yer fat butt up or I'll put a sling into you!"

Jed glanced back at me and the Sheriff, realizing that he may have given an unwarranted admission of guilt for what had happened with the window and quickly turned and walked toward the saloon. Percy rolled to his stomach and with a grunt and a heave, lifted himself off the ground and stood up. Dust covered his clothes and clouded the air around him as he pulled up his pants and jogged to catch up to Jed and the others. Cappy walked up to me. The man holding the shotgun lay it across his shoulder, comfortable that the threat of having to use it had passed. The other man looked to the porch where the women were cleaning.

"Wee doggie! That was a close one! Heeye heeye!"

Cappy smiled and stuck his thumbs in his belt loops, pulling his pants as he rocked back on his wobbly heels. He got what he'd hoped for after all. Just enough excitement to embellish on later, but not enough to give him reason to check his britches.

"Cappy!" The Sheriff barked and gave him a stern look. Cappy's smile curled downward with the wrinkles on his cheeks. He released his grasp on his pants and walked to his wagon.

"Ehhh! No fun a'tall," he said.

He limped over and rumbled into his wagon seat, banging his knee on the wood slats of his seat.

"Ooooo! Dang if that don't hurt!"

The man with the shotgun laughed and shook his head, as did the other man, his attention no longer on the girl's chore of cleaning up the porch. The Sheriff was indifferent. He looked at me, still unsatisfied as to my business.

"What's yer name, stranger?" he asked.

I looked back at the Sheriff

"Rowdy, sir. My name is Rowdy," I answered.

"Okay, Rowdy. I've known Samuel McAlister for years. Cappy knows the way, but you may be goin' on a wild goose hunt. Ol' Sam was always a good man. Still is somewhat, but he ain't been right for a while, especially since he got news about his boy dyin'."

My eyes opened slightly, and I was caught off guard by the Sheriff's comment. I knew instantly that he was talking about Boone. I still hurt for him, too.

I thought back to the fight the night he was killed. The tomahawk sticking from his bloody chest, the rage and hurt building as I looked at his lifeless body on the ground next to me. He saved me. He put me on this path. Now I was about to meet his family, and who knows how that would go down.

"You alright there, Rowdy?" the Sheriff asked.

I snapped back to the moment. Inadvertently, I had dazed into memory, one I would like to forget, but one that would haunt me for a lifetime.

"Oh, yes, sir."

I'd managed to catch the Sheriff's suspicion after all, but Cappy broke in.

"Well? Are ya comin' or ain'tcha?"

"Thanks," I said, extending a hand to the Sheriff.

He shook my hand.

"Rowdy, you stay outta trouble now. Cappy'll show you the way to McAlister's."

I stepped into the stirrups and hoisted myself up to the saddle. Pulling on the reins, Delilah backed up a step.

"Good to meet you, Sheriff," I said.

He didn't answer but gave a small courtesy nod and walked away. Cappy headed off in his wagon and I turned to follow. The man with the shotgun followed the Sheriff down the street, but the other man remained and was looking directly at me. He glared, a small turn in his lip, watching me as I rode by. I didn't like his look. I wondered why suddenly he was interested in me and what made his demeanor so foul. His glare stuck as I went.

"Dog?" I said.

Dog followed. If I needed to remember anyone from today, it would be him.

Dust rose from the Cappy's wagon as we made for the edge of town and McAlister's place. The sun drifted lower in the sky and I was glad to be getting through today in one piece.

CHAPTER 37

I rode next to Cappy and listened to him ramble on about the town, the sheriff, his favorite spot at the saloon—anything that came to his mind in fact. He spoke in segments, switching topics randomly as he went. Dog ambled alongside Delilah, looking up every so often. His tongue flopped from his mouth and bounced as he trotted along.

It wasn't long before I saw a small homestead in the distance. Cappy pointed and told me that it was McAlister's place. He'd been there for years and had a sizable amount of land attached to it. Cows stood in groups under a limited grove of shade trees. A dead calf lay rotting in the sun, flies buzzing around its flaccid body. Where was his help? Not a hired hand in sight. I was concerned that Dog may wander off and stir up trouble with the cattle, but was glad to see him staying close by, uninterested for the time being. It became easier to see the ranch as we approached. The sun was relatively low, and evening was on its way. The stead consisted of the ranch house, a ram-shackle barn with a small corral fenced off to its right, an open dirt area in-between the house and the corral, and a small cedar fence outlining a stretch of trees, grass, and dirt from the front of the house to the main ranch entrance. A board was nailed to one post that read *McAlister's*. Below it, the McAlister brand symbol—a large 'M' with a smaller 'A'—formed in the center at the bottom, a simple representation of McAlister property, but not easily duplicated.

We rode closer to the house. I figured Cappy would anchor his wagon and introduce me to McAlister personally, so I had little concern. That soon disappeared, starting when the front door flew open. A man ran out to the porch raised a shotgun to the sky, fired one shot, cocked the barrel, and aimed it straight at us. I was caught totally off guard and jumped in my saddle at the noise.

"That's close enough," he ordered.

He held his position and his aim. I looked over at Cappy, who was standing up, wobbling.

"Heavens to Betsy, McAlister! Don't you knowed who I is?" Cappy's voice cracked as he spoke.

McAlister looked over the barrel of his shotgun.

"That you, Cappy? What in the Sam-hill you doin' out here, and who's the stranger?"

"I'm—"

BLAM! The sound of his shotgun overpowered anything I tried to say; its report echoed beyond the ranch. Smoke smoldered from the barrel as he lowered it from its skyward position once again.

"You'll do good to keep yer tongue," McAlister warned.

He was certainly edgy. I wondered if that's what the Sheriff had meant when he said he hadn't been *right*. I swallowed the lump that had formed in my throat and kept my composure.

"Calm down there, ol' Sam. This here's a friend of mine. Names…uh, his names…"

Taking the chance, I whispered Rowdy.

"Rowdy," Cappy finally replied. "Just got to town. Said he heard you was lookin' for a hand."

"Just got to town, huh?"

He lowered his shotgun slightly and laughed.

"Well Hee-haw, Cappy. You must knowed him real well, seein' he just got to town and all."

A smile accompanied his laugh. Cappy chuckled along with him. I sat and watched these two and began to agree whole heartedly with their reputations. They were both off their rocker a bit. Cappy seemed harmless enough, but I wasn't so sure about McAlister. A smile escaped my lips and I shook my head. McAlister noticed, his laughter and smile disappearing instantly.

"Somethin' funny, boy?"

I looked at him but didn't answer.

"Well?"

He stepped down from the porch, the shotgun resting across his body. I raised my hands slowly.

"Beg your pardon, sir, but I'm not aimin' to get my head blown off tonight."

McAlister looked me up and down and grunted.

"I'd like to talk to you about workin' for—"

He cut me off, thankfully not with another blast, but simply raised an open hand to me.

"Cappy, why don't we go inside and grab some coffee."

Cappy smiled. "Don't mind if I do."

He stumbled down from his wagon seat.

"What about him?"

Cappy gestured to me over his shoulder with his thumb, his arm bounced as he waited for a response. McAlister took another step closer.

"Don't know'im yet. He can stay in the barn tonight and I'll deal with him in the mornin'."

He looked and nodded towards the barn door.

"Take yer dog and yer horse and settle in. There's water in there, but that's about it."

He turned and stepped back up onto the porch. Cappy looked at me and shrugged his shoulders. He laughed. There wasn't anything I could say that would improve my situation. I shook my head and dismounted.

"Thanks, Cappy," I said sarcastically.

"Oh, it's not so bad. Ya still have yer head. Heeye, heeye, heeye!"

He laughed and limped up the steps and into the house. I looked around. It wasn't too bad a place.

CHAPTER 38

An orange glow painted the horizon as evening settled in. Light blues blended with darker blues, turning purple on the opposite side of the sky. It was a beautiful end to a whirlwind day.

I led Delilah to the barn and opened the main door. It creaked as it swung open. A dank smell of musty air filled my nose as I stepped into the dark of the barn. Dog followed and promptly found a soft patch of hay to lie on. Turning circles and nuzzling the straw with his nose, Dog made a suitable resting spot and plopped down, an exhausted grunt escaping as he relaxed.

I undid the straps holding my saddle to Delilah and gently removed it from her back. I took the saddle blanket and tossed it next to Dog, staking my claim on a portion of hay next to him. I closed the door to the stall and offered Delilah a handful of hay. She nibbled thankfully. As she chewed, I looked around for a watering trough. It was getting quite dark, but what light remained shone through the open barn door providing just enough illumination for me to find what I was looking for. I filled a bucket at the trough and brought it to Delilah. She didn't drink right away, but it was there for her when she was ready. I closed the small door of the stall securing her inside and returned to the trough.

I dipped my hands in the water and quickly brought them to my face. The cool wetness dripped from my forehead, past my nose, and off my chin. I brought another splash to my face, this time letting some of it trickle into my mouth and down my throat. I felt safe enough and was able to enjoy a bit of relief from my hard travels. I wiped my chin with my sleeve and walked over to the barn door.

Somewhere in the pasture a cow mooed. Stars were already starting to dot the sky overhead. I could hear Cappy and McAlister inside. One would let out a laugh and the other would follow suit. It seemed like there was more than just coffee that they were enjoying. Somehow, I felt that everything was going to be alright. I closed the creaky barn door and walked through the shadows to the hay where Dog was.

"Asleep already, huh?" I said aloud, looking down at Dog.

I sat down next to him, spread out the saddle blanket, and rolled over on top of it. The hay was soft enough and cushioned me from an otherwise hard ground. I removed my boots and placed them next to me. I closed my eyes.

"Dog, you got the right idea," I whispered.

I tipped my hat to cover my face. Sleep came quickly, my body and mind spent from an arduous journey. I slept soundly, undisturbed until the dreams crept in. Vivid as the day they happened, but twisted and uncomforting. I couldn't wake up. The terrors of my past rained down on me, forcing me to relive and remember the darkest times of my life.

CHAPTER 39

Light shone through the cracks in the porch as I lay on my stomach in the dirt, shaking, trying to remain quiet as blasts of gunfire cut my father down right before my eyes. The yips and hollers of the murderous band of men tormented me. I was unable to move as I watched my father crumple to the ground, blood seeping from his lifeless body. Their horses pranced in a circle around him, sending dust into the air with each step.

Time seemed to slow. The CLOMP of their hooves sent echoes, blending with the grunts and banter of the riders atop them. I reached out to scream, but as I opened my mouth, water poured in on me, filling my scream with a gurgled wave of wet. The sky went dark and water poured in through the cracks above me. I started sinking in the sloppy ground beneath me. Each grasp useless as there was nothing to hold on to. The porch collapsed around me with a loud crash as lightning flashed and thunder clapped. I couldn't breathe. I sank into a muddy current and was swept away. I panicked and flailed my arms and legs trying to find my way. The muffled sound of thunder faded as I tumbled.

With a sudden thud, I washed onto a rocky surface. Sand scratched my face and filled my mouth. I spit, coughed, and crawled on my hands and knees, not knowing where I was or what was happening. I slowly rose to my knees, my hands outstretched in front of me. My palms hurt, my joints throbbed, my skin tingled. I looked in front of me and saw Boone lying on the ground, the stump of an Indian tomahawk sticking from his chest. I tried to stand but didn't have the strength. I stared ahead in horror as Boone began to roll over. Slowly he stood, shaky yet rigid. His eyes dark as ink, his skin pale, and his clothes drenched in his own blood. He opened his mouth to speak. A crackled "Roooowwwwdy" escaped his colorless lips.

As he spoke, a pair of eyes appeared in the dark behind him. A low growl sent shivers down my spine. The hairs on my neck stood as I watched an unnaturally large wolf leap at Boone. It tore at him, but still Boone stared at me. The wolf ripped through him. Boone collapsed to the ground, one hand outstretched to me, his eyes now as clear as the day we met. He never screamed out in pain or asked for help. The wolf straddled him, preparing to attack again. Blood filled slobber dripped from its lips. Its claws gored into Boone's back, holding firm to protect its prize. Tears streamed down my face. I couldn't run. I couldn't fight. Helpless, I suffered. A final word slipped from Boone's mangled body in a fading whisper, "Burn…"

With that, a swirling column of flames surrounded Boone and the wolf. Sparks filled the air. A scorching wind blew past me. My skin was hot, my eyes stung from its brightness. The towering fire twisted faster and faster. An orange glow engulfed Boone and the wolf and with a final howl, the flames collapsed on itself and disappeared. Boone was gone. The wolf was gone. And the night was silent.

I remained kneeling. I looked at my palms then pressed them to my thighs, wiping them back and forth. I had control of my body again. I placed one foot on the ground and prepared to stand. Unsure of myself I pushed down with my foot and rose to both feet. I gazed into the dark. Cold sweat formed on my forehead.

"Boone…" I whispered.

From somewhere in the dark a voice echoed.

"He can't help you now."

CHAPTER 40

I awoke abruptly, lunging forward with both hands. Reaching out, I clenched my fists. A frantic flutter of wings sounded off above me, startled by my sudden movements. It was still dark. I looked around. Beads of sweat clung to my brow. Forgetting where I was, I found myself in the hazy confusion between sleep and reality. Everything had been so real, as if I truly experienced each agonizing moment in my twisted dream. My mouth was dry. I rubbed my eyes. I could hear the rhythmic breathing of Dog nearby and slowly came out of the dreamy fog I was in.

I reached for my boots and put them on. The door to the barn was slightly cracked, a dull light invading its edges. I stood up and walked towards it. I grabbed the latch and gently pulled, swinging the door towards me, its hinges creaking all the way. Moonlight poured down on me as I stepped out of the barn.

All was quiet in the night. I moved from where I was to the fence surrounding the corral. Leaning on the top cross beam, I inhaled deeply through my nose, taking in the smells and aromas from the ranch. The crisp night air filled my lungs, reviving me. The ranch was a peaceful place. Cattle rested just beyond the corral in the pasture. The random chirp of night bugs played under the trees beyond the house, and an occasional lightning bug blinked, showing itself briefly, only to disappear again.

"I could get used to this," I said to myself.

I lowered my head, looking at the ground, and let a comforting breath of air escape my lips. I was relaxed again, and wide awake.

Click!

The sound of a hammer engaging for action chilled my spine. I slowly turned to find myself, once again, on the wrong side of a gun barrel. McAlister stepped towards me, his shotgun raised and aimed at my chest. Moonlight reflected in his eyes. His body cast a growing shadow behind him as he approached.

"What are you really doing here?" His voice pierced the calm.

I stood motionless and watched him draw closer.

"Cappy seems to think yer fine, but I ain't told no one that I'm lookin' for help."

He stopped directly in front of me, the barrel of his shotgun so close I could reach out and touch it.

"So, I'll say it again, what are you really doing here?"

His aggressive tone demanded answers. I had no reason not to be forthcoming with him, but I worried how he might react. With no other choice I answered.

"Boone sent me. Said you'd—"

He cut me off.

"Boone?"

He lowered his aim a bit and looked to the sky. Then, as quick as he drifted off, he refocused and moved one step closer, pushing the shotgun barrel to my chest.

"Boone is dead."

"I know, and I am sorry for that."

"You kill him?" he shouted.

McAlister's hands started to shake, his finger dancing uncomfortably close to the trigger.

"No," I quickly answered, trying hard not to move. "Boone saved my life."

McAlister stared at me, searching for lies in the pits of my eyes.

"Please. In my pocket there is a paper with your name and where to find you."

I glanced to my shirt pocket.

"Boone gave it to me just before…"

I paused. I looked at McAlister and could see his pain, although I had no idea what it was like to lose a son. His face seemed to droop, his eyes glazing over with the moisture of rising emotions being held back, but ready to flow at any moment.

I slowly raised one hand to my short pocket and undid the button. I pulled the slip of paper out and held it between two fingers in front of my chest.

"He gave this to me the night I left Dodge City."

McAlister reached for the paper. One hand held the shotgun while the other unfolded the note. He squinted as he read.

"Sam McAlister… Lincoln, New Mexico."

225

He read the words over again and again, whispering to himself, as if talking to Boone, trying to figure everything out. The pressure of the gun barrel against my chest lessened, and then was gone altogether as he lowered the weapon to his side. I had no idea of their relationship. I gathered there was one, but more than that there seemed to be a mutual respect between them as men, not just father to son. McAlister switched his attention from the note to me again.

"It's early, but not too. Follow me to the house. We've a conversation ta have."

With that he turned and walked slowly towards the house. Easing my tensed muscles and letting out a quiet breath of relief, I followed McAlister, wondering what he would ask and where I would start.

CHAPTER 41

The taste of fresh coffee and feel of a sturdy chair was a welcome change to my usual trail mess. I sat across from McAlister at his kitchen table and sipped my drink. He looked smaller and older sitting across from me, but his confident tone and aged rasp in his voice was a reminder that he was tough as nails, regardless of how he seemed to me at the time. He sat back in his chair, legs crossed. His boots, aged and worn like him, pointed out from under the table. He looked at me with an inquisitive stare, seeming to wait for me to talk first. Under the circumstances, I still felt the need to be cautious with what or how I explained myself and my situation.

Outside, a rooster announced it was ready for a new day. Wasn't this what I was hoping for? A new start? Again. I swallowed another bit of coffee and began to explain myself to McAlister. He listened, never once interrupting. His eyes never failing to keep focused on me. We sat until the sun came up, me talking, McAlister taking it all in. The more I talked, the more comfortable I became. It felt good to tell my experiences to someone. It would have been a great story to tell my father if he was still around. I ended with Cappy bringing me here. I finished telling what I had to tell and sat back in my chair. McAlister shifted in his seat and leaned on the table between us. He folded his hands and placed them beneath his chin. His wrinkled face and aged eyes focused on me intently.

"Boone sent you to me, so I'll take what you're sayin' for truth. He was always a good judge of character. Sounds to me like you've had troubles. Made the most of 'em from what I am hearing......'til now. Runnin' may have gotten you outta a bad spot, but you can be sure this Byrne fella will be lookin' for ya." McAlister's gaze stuck. "I know I would."

Silence filled the small kitchen. I had no response, other than to nod. McAlister got up from his chair and brought his empty cup to the pot of coffee keeping warm on the stove. He poured a fresh cup and took a long sip, then set it down in front of him. Steam rose from the lip of the cup. He wiped his mouth with his sleeve.

"I could use you 'round here awhile. Got some things that need fixin'. You up for that?"

A sense of relief filled my chest, as if I had held my breath, waiting for a fresh gulp of air to arise.

"Yes, sir," I answered.

"You'll stay in the barn 'til the roof on the workers quarters gets patched up. Wind ripped through here last fall and did quite a number on the place. Meet me round back in a half hour. You can find a place for yer horse in the barn or pasture. Up to you."

He turned and walked out of the kitchen. His footsteps echoing through the small ranch house as he went. I sat a moment longer, finished what was in my cup, and thought about the things he said. Most were agreeable, but one thing bothered me still. McAlister was right about Byrne. He wouldn't give up so easily. Chances were that he'd already been searching, but how close was he getting, and to what lengths would he continue? Was it coincidence that Santiago found me? Helped me recover? Did he have connections to Byrne? I had no idea. It was clear his motivations were questionable, and had I not left as I did, I may have been in a much more dangerous situation. Now here I was in Lincoln at the very place I set off to find. Sam McAlister was cautious yet seemed to be a trusting man. Going forward I planned to be cautious as well, especially around the people of Lincoln. It would be hard to know who to trust.

CHAPTER 42

A little over a month passed since my arrival at the McAlister ranch. The roof on the workers quarters, my roof now, was patched and holding well. We had just barely finished the last of it when we were hit by a strong thunderstorm. Water fell harshly from the darkened, often flashing clouds above, but not a drop found its way through. I felt good working and living here. My life has always been about new beginnings, but I truly hoped this would be the last 'fresh start' for a while.

We traveled to town every couple of days, mainly for supplies—materials for patching the roof, flour, beans, coffee, a bag of rice, a small barrel of gun powder. I decided not to ask McAlister's reasons for that. I figured he'd let me know if I needed to, but I kept a careful eye on where it was stored. Today, we were headed in to meet Cappy at the saloon. "Wet our whistle," as McAlister had put it. I rode Delilah and McAlister drove a small wagon to town. Dog stayed at the ranch and slept on the porch near an old rocking chair. It seemed to be a spot he returned to often. Maybe a new favorite resting spot, and on a day like today he made the most of it.

A pleasant wind blew at my face as we entered town passing by the Lincoln's Livery. Jameis Duncan was at work feeding the horses that were stabled there. He saw us and gave a wave but went right back to his work. *Best one in town,* I thought and chuckled aloud. It was in fact, the only one in town, but it was a great line and Jameis used it on every new folk that came his way. A little further down the road, we came to the Saloon where I first met Cappy. Nothing special about the place except that things felt different today. I wasn't sure why, but my heart pounded my chest. I looked around and saw the Sheriff's office, doors closed, but the front window was open. Miss Molly's store was open but didn't have its usual customers coming in and out. The women of Lincoln loved shopping there it seemed. Miss Molly always had a taste for unique and fashionable items. A few people milled around at the far end of town, but that was it. I dismounted Delilah and tied her to the hitching post. McAlister parked his wagon and stepped down from his seat.

"Anything seem strange to you, Mr. McAlister?" I looked around again, surveying the town from one end to the other.

McAlister looked around. "Don't see nothin' too out of the ordinary," he replied.

He walked up to the walkway just outside the saloon.

"Come on, Rowdy, let's cool off a bit. Cappy should be along soon anyhow."

With an uneasy feeling in my gut, I followed McAlister inside. I found a table while McAlister got what he wanted from the barkeep. He returned with a small glass of whiskey with one lump of ice. Ice was a commodity that was hard to come by but a necessary part of McAlister's favorite drink and was well worth the extra five cents. He brought me my usual glass of spring water, or so they called it. It was wet and quenched my thirst, but I'd be a suck-egg-mule if this was truly spring water.

McAlister sipped his drink as we waited for Cappy. I hadn't touched mine. I usually anticipate another one of his far-fetched stories of Indian encounters, or of his "private meal" with Lucy Belle Masters, or any number of retells that he enjoyed spouting off. He always had something to say. Ol' Cappy was a character, but I liked him. Today though I was too busy trying to sort through the feeling I was having. Something wasn't right. I just knew it. I'd been to town a few times now, but something was missing. I retraced our path in my mind, trying to figure out what it was. The edge of town, Jameis and the Livery. The Sheriff's office. The general store. Miss Molly's. The saloon. Jed, Percy, and their group of miscreants hanging around close by.

"What's on yer mind, Rowdy? Somethin's got you all riled up."

McAlister took another sip of his drink and then set it on the table.

"I don't know, Mr. McAlister. Just got a feelin'. Like…"

"Like troubles brewin'?"

"Yeah, something like that."

"If yer thinkin' that—"

McAlister was interrupted as Cappy surged through the swinging doors of the saloon, each one slapping the wall on either side, flapping wildly to a close. Cappy's sudden entrance only fueled my instincts that something wasn't right. Looking at McAlister, I could tell he was suspicious as well. Our eyes met, seeming to agree instantly that Cappy had news of his own to share. Somehow, through all the stories and embellished adventures, Cappy did seem to have an inside track of the goings on around town. You just needed to know which part of the stories to filter out and which were the most important to remember.

Cappy saw us and stumbled over, knocking a chair down on the way. He made it to our table and leaned over, placing both hands on the table between McAlister and me. Sweat covered his forehead.

"What's goin' on there, Cappy?" I said.

He slowly tilted his head to look at me but didn't answer. He then turned his look to McAlister, sweat dripping onto the table in front of him. Cappy had something to say and I wished he'd just get on with it. He'd only been here a moment, but I was ready to shake him and tell him to spit it out already!

"Cap?" McAlister said softly.

"We need to talk, Sam. You, me, and Rowdy." He glanced at me again. "But not here."

Calmly, McAlister stood up.

"Lead the way, Cappy."

Cappy turned and walked past the chair he knocked over. McAlister followed, as did I, stopping briefly to right the chair before we left. We stepped onto the porch just outside the entrance to the saloon. Cappy hobbled down the walk to his wagon, McAlister mounted his, and I headed for Delilah. They headed off down the main road towards the Livery. I stepped in my saddle and pulled the reins to lead Delilah away from the hitching post.

The door to the Sheriff's office was wide open now, and the two town Deputy's stood there looking directly at me. They didn't move but stared enough to heighten my sense of security. I looked back and slowly led Delilah away and out of direct eye contact. I wanted to look back, but I dared not. I caught up to McAlister and rode alongside him. I glanced at him and gave a nod, to which he responded with a nod of his own. In that brief instance, I noticed that he drove his wagon with one hand, his other hand holding a shotgun across his lap. It became clear that Cappy was leading us back to the ranch.

CHAPTER 43

The gentle breeze that welcomed us to town had now changed direction and a cooler crisp air bit at me. We were a few hundred yards away from the ranch when Cappy came to a stop under a large, dead tree. The bark of the tree was dusty and brittle, and its craggy limbs sagged and cracked in the growing north wind. I could see the ranch house just beyond the grove of trees standing in line at the entrance to the property. A small dust devil swirled through the pasture, dust and dry grasses flying around in a whirlpool of air. Cappy grunted as he stepped down from his seat. McAlister was already standing next to his wagon when Cappy got to him, the shotgun still in his grasp. I dismounted Delilah and walked over myself.

"What's this all about, Cappy?" McAlister asked.

Cappy took a breath, then looked at me, his eyes concerned and suspicious.

"I was over near Gentry's at the other end of town gettin' some irons filed fer Ms. Lucy Belle's mare. She'd threw a shoe. Anyhow, whilst I was waitin' I heard these men talkin' out back. Somethin' about 'he's the one' and 'been lookin' for him'. Didn't pay no never mind, except when I heard yer name come up."

Cappy motioned to me as he said this.

"Go on, Cap. What else did you hear?" McAlister asked calmly, inquisitively.

"Right. So, I made my way to the window near the back of Gentry's. It seemed the best place to hear without lookin' like I was nosin' into their meetin'. I heard Jed's voice say, 'That Rowdy fellers stayin' at 'ol McAlister's. Been there about a month.' The other voice I didn't recognize, but he said something else. Somethin' like, 'Mr. Byrne will be happy to hear the news.' Mean anything to ya, Rowdy?"

A hot flash of anger and frustration filled my head and shot down the back of my neck. My hands began to tingle, and I realized I was clenching my fists. My knuckles were white from the pressure. I held my breath, igniting memories from Dodge City, the fort, losing Boone, all of it fell on me at once. I must have been in quite a daze because I jumped when McAlister placed his hand on my shoulder. His grip was firm, and although I jumped, he didn't let go.

"Easy now," he calmly said, his hand still clenching my shoulder in a comforting, supportive way.

"Mr. McAlister. You were right. Byrne is lookin' for me. I'm sorry. I've met some bad men in my past but this guy'd lick 'em all and send their bodies back to their relatives in separate bags. And now he knows where I am! I've gone and put you in a bad spot, Mr. McAlister," I rambled.

So many thoughts were flying through my head. When I should leave. If I should leave. Either way, they'd still come for McAlister.

"Rowdy!"

McAlister dropped his hand from my shoulder and spoke very firmly.

"Listen up, son. Calm yerself. We'll figure this out. One things fer sure, if one of those Byrne men step foot on my property and use so much as bad manners, the only thing they'll see is a bright light taking 'em to wherever they deserve to go. Mount up and let's get back to the ranch and think this through."

He turned to Cappy.

"You go back into town and see if you can dig up anything else. Carefully! Don't go makin' a scene or try to be too smart about it. Come back out tonight but be here before it gets dark. I wouldn't want to shoot an old friend by mistake."

Cappy smiled oddly. Almost happy to be in on a big 'to do'. One way or another, it would be a new story for him to yarn on about down the line. He quickly hobbled back to his wagon and climbed aboard. With an energetic, "He-Yah!" he headed back the way we came.

McAlister and I continued in. Dog was asleep where we'd left him and only slightly lifted his head to acknowledge our return. I led Delilah into the barn and removed her saddle. She grunted her approval and walked to the water trough in the corner of her stall. I stayed and watched her drink, falling captive to the past once again. Delilah had grown into a beautiful horse. Strong, smart, and very capable of following commands on the trail. She was all I had in the world that remained constant, and I was more than prepared to keep things that way. The barn door creaked as McAlister brought his wagon horse, May, to her stall. She was older, but got the job done. He slid the stall door to a close and tossed a handful of hay into a bucket hanging over the rail. He brought another handful over for Delilah and placed it in a similar bucket.

"She's a fine animal, Rowdy. She'll be safe here."

"Don't know what I'd do without her," I replied. "Byrne... I should have known he'd come lookin' for me. Boone told me to come find you, but maybe I should've kept headin' west."

McAlister had been leaning on the rail next to me, one foot balanced on the lowest cross beam, arms crossed at his chest. He straightened his stance.

"Let me tell you something, Rowdy. I trust you. You've proven yerself to me and I've got no reason to think otherwise."

He shook his head.

"Boone sending you to me? I think he knew somethin' you didn't. Somethin' that yer finding out right now. He worked for that man and knew what he'd do. Knew what he is capable of."

I looked at McAlister and saw a fire light in his eyes. You could tell just by his look that there was more. He spoke again, firmly this time, yet softer than before. His teeth clenched.

"That man...Byrne...the reason you're here now...I hold him responsible for Boone's death, and as God as my witness he will be avenged."

McAlister walked out the barn door. I could hear his footsteps as he leapt up the few steps to the porch. Silence found its way around me once more, but my mind raced. Those few words spoke volumes. I was ready for whatever came at me. Ready to stand with McAlister. Ready to see this to an end. I turned and walked out the barn door, the afternoon sun starting to sag in the sky. Cappy would be back soon. McAlister sat near dog on the porch, still as stone. I looked out to the trees guarding the entrance to the ranch, their shadows stretching towards the house. I joined McAlister as we watched and waited for Cappy to return. He hummed a tune I was unfamiliar with as we sat, but never said a word.

CHAPTER 44

Twilight approached and still no sign of Cappy. The air breathed cold. Sporadic gusts invaded the ranch, spreading dust and chill with every wisp of wind. The horizon turned crimson as the sun disappeared from the sky. Purple and grey, orange and black, mixing together in colorful streaks across the sky, stretched overhead like open hands pulling at the night.

McAlister sat in his chair, a place where he'd been most of the afternoon. He'd stepped into the house for coffee and disappeared into the barn for a while, but returned to the porch, something brewing on the inside. He was surprisingly quiet. I had finished my afternoon duties and returned to sit with him.

"Where is he?" I said.

No answer.

"Mr. McAlister? Everything alright?"

No answer.

I sat back and looked across the darkening plains. Cactus stood out like blackened figures standing watch over the terrain. The chirp of bats on the move circled overhead. The pastures were quiet with looming shadows of McAlister's few cattle grazing nearby. Beyond the rise, past the tree line at the front of the ranch, a flock of night birds took flight, swooping and screeching as if suddenly startled. Dog's ears flinched and then stood up, alert. He got to his feet, eyes wide and searching.

"Easy, Dog. Whatcha see?"

McAlister spoke up, "Riders comin'."

Sure enough, a pair of riders followed by a horse drawn wagon approached the ranch. The dim light was enough to see our visitors' approach but was insufficient to make out any details of who exactly it was.

"That Cappy's wagon? Who'd he bring with'em?"

McAlister reached beside his chair, picked up his shotgun, and stood up. I hadn't noticed the shotgun until now. He must have brought it out of the house earlier while I was closing the barn for the night.

"Let's go find out."

McAlister stepped to the front of the porch. I was unarmed but followed him down to meet the riders. They showed no hurry in their arrival and made no friendly signal yet either. As they passed the last of the trees and entered the clearing just beyond the house, McAlister cocked his weapon and fired one shot into the air.

"BLAM!"

The shot echoed through the barnyard, across the pasture, startling the otherwise quiet grazers, and disappeared into the falling darkness. My ears rang, but I clearly heard the hollers of the men riding in. One stood out most of all.

"Holy Hell, Sam! You done 'bout sent me flyin' off this wagon! My dern horse can't take a crack like that!"

"Cappy? Thought I told you to be back before dark. Yer lucky that was a warning shot."

"Dag nabit, Sam, I done the best I could. Got Sheriff Campbell and one of his deputies here, didn't I? We got news but you ain't gonna like it."

"Sheriff Campbell?" McAlister spoke firmly.

"Yep, it's me, Sam. Got Roberson with me, too. We're gonna come in now. No need for that howitzer though. I'm thinkin' we're on the same side. You mind?"

Sheriff Campbell gestured to McAlister with open arms. McAlister paused. I looked at Cappy, now barely visible in the waning light. He stumbled down from his wagon, pulled his pants up under his overgrown belly, and started hobbling towards us. Sheriff Campbell and Roberson dismounted. Roberson reached for his rifle sheath but stopped short at McAlister's insistence.

"You won't be needing that, son. Walk your horses in, tie 'em up, and meet me inside. Rowdy, come with me. They can handle themselves."

I could hear Cappy muttering under his breath, "Some thanks I get…The things I do…Warm welcome too." He went on, but I ignored the rest and followed McAlister inside.

"Come on, Dog."

It was dark inside the house. Dog trotted in and I stepped through the door when McAlister pulled me by the arm.

"Quickly!" he said. "We need to be very careful these next few moments. Sheriff or not, listen closely to what he says and how he says it. Cappy ain't an issue. I'll keep my eye on Roberson. He's new to town. Only been with the Sheriff about a month before you got here."

McAlister released my arm.

"You don't think we can trust them?" I was confused and curious.

"Probably can, but let's not take any chances. The way things are goin' down we need to be very selective in who we trust. Let 'em earn it."

There were four wooden chairs around a square table in a corner closest to the fireplace. McAlister walked to it, struck a match, and lit the wick on a lantern that sat in the middle. I did the same with two more over the fireplace. The flame growing, dancing, almost teasing, flickered in front of me. I stared into the light, my eyes fixated. Falling out of focus, my mind wandered to the past. Blackened eyes reflecting the fiery anger of a lunging river pirate, a warring Indian, a wild wolf each jumped at me in memory as I stood mesmerized by the light. The room filled with a yellow glow, shadows mixing across the room. Startled by a rap on the door, I came to my senses and peered out the side window.

"Comin' in," Cappy said.

"Come on then," McAlister answered.

The three men entered the house and stood between me and McAlister.

"Let's take a seat and hear what you have to say."

Cappy, McAlister, and Sheriff Campbell took a seat around the table. I pulled the fourth chair to one side and sat myself. Roberson leaned against the wall near the window listening in.

"What's this bad news yer talkin' about, Cap?" McAlister questioned.

"Well, I go'd back to town like you said. My plan was to go to the saloon fer a spell, like usual, then make my way back to Gentry's on foot. Listenin' fer anything familiar to what I heard earlier. Well, I hadn't been settin' but fer a few minutes when Jed, Percy, and some stranger walk through the front and straight to the bar. Jed and Percy was all smiles, which made perfect sense as the man that was with 'em paid fer their drinks. They soaked up plenty over the next little while, although the man they was with didn't touch a glass. Musta been a least an hour before they walked out. Percy seen me settin' across the room and stumbled by as the others left. He placed his hands on the table in front of me, smiled, and told me to 'tell that Rowdy fella bye.' He laughed as he stumbled through the swinging doors and out to the street. I got up from my chair and watched them go, loud and obnoxious as ever. I stepped outside and saw Flynn step into the street and confront the three men. I couldn't hear what was said. They spoke for a while, but only Flynn and the stranger. Jed and Percy never got a word in edgewise. I figured he'd come to see what the ruckus was about, but that thought left quick as they walked together up the way towards Gentry's."

"Did you see any of this, Sheriff?" McAlister interrupted.

"Nope, Roberson and I were out lookin' into a problem at the Morris place."

"Can I finish?" Cappy said, almost in a whiny tone.

We all looked at Cappy.

"Alright, finish up then," McAlister said, somewhat irritated.

"Like I was sayin', they walked up town towards Gentry's Then past to that small boarding house. Gill's place, just across the way from Gentry's. Makes sense now that I think about it."

Cappy paused in thought.

"Cappy? How'd you find Sheriff Campbell?" I asked.

Cappy was startled back to the moment by my question.

"The Sheriff? Right. Well wouldn't you know it, but Deputy Flynn must'av seen me followin'. The group had turned the corner towards Gill's, but Flynn was waitin' fer me when I came up to the corner. He stepped out in front of me, cutting me off, and started askin' all sorts of questions. What's my business…Why I was following them…Where you were."

Cappy pointed to me.

"I told him I didn't know nothin', but I'm guessin' my poker face isn't what it used to be. He called me a liar and accused me of being up to somethin'. I told him that was crazy talk. He didn't like that much because he hauled me down to the sheriff's office and locked me up. He left me there alone, at least 'til Sheriff Campbell and Roberson showed up. Got lucky though."

"How so?" McAlister asked.

"Cause the last thing Flynn said to me as he left was that he'd deal with me after he and some other guys paid you a visit. Said he'd be back after the job was done. Tonight!"

The fire inside me was back. Again. I looked around the

room. McAllister's brow was furrowed and stern. Roberson's face was blank, emotionless, but seemed ready to follow the Sheriff's call. Sheriff Campbell looked up at me. I was breathing heavily.

"When you first came to town, I sensed trouble, Rowdy. Maybe you didn't start it, but it looks like it followed you here."

I waited, growing tenser as he spoke. What would he do? Arrest me? I wanted to lunge out the front door and track down Byrne before he had the chance to come here. I wanted this behind me. I'd had enough.

"Look Sheriff—"

"Calm down, son," he interrupted. "As things look though, it seems you've helped me get the fox out of the hen house. Flynn? Rough guy, but never figured him to flip on me. Guess there's some money in it for him. Either way, Roberson and I came out here to back you up. Never heard of Byrne, but if he's gone to all this trouble to find you, well, I know the kind. I've known McAlister for years though. Cappy, too. Never once did I question their character or integrity. If anyone tries anything, we'll straighten them out. One way or another, we're behind you."

"Thank you, Sheriff."

Relief poured in on me, brief as it was. I reached out to shake his hand. He stood and grasped my hand firmly. McAlister stood up as well. Cappy, the only one still sitting, tapped his hands gently on the table, proud of his contribution.

"What's next?" he questioned.

Cappy's timing couldn't have been more perfect, for at that

exact moment Dog let out a warning bark from the porch, followed by a low growl. Something wasn't right.

CHAPTER 45

An orange glow grew in the window that overlooked the porch. Roberson, who was the closest, pulled the shade to one side and peeked out.

"You better take a look, Sheriff," he said still looking outside.

Both McAlister and Sheriff Campbell went to the window. Roberson backed away making room for them. A quick peek was all they needed. McAlister stepped back as did Sheriff Campbell.

"How do you want to handle this?" Campbell asked.

"This is my place. I'll take care of this," McAlister answered, stepping for the door.

"Whatcha see?" Cappy asked. He stood up and started across the room.

"You stay put, Cap." McAlister pointed at him.

"Rowdy, you too. Stand by the window and cover me from in here."

"Cover me?" Cappy questioned, whining once again.

"Cover us," Sheriff Campbell added. "I'm not about to let you go out there alone. This may be your place, but it's still my jurisdiction."

He turned to Roberson.

"Roberson. Walk out behind us but stay on the porch. Keep an eye on things."

Keep a watchful eye...

A learned skill from time spent on the water. Those words echoed in my head. River pirates lurking, cargo and crew to protect, through day and night. Always keep a watchful eye. I shook my head as I remembered these words Captain Hennessey told me so long ago but remained as important as ever. Even more so now.

McAlister stepped to the door and picked up his shotgun that leaned on the wall just at the doorway. Sheriff Campbell moved next, and then Roberson, each adjusting their gun belts, just in case. McAlister reached for the doorknob but stopped short of opening the door. He turned and looked at us all.

"This could go one of two ways but prepare for the worst."

Sheriff Campbell nodded, and McAlister opened the door. The three men stepped outside and closed the door.

"The worst?" Cappy exclaimed.

"It'll be alright, Cappy. Just keep your head."

"Exactly," Cappy shouted. "That's what I'm worried about. Keepin' my head!"

"Shhh!"

I walked to the window and peered outside. What I saw caused me to shudder. Maybe Cappy's worries were well founded.

Six riders sat atop their horses twenty feet or so away from the porch. The riders on each end held torches, the source of the glow that filled the windows of the house. I immediately recognized the other Sheriff's deputy, Flynn. He led the group and was front and center. He wore a serious look upon his face. To his left sat Jed and then Percy, who was holding one of the torches. To his right were two men I didn't know. The third man holding the torch took most of my attention when I saw him though. He slouched in his saddle, aiming the torch to his side. The firelight that lit up his surroundings found darkness in the cavernous scars lining each of his cheeks. His crooked wrinkles and leathered face pulsated as the torch light danced with the cold breeze. He stared up at the house.

"Santiago," I whispered under my breath.

I quickly scanned the scene for any signs of Juan Diego, but he was not here.

McAlister was first off the porch. Sheriff Campbell followed. They walked only a step or two towards the band of men.

Holding his shotgun with both hands, McAlister spoke up loudly. "Flynn! You mind tellin' me what business you have comin' here and showin' up like this? Looks to me like yer goin' on a raid."

Flynn sat sternly in the saddle. Smiles crept out on the faces of Jed and Percy though. They were excited about something, which gave me an uncomfortable feeling. Moments passed with no reply from Flynn. Sheriff Campbell spoke up.

"The man asked you a question, Flynn."

"I heard him, Sheriff. I don't think he is gonna like what I got to say," he answered in a sarcastic tone.

Each of the men's eyes fixated on each other. Another cold gust of wind swept through causing the torches to bend and flicker in its wake. Shadows bounced about the yard, leaping and hiding until the air grew calm again.

"Why don't you get down off your horse and come talk to us about it then?" McAlister said. "We'll listen to what you have to say and then you can be on yer way."

"Like it to be that easy, wouldn't ya old timer? You see, I didn't come all the way out here to talk things through. Yer going to do what yer told and that's that."

He looked at the Sheriff. "Campbell, you can saddle up and head back to town. No need for you to get all tangled up in this."

"Like hell," Campbell replied. "Flynn, you listen real good. I don't know what yer thinkin' or where you come off half-cocked talkin' the way you do, but I do want to know if yer willing to pay the price for what yer doin' here."

"The price? Don't you worry, Sheriff. For what I'm getting, I couldn't care less about any price you want to throw at me."

The man on the horse next to Flynn interrupted. He spoke well but was impatient. "Gentlemen, this is going nowhere. All we want is that horse thief, Rowdy, and his horse, then we'll be on our way. You tell him to come on out. I can see him peeking through the window."

He pointed directly at me.

What do I do? I couldn't very well hide out here, and I was never one to walk away when challenged, but this was serious. I stepped back from the window and closed my eyes. In the past, my father's voice would question my manhood, my actions or reactions, but not this time. My mind raced. Byrne chided me. Santiago threatened me. Mac cautioned me. Pierre challenged me. Wolves growled at me. Indians charged at me. Cappy called to me…

"Rowdy…Rowdy?"

My head spun like a whirlwind in the desert, picking up portions of dust and sand and grit, things that stung the most, and hurled them around through the air higher and higher until piece by piece they fly free.

"Rowdy?"

At once the spinning stopped. My mind went blank except for one thing, the image of a light shining through the cracks of an old wooden door. The door slowly swung open revealing a night sky shining brighter than I have ever seen. Stars blinked, displaying their beauty and mystery from the heavens. Calmly they shone, their light filling the void between me and the darkness I was surrounded by. I breathed deeply and opened my eyes. I looked up at Cappy.

"You okay?" he asked.

I didn't respond but headed straight for the front door. I reached for the handle, turned the knob, and before Cappy could get a word in edge wise, I was outside standing next to Roberson on the porch.

"Well, look what the cat dragged in," the strange man said, raising his arms as if he was surprised by my arrival.

I started to walk down the steps, but Roberson grabbed my arm to stop me.

"Are you crazy? Where do you think you are goin'?" he whispered.

"That's right," the man continued, "Come on down and join the party."

"Mister," McAlister said. "I didn't catch your name."

"I didn't offer it, but if you must know, it's Beringer. Nick Beringer. My employer has some unfinished business with our horse thief here and now that I see that he is in fact who I am looking for, we'll be asking him to take a ride."

He smiled a discourteous smile at McAlister. Flynn was still stern in the saddle, but the other riders chuckled, all but Santiago. He hadn't taken his eyes off me since I stepped into view.

"Asking?" Sheriff Campbell said.

"Sheriff, we both know what I mean, and we both know what'll happen if he doesn't come. Let's keep cool about this and it will all be over soon. No harm, no foul. Just me retrieving what I was sent to get."

"Don't make a move," Roberson whispered.

"You've made your point, Mr. Beringer, now let me make mine." McAlister spoke firmly and with authority. "You and Flynn and the rest are going to turn your horses around. You're going to get off my property, nice and calm like. No harm, no foul. Just doin' what yer told by a man holding a gun to you."

With that, McAlister pointed his shotgun directly at Beringer. Flynn pulled his pistol, aiming it at McAlister. Sheriff Campbell pulled his and aimed it at Flynn. The man next to Santiago, raised his hands, exposing a rifle, and pointed towards the porch. Jed and Percy looked at each other and nervously pulled at their gun belts. Santiago did nothing. He just sat and stared at me, holding his torch.

The air seemed to be sucked out of the place. What had been a breezy evening turned stale, cold, and dank. The torch light ceased to jump as it had, smoke trailing above and disappearing into the darkness. Sweat trickled down my neck, giving me a chill. Roberson had a hand on his gun belt and was slowly unfastening the strap that held his sidearm in place. Solid as stone, the men on horses kept their aim, as did McAlister and Sheriff Campbell. Not a flinch or waver in their resolve to see this through...and then it happened.

Dumb as they were, and obviously in over their heads, Jed and Percy still fumbled to get into the showdown. When Jed finally un-holstered his weapon, Percy tried to hand him the torch so he could pull his, but instead dropped it on Jed's saddle. Sparks flew as the torch bounced off the leather and into Jed's lap. Jed let out a scream and quickly pushed the torch off his saddle and onto the ground, not before pulling the trigger of his gun.

BLAM!

The shot rang out through the yard and ignited a firestorm of blasts and bullets. McAlister and Sheriff Campbell fired as did Flynn and the man next to Beringer. Beringer's man was hit by McAlister's blast and was sent flying off the back of his horse. Flynn fired twice at McAlister, and jumped off the back of his horse, using it for cover. I wasn't sure if either had been hit by their exchange in gunfire or not. Roberson shot as I jumped from the porch and took cover near the hitching post. Jed and Percy's true colors came out, as they turned tail and ran as soon as the gun fight started. McAlister and Sheriff Campbell retreated to the porch and lumbered up the steps. Santiago slid off his horse and reappeared under its chin with

a shotgun. He blasted once, the powder exploding and emitting a bright fire from its barrel, followed by a spray of shot that tore across the open area between the two fighting groups. Santiago's horse reared and bucked away leaving him vulnerable. He fired again, then dodged to his left. Beringer found cover by making his way to the side of the yard near the corral. Each torch had found its way to the ground, but still burned bright enough to light up a portion of the area between us
and them.

I had left the house unarmed and found myself in a bad spot. I looked back to Roberson as he fired a shot. I pressed my lips together and whistled, hoping to get his attention. He heard me, saw my empty hands, and knew immediately what my signal was for. He reached to the left side of his gun belt and pulled a second pistol from it. He showed it to me, and I nodded. He fired one more shot and then tossed me the pistol. I was able to catch it but had to scramble to dodge bullets that traveled my way.

I dove behind a water trough near the corner of the house. The corral was ahead and to my left. Flynn crouched in the shadows somewhere behind his horse. Roberson whistled to me, then motioned for me to run on the count of three. Santiago knelt near the corral fence only 20 feet from me. I spun the chamber. Six shots, that was all.

I looked at Roberson and was about to make a break for it when I saw Santiago's face change from vengeful concentration to careful listening. Beringer crouched next to him, paused, then slowly slid between two lower rails of the corral fence. He wasn't the least bit graceful and flubbed to the ground on the other side. I heard a slight grunt as he bounced on the uneven ground of corral dirt. Santiago turned his head, stood slowly, and lumbered over the fence and into the darkened corral to join Beringer. I looked back at Roberson. He waved me on again. I shook my head and returned my attention to the corral.

Their two dark figures slowly sank from view into the pit of the corral. Engulfed in shadow, I was unable to follow their movements. I slowly stood, crouching a bit and stepped towards the edge of the house at the end of the trough of water. Shining up from the smooth reflective surface in the lingering water, the moon brightened my face. The torches were mostly burned out and smoldering on the ground, but moonlight had overtaken the ranch, illuminating the yard. I looked again for Santiago and Beringer. There was no sign of either of them. And where was Flynn?

"Rowdy!"

Roberson raised his voice to a loud whisper, but his tone worried me.

"Get over here!"

I glanced around the side of the house again, then slowly retreated to the porch. Roberson opened the door but blocked my way.

"McAlister's been hit."

CHAPTER 46

I pushed by Roberson and entered the small front room of the ranch house. McAlister lay on his back on the floor to one side of the room. Darkened blood soiled his shirt below the rib cage. His breathing was shallow. Lantern light paled his face making it look chalky white. He was in bad shape.

"We need to get 'im to town. He'll die if Doc don't fix him up quick." Cappy fumbled his fingers as he talked. "I'd go, but I ain't near as quick as one of you. An' who knows where they are now?"

Roberson peered in the door. "I'll go. My horse is close enough to get to. I haven't heard a peep from Flynn since he crawled behind the tree line."

"But the other two are out back somewhere." I spoke up, realizing I hadn't moved since I caught sight of McAlister. I stared at him as I spoke.

"Yeah, but if one of us don't go soon…"

"We know, Cap!" I snapped at him, not meaning to.

Campbell's voice took charge and calmed us at the same time.

"Roberson, you make a run fer town. Rowdy can cover you til yer safely away. Cappy, grab a blanket from the bed and bring it

257

here. McAlister's shiverin' and needs to be looked after. I'll watch out the side window and blast anything that tries to sneak up from the back side of ya, Roberson."

Roberson nodded.

"Ride fast to fetch the doc but be careful on the way back. You won't know where we stand at all til yer right close by again. Got it?"

He looked to me.

"Rowdy?"

"I got it, Sheriff."

Roberson and I shared a ready glance and headed for the front door. Everyone went to work. I slowly opened the door and crouched out onto the porch. Crickets played a tune in the distance. Roberson crouched next to me.

"Ride fast and hard," I said.

"There another way?" Roberson answered in a sarcastic yet serious tone. He took a deep breath and then launched off the porch, high-tailin' to his horse. He made it, mounted up, and was off. He galloped out the front of the ranch and disappeared into the dark. I surveyed the yard, the tree-line, and as much of the corral as I could see. I started to retreat indoors when a loud blast erupted from Roberson's direction. Its report was not from a weapon that Roberson carried. Sheriff Campbell was next to me in in instant.

"Where in the Sam hell did that come from?"

He looked concerned and agitated.

I pointed.

"Roberson just passed that way."

Campbell spit.

"Back inside," he said.

I backed my way through the door and headed for the window on the side of the house. "Get back quick!" I whispered to myself.

Cappy knelt beside McAlister, covering him with a blanket. He stayed there still and quiet, as if in prayer. McAlister wheezed and coughed, startling Cappy, sending him backwards off balance. He thumped to the floor.

"Should've stopped drinking years ago, Cap."

McAlister's voice crackled as he spoke, his mouth barely moving. I couldn't help but smile a little. I walked to McAlister and crouched near him.

"How you feelin'?" I asked.

"Like I've been shot, Rowdy." He paused, then reached out and grabbed my arm. "You know he ain't gonna stop comin' after you until he gets what he wants. Seems like the kind of man that doesn't quit fer spit. You need to stand tall and finish this. Here. Tonight. Dangerous as it might be, you may not have a better chance than now." McAlister wheezed, coughed, and clinched his side in pain. Blood dripped from his lower lip and ran down his chin.

I turned to Sheriff Campbell. My eyes telling the whole story. My hurt, my anger, my needing to do…something, anything. I stood up, looked at Cappy across the room, and took two steps to the door.

"Where you goin', Rowdy?" Sheriff Campbell asked, a little too authoritatively.

Frustrated at the world I answered, "Out. They went around through the corral, probably to the barn and stable. Maybe even to find Delilah. They won't kill me. Beringer said it himself. They aim to take me back to Dodge City. To Byrne himself. I'll draw 'em out and you be ready."

"That's crazy talk," Cappy said.

"Maybe, but waitin' in here ain't gonna solve anything."

I stepped to the front door. Campbell walked up behind me and put his hand on the door, preventing me from opening it.

"Rowdy..."

"Campbell, I'm goin'. Don't try an' stop me again. Please."

"I'm not gonna stop you." His hand slid off the door. "Here," he said. He handed me a pistol.

"Had that gun since I came to Lincoln. Tuck it in yer belt for now. Use it if you have to. I'll be watching out from the corner of the porch, but I'll wait til yer round back before I move into position."

His look was serious and compassionate. He wanted justice as much as I did, but he knew deep down that I had to settle this in my own way.

I tucked the pistol into my belt above my backside, concealing it from a forward approach. I stepped onto the porch letting the door ease shut behind me. Any other night I would have enjoyed the crisping air, its gentle breeze as it whispered its way through the branches of the trees across the yard. But not this night. This night was as forgettable as they come and wasn't even close to being over. I walked slowly to the head of the steps glancing briefly over my shoulder at Campbell. His face was stern and focused. He gave me a nod, which I returned and then stepped down off the porch. Dirt crunched under my feet. I walked cautiously to the side of the house and made my way to the corner. I could see the portion of the corral fence where Beringer and Santiago slipped away, but no sign of them in the blackened nothing beyond the rails. The barn door creaked to my left, startling me a bit, but no other sounds accompanied its eerie night call.

They're in there somewhere, I thought to myself.

I stepped toward the barn door, leaving the protection of the ranch house walls behind. My breath was shallow, my heart thumped in my chest, my steps as light as could be made. Each movement in each moment saw me gain ground on the creaking barn door. Halfway there. Ten paces now. Five paces. At once, a loud, whinny and angry snort echoed from inside the barn. Delilah! Throwing caution aside, I leapt at the barn door. Unafraid, filled with anger and frustration, I burst through the door. Bats scuttled out the door above my head and raced out into the night sky. Their dark shadow rising and flowing in the air as they headed out to hunt.

Inside the barn, I skidded to a halt and knelt down trying to see anything. Delilah continued to snort, and I could hear her stomping her hooves defensively. I slowly stood as my eyes adjusted to the darkness of the barn when I heard the click of a hammer setting its place in action on its revolver.

"Don't ya move another step there, boy." Beringer's voice was raspy, his breathing labored. "All I need to do is pull this trigger and end you, but that would take the pleasure away from Byrne doing it himself. I can wait, can you?"

Motionless, but fighting the urge to leap at Beringer, I remained silent.

"Seems to me all this could have been avoided. Probably handled back in Dodge City. But then you had to go off and involve the Colonel. Bad move. Life changing actually if you ask me."

Beringer stepped forward.

"Life changing for you, you mean," I replied.

Another hammer clicked. Beringer glanced beyond me.

"Santiago…go ahead and come out. He ain't goin anywhere. And no one is coming in for him either."

Santiago hobbled over. His left leg dragged a bit as he moved. His pant leg looked moist. He'd been hit. I couldn't tell how badly, but he had been injured in the gun fight.

"You think you preeety smart. I lose big money over you."

"Where's Juan Diego? I swear! If anything happened to him…" I glared at Santiago. Beringer walked around in front of me.

"You can talk as big as you want, Rowdy, but the fact remains that you are in a no-win situation. The best thing for you is to help us all get out of here without any more trouble. Take your chances with Byrne. Who knows, if you return his property, he may go easy on you," Beringer said with a sly grin.

"Kill heem quickly you mean." Santiago laughed out loud. It was a deep raspy laugh that ended in a muffled groan. He reached down to rub his wound.

"Here's what's going to happen," Beringer said. "We're gonna walk outside real quiet like. Just you and me. You're gonna collect two horses from the yard and we'll ride out."

He talked over his shoulder at Santiago.

"Get the horse from the stall and take her to the meeting point. You'll get your money and a little extra when we meet up."

"All of my money, Si, Señor. I go."

I took a step towards Beringer, but his glance towards Santiago refocused on me.

"Don't be stupid, kid." Beringer stepped closer and pressed the barrel of his gun to my neck.

"You are one big headache, and if I wasn't under specific instructions not to kill you outright, well, let's just say this would have been over long ago."

I stared at Beringer. Santiago turned to move in the direction of Delilah's stall. From the blackened pathway between us and Delilah, a low rumble started to rise from the darkness. The rumble tuned noticeably louder and changed to a wet, angry, growl and was getting closer. On the precipice of darkness, two black eyes emerged. I looked past Beringer to see Dog slowly step into view, teeth bared and ready for flesh. Beringer turned his attention from me.

"Shoot that mutt, Santiago," Beringer ordered.

I looked at Santiago, then back to Dog. No time to think or waste. I pressed my lips together and let an air piercing whistle escape my mouth. Without hesitation Dog leapt at Santiago. Santiago tried to raise his shotgun but wasn't fast enough. Dogs front claws ripped at Santiago's chest as his jaws snapped and caught Santiago's forearm. Dog shook his head ferociously, sawing and grinding until his fangs touched bone. Santiago fell backwards onto the ground, struggling to get free.

Santiago screamed out in pain. His arm bled profusely, his leg wound, now aggravated by the fall, opened and gushed warm and red. Dog didn't let up.

Time slowed dramatically. Dog was in full force with Santiago. Beringer turned from me to take aim at Dog, giving me my opportunity. I tackled Beringer from behind, slamming my arms down on his, preventing his shot at Dog. I reached down his arm and wrestled to get his weapon. Beringer grabbed my arms and we rolled in the dirt.

The barn, a quiet place for animals to escape the outside world, to rest and recover from a hot day, to recover from the grind of ranch life, now echoed with anger, fear, determination, screams, and growls. Delilah snorted and grunted. Her whinnies trailed through the air like pleas for us to stop. Dog's relentless attack on Santiago was malicious. Dog was punishing Santiago with each bite, scratch, and claw, none of which were a true kill shot. Santiago bled.

Beringer yelled and grunted as we struggled. I gritted my teeth as my grip loosened from his fist at the hilt of his pistol. Beringer rolled under me, our arms entangled and straining. One blast fired from the barrel as we fought, the bullet splintering the wall of the barn and flying off into the empty pasture beyond. The blast startled Dog which allowed Santiago to slip back just enough to kick out. He struck Dog once on the snout and once in the ribs, knocking him back on his side. A yelp followed by a shallow whimper escaped from him as he slowly tried to stand. Baring his teeth again, he wobbled in front of Santiago. Santiago grabbed a wood slat and pulled himself to his feet. His ruined body swayed as he stared angrily at Dog. Beringer, still beneath me, raised his knee abruptly, connecting with my groin. All the air pressed from my lungs and my midsection pulsed with pain. I lost my grip on his hands and fell to my side. Beringer pushed away from me and aimed his gun at my face. Slowly he stood, catching his breath. Dog's guttural warning vibrated behind him. I looked at him bravely standing his ground, injured, but ready to fight no matter the cost.

"Kill that dog! Shoot her now!" Beringer yelled.

Santiago didn't hesitate. He raised his shotgun, arms throbbing, bleeding.

"Vaya con Dios[8] dog!"

"No!" I yelled.

The shotgun blast roared through my ears, through my head, through my heart. The smell of gunpowder burned my nose. My eyes squeezed shut and my fists clenched, leaving my palms to bleed beneath my nails. In rage I opened my eyes, filled with sweat and tears. Beringer's eyes were wide, but he wasn't looking at me. I followed his gaze and watched as he raised his weapon and fired beyond me.

"Stay down, Rowdy!"

That was all l heard before the second shotgun blast.

CHAPTER 47

I covered my head and dropped from my crouched position to the ground. Lead pellets split the air above me, spreading out as they traveled. I rolled away from Beringer and looked up. His face was white. His expensive suit, covered in dirt and sweat, now absorbed blood as it spewed from his chest and midsection. His white shirt turned a murky red as he staggered backwards against the wood railing that separated stalls from the barn walkway. His throat gurgled, and then he fell.

I turned to look towards the barn door opening. There stood Sheriff Campbell, shot gun still raised to his shoulder, sweeping right and left.

"You okay, son?" he asked as he stepped further inside.

I looked to where Santiago had been fighting with Dog to see him crumpled on the barn floor, motionless. One boot was missing from his left foot, his other leg twisted unnaturally to the right. His arms flailed out to his sides and his face was buried mouth first in hay spattered dirt. I could see from the corner of his face that his left eye was open. Dead as he was, Santiago's body oozed creating a nasty mixture of dirt and blood beneath him.

Dog!

Just in front of Santiago, Dog lay on his side. His breathing was shallow, but he was alive.

"I'm okay, Sheriff."

"Let's get you and Dog inside while I decide what we do next."

Aching, I slowly rose and walked to Dog. I knelt and gently rubbed his side. His fur was soft, but he was still tense from action.

"It's okay now, boy."

He tilted his head and stretched enough to lick my hand as I stroked him.

"Be right back."

Dog laid his head down on the ground again, his chest rising and falling, calm.

I stepped into the darkened path to Delilah's stall. She stomped the ground nervously as I approached. I clicked my tongue.

"Shhhh. Everything's gonna be fine," I soothingly whispered.

Her shadow stood across from me. I reached my hand to let her catch my scent. Slowly she stepped towards me, her muzzle bumping my hand. Her nostrils were wet with anxiety, her breathing vibrated through her lips. I slowly stroked her nose, between her eyes, then behind her ears. She stepped forward again and brushed her whole head into my chest and arms.

"At-a-girl. I'll come check on you shortly."

I patted her head again and she nodded hers as if to say, 'Don't go.'

Delilah was safe as can be and no worse for wear. I walked back to Dog.

"What'll we do with this mess?" I asked Campbell.

"A-yuh, that's the question, ain't it? Well, they ain't goin no where's and I don't suspect anyone's gonna miss them for a least a day or two. Let's head inside and regroup, see how McAlister is doin'. Roberson should be back anytime with the Doc."

"Okay."

Carefully, I placed my hands under Dog's side and lifted him into my arms. I cradled him as we walked out of the barn. Campbell rested the shotgun on his shoulder, and he caught me looking towards Delilah's stall.

"She's fine, Rowdy. A little shook up, but fine. Let's get settled and you can come check on her later." Sheriff Campbell followed me out of the barn as we walked back to the house. The quiet, stillness of night had returned just as quickly as it had been interrupted. A nightingale sang a tune just beyond the corral. The moonlight cast long shadows from our bodies as we moved. I stopped for a moment.

"What's on yer mind, Rowdy?"

I turned to Sheriff Campbell. "McAlister said I should end it. Tonight. But this ain't over. Won't be long til Byrne gets word of what happened."

Campbell huffed a sigh but didn't say a word. I knew what he was thinking.

This could be far from over.

Instead he said, "Sure do have a lot to clean up round here."

I looked around the yard. The moon still unobstructed overhead cast enough light for me to see our battle zone. Two smoldering torches lay in the dirt. Three horses gathered together near the corral fence, saddled and ready for riding, not knowing their riders weren't going to return. The man who rode with Beringer lay face up at the edge of the yard, legs sprawled open, arms flailed above his head. His mouth was open as were his eyes. His chest was dark and wet with blood and the top of his right shoulder was missing.

"Gonna have to do somethin' with these bodies before too long, I reckon. We'll have ki-yotes or who knows what comin' round for the nighttime buffet if we ain't careful," Sheriff Campbell said.

I cringed at the thought, remembering the wagon train I came across. I looked down at Dog.

"That's when you saved me. Looks like you're getting pretty good at that." I smiled. Dog continued to rest in my arms. I started for the house again when Campbell reached out and placed a hand on my shoulder.

"Hold up just a minute, Rowdy. We got riders comin'."

I looked to the trees beyond the house which bordered the path leading to and from McAlister's property. Sheriff Campbell raised his shotgun.

"Git behind me," he said slowly between his teeth.

He stepped forward and I stepped behind him, following his cautious pace across the yard. The silhouettes of two riders came into full view. Gun raised and ready to throw down again if need be, Sheriff Campbell fired one warning shot into the air.

BLAM!

"Hold it right there or the next one will split you in two!"

My spine tingled with anticipation.

"Whoa there, Sheriff. It's me, Roberson. I got the Doc."

Relieved, I walked past Campbell. I could feel the warmth of his shotgun barrel as I went by. Roberson and Doc rode up and stopped in front of me. Roberson looked down at me holding Dog.

"She gonna make it?"

I nodded. Doc slipped off his horse and headed straight for the house. Roberson dismounted and took the reins of both horses and tied them to the hitching post.

"You have any problems findin' Doc?" Campbell questioned.

Roberson looked at Doc, his face changing.

"Flynn's dead," he said.

I looked at Sheriff Campbell.

"He took a shot at me as I headed for town. Missed though, then gave chase. Wasn't himself, all yelling and hollerin'. Seemed to have lost himself. Let off a few more rounds as we got closer to town. I had no choice but to fire back. One shot. One lucky, unfortunate shot. I'm real sorry, Sheriff."

Sheriff Campbell looked at the ground and then up at Roberson.

"As far as I'm concerned, he gave up his deputy badge the moment he agreed to ride against us. Where is he now?"

"He's layin' in some bramble just past Lincoln cemetery," Roberson answered.

"Well, won't have to move him very far then," Sheriff Campbell said and walked past us to the house.

Flynn had been with the Sheriff for a while, so I can't imagine what Campbell was thinking. Betrayal? Frustration? Sadness? He was too chiseled a man to let his emotions show, let alone get the better of him, but you could just tell that he'd had enough for one day.

"What about you?" Roberson asked. "You gonna make it?"

"Yeah, just trying to decide if we've put out the fire or poured kerosene on the flames. Ain't no way Byrne lets this go. It's just a matter of time 'til he gets news of what happened here."

Roberson nodded. There wasn't much else he could say.

"Let's go check on McAlister."

We finished walking to the house in silence. Cappy met us at the door and held it open as we walked inside.

Time would in fact be an ally and an adversary, but there wasn't anything I could do about that right now. I wasn't afraid of Byrne. Never was. I just wanted to see an end to his pointless pursuit. That man must be extraordinarily proud, or angry, or just a damn fool to think he needs Delilah back and to see me punished or worse.

Yeah, I stood up to him, more than once now, and I don't plan on giving in to any of his ridiculous threats or demands. Does that make me just as stubborn? Or does that go along with what the Captain said so long ago.

Pick yer battles, don't let 'em pick you. Once ya commit, see it to the end and make sure that ya leave a mark of remembrance so that it is known that you are not to be taken lightly...

Either way, I may have to decide one day. Stay here, live life, and deal with his backlash when he discovers that I have yet again eluded his capture, or pack a bag, saddle up and meet him head on? Those were questions I couldn't answer right now.

CHAPTER 48

The house was still. The door closed quietly behind us as we entered the room. I placed Dog on the floor in the corner. He laid his head down and panted softly. Doc was kneeling next to McAlister. Sheriff Campbell, standing nearest, wiped his brow and then turned to look at us. His frustrated look remained, but his eyes told a different story. I stepped closer, but Campbell put his hand up, motioning me to stop where I was.

"What's wrong?" My voice was hoarse and tired, quivering with worry.

Doc stood up and walked over to me. He placed a hand on my shoulder and gave me an empathetic look.

"Is he going to be okay?" I asked.

"It's hard to tell. He's losing a lot of blood. I was able to remove one bullet from his shoulder, but he took another to the abdomen. I can't find that one. If we can get him to my office in town, he might have a chance."

Doc removed his hand and went to gather his things.

"We have to get a move-on. He doesn't have much time."

A chill ran through my spine. My fingers and hands started to go numb. Was this really happening?

"Okay," I said to myself.

I turned to look at Roberson. Cappy stood next to him and they both looked spent.

"Cappy, go get the wagon."

I turned to Sheriff Campbell.

"Help me get him up, Sheriff."

I stepped towards McAlister but stopped in my tracks. McAlister held his right hand up, palm facing me, signaling me to stop.

"Rowdy."

His voice was low and weak, almost to a whisper.

"Rowdy, come here and listen."

I stepped over and knelt next to him. He grabbed my hand in his callused palm. He squeezed and closed his eyes.

"We've got to get you to town," I said.

McAlister wheezed and cough, his lips moist with fresh blood.

"Ain't no time for that now."

"But Doc says—"

"I know what Doc says," he interrupted. "Listen closely, Rowdy. When you showed up and told me about Boone, it hurt deep to the bone. I wanted to blame you. But truth be told, I never did. It was those men that came. They were to blame for his dyin'. Maybe they weren't the ones to do it, but they ran with the man who gave the order."

He coughed again, wincing with pain.

"Campbell told me that you got the last of 'em."

He took a slow breath.

"I never wished trouble on any man, but they got what they deserved. You stood up for yourself, Rowdy, and in doing so stood up for Boone, too. I want to thank you for that."

He paused.

"Boone was my only son. He was tough, but he always did what was right."

He looked at me like a proud father might look at his child.

"Yer just like you him, Rowdy."

My eyes welled with emotion. My stomach turned with frustration. All I wanted was to get him to town, to help him. And now, lying here on the floor, in the shape he was in, I knew where this was going. I was helpless.

"What should I do?" I asked him.

The room was quiet and seemed to grow cold. I looked at McAlister, tears starting to carve their way down my cheeks.

He looked me straight in the eyes and tried to lift his head. Sheriff Campbell moved around McAlister and supported his neck and shoulders.

"Live," his voice whispered. "Live your life. Don't worry about the things you can't control. Keep this place goin'. The ranch, I'm givin' her to you."

His eyes rolled back.

"Campbell, you make sure things get handled right for 'im."

Campbell nodded. "You can count on it," he said.

"Bring me down, would ya?" McAlister said through a burst of coughs.

His stomach seeped, adding to the stains of red on his clothes and bandaged belly. Blood and spit ran from the corner of his mouth. He closed his eyes and breathed very shallow now.

"Doc," I said. "Is there anything at all you can do for him?" My lip quivered as I asked.

Doc looked down to the floor, rubbing his hands nervously together. "I wish there was, Rowdy."

Roberson stood off to one side of the room, leaning against the wall near the window. He stared through the glass as if he'd seen something off in the distance. He was here, but his thoughts carried him far away.

Cappy still stood nearest the door, his hat in his hands now, crumpling under his fingers. His nose ran, his eyes were full of sorrow. I can't say how long he and McAlister had known each other, but I know they had quite the history. It seemed like one of them always had some story to share about the other.

Doc slowly packed his bag. His medical tools clanked as his tossed them carelessly into his satchel. Sheriff Campbell raised himself to one knee but stayed close to his old friend. His left hand rested on McAlister's shoulder. He gently flexed his fingers over and over, trying to bring some comfort to his friend. His head bowed in silence.

I remained on my knees next to McAlister, his hand still enclosed in mine. I felt like a child again. I felt sadness that I hadn't experienced since I watched my own father gunned down, since my brother was murdered protecting me. I felt alone. I was on that dark river once again, alone and afraid, uncertain of what was going to happen next. My throat was raw. I wanted to say something to him, but what could I say? And then I knew. All at once it came to me. A clarity like the sunshine on your face after walking through the pouring rain.

"A man acts like one because he has to. A boy acts like one when he wants to. What are you?" I whispered this to myself.

Then, squeezing McAlister's hand, I leaned forward and whispered near his ear.

"I'll live," I said. "I'll live for Boone. I'll live for you. And if anyone else rides in here and tries to take me or this place down, I'll send them along for you to have a word with them."

His eyes opened slightly.

"You do that, son," he breathed.

McAlister exhaled quietly, and then he was gone.

Outside, somewhere beyond the barn, past the corral and the pastures where the cows lowed amongst themselves, echoing in the distance, a lone wolf's howl rose to the moon. Its single cry seemed to hang on the quiet breeze, traveling upward to the heavens and stars above.

EPILOGUE

The next morning Sheriff Campbell and Roberson caught up with Jed and Percy. They were hanging out behind the Waterin' Hole Saloon, arguing, as usual, as to where they were going to go once they left town. It seemed that even between the two of them they didn't exude enough acumen to know that they should already be out of town. Campbell informed them, in no uncertain terms, that they would be cleaning up the mess from last night before heading off to the town jail. He said the judge might show leniency for their "civic contribution." Doubtful if you ask me.

It took them the better part of a day to retrieve the bodies, haul them to the town cemetery, and dig the graves. The dead were buried in a rocky corner of the cemetery where the ground was the most tough to excavate. It was a hellish place for them, but it was more than they deserved. Each eventually had a simple headstone placed with only their name chiseled into it. I'm not even sure that they were placed on the correct spot, but hey, you get what you pay for.

Doc returned with the Undertaker to handle McAlister's remains. It was tough watching them work, but I stayed close by in case they needed a hand. It was the least I could do. His closest friends were the only family he had left, so Cappy and I decided that a spot down by the creek, next to an old shade grove, was as good a place as any for McAlister to be buried. It was a quiet spot beyond the pasture, still on McAlister property, but secluded enough as to not draw too much attention.

I dug the hole myself. Dog laid close by, watching as I scooped and tossed the sandy dirt aside. It was emotional work, not hard on the body, but kept me thinking about how he acted as a man. It had me continue to ask myself the question of what kind of man I would be. My father raised me, but so did the Captain. Colonel Forsythe, and even Byrne had impacts on my life that sculpted and carved away at who I was, but it was McAlister who helped me bring all those pieces together. He wasn't my father, but I'd loved and respected him for the man he was. Even at the very end he taught me a very valuable lesson. No matter what is going on in my life, the good or the bad, a man must live his life. It was really that simple.

We laid McAlister to rest the next day. The minister from town presided over the burial. Sheriff Campbell, Cappy, Roberson, and I stood up front. Jameis Duncan from the town Livery stable and Miss Molly were there too, along with a handful of others from town that knew McAlister. It was a short service and most everyone was gone by the time the sun began to set.

The sky was painted with color. Reds and oranges bled together, spilling into the darkening purple in the eastern sky. Slowly these colors converged together creating what was probably the most memorable evening I'd had since I laid on the deck of the Delilah and watched the sky bend the night into view. Tonight, I sat rocking back in a chair on the porch at the front of the house. Roberson sat with me, but we didn't talk. There was nothing more to say right now. The sun sank below the horizon. The evening air was fresh, filling my nose with a calm, cool sensation. A night owl chirped and hooted. Dog slept by my feet and Delilah was safe.

"*Past the water, following the moonlight son,*
Along the water and I'll soon be home."

I smiled as I hummed this forgotten tune because I knew I was already there.

TRANSLATIONS

1. Go on! Didn't I tell you to stay put? You want this man to get loose and kill us?

    (Vamos! No te dije estes listo? Quieres que el Hombre se suelte y nos mate?)

2. Bring water and bandages.

    (Traé agua y bendajes.)

3. Pour it now?

    (Poner agua?)

4. Yes, only a little.

    (Si, solo un poco.)

5. Enough.

    (Sufficiente.)

6. Go care for the horses.

    (Cuida los caballos)

7. Bring food. We are hungry. Hurry up!

    (Traé comida. Estamos ambrientos. Apurate!)

8. Go with God

    (Vaya con Dios)

ABOUT THE AUTHOR

Chris Mullen is an up and coming novelist and writer. His book *Rowdy: Wild and Mean, Sharp and Keen* is the first installment in his *Rowdy* series. He lives in Texas with his wife and two teenage sons.

Connect with Chris via Twitter and Facebook @**Rowdy2019** or Instagram **@chrismullenwrites**. Find out more about him, the *Rowdy* series, and his other projects at **chrismullenwrites.com**.